ANNA KARENINA ISN'T DEAD

(The Rewritten Lives of Literary Legends)

EDITED BY
ATLIN MERRICK

Improbable
PRESS

First published by Improbable Press in 2024

Improbable Press is an imprint of:
Clan Destine Press
www.clandestinepress.com.au
PO Box 121, Bittern Victoria 3918 Australia

National Library of Australia Cataloguing-In-Publication data:

Atlin Merrick
Anna Karenina Isn't Dead
(The Rewritten Lives of Literary Legends)

978-1-922904-68-3 (hb)
978-1-922904-69-0 (pb)
978-1-922904-70-6 (ebook)

Cover artwork by © Claudia Caranfa
Cover text by Willsin Rowe
Layout & Typesetting by Dimitra Stathopoulos

Improbable Press
improbablepress.com

For all the women who are writing their own stories

For all those who didn't have the chance

And always, for Joseph Merrick

CONTENTS

COUNTERSTORIES: ANNA KARENINA ISN'T DEAD

"You read something which you thought only happened to you, and you discover that it happened 100 years ago to Dostoyevsky," said James Baldwin.

For me, it was always Tolstoy. The first time I wrote about *Anna Karenina*, I saw myself in Kitty, whose infatuation with Anna reminded me of my adolescent fascination with a girl whose dark curls, like Anna's, escaped her ponytail and fell into her face. The story I wrote for this collection, *Lilac*, first took shape then, as a self-indulgent fantasy that every desire Kitty and I shared could be fulfilled.

Since then, I have written about *Anna Karenina* many times, as a lover, a scholar, and an activist. The irony of my self-discovery through the works of an inveterate homophobe and misogynist was not lost on me. In an attempt to square the circle, I scoured biographies of Tolstoy's wife, Sophia Tolstaya. What I found were *counterstories*.

In 1889, Tolstoy wrote his infamous novella *The Kreutzer Sonata*, a violent denunciation of marriage, sexual desire, and even love itself. Sophia Tolstaya hated the story. In the following years, she wrote two counterstories in response to it: *Whose Fault?* and *Song Without Words*. Both stories revolve around the suffering of a wronged wife under the hand of a cruel, jealous, and bigoted husband.

Anna Karenina Isn't Dead is a collection of such counterstories. Like Sophia Tolstaya's counterstories, this anthology takes inspiration from male geniuses' uninspired mistreatment of female characters. It is about indignation in the face of bigotry. It is about reviving the corpses strewn across the literary canon and making them speak. It is about expanding the potential for self-recognition and connection exponentially across time and place.

A counterstory is more than a counterargument. All of us, Sophia Tolstaya included, care deeply about the stories we are responding to. When *The Kreutzer Sonata* was banned by government censors, Sophia Tolstaya personally begged the tsar to allow its publication. A counterstory celebrates what was done well, and imagines a better world rising from the ashes of what was done badly. The worlds these authors created have inspired us to create in return; and so the unbroken golden thread of human creation spools outwards.

James Baldwin said, "Art would not be important if life were not important, and life is important." This anthology reckons head-on with the inseparable bond between art and life, and cherishes the best of both.

Béatrice de Charmoy
Winter 2024

HOW IT BEGAN: A SHORT PREFACE
ATLIN MERRICK

The story that ends this collection is the reason this book began: Béatrice de Charmoy's wonderful Anna Karenina tale *Lilac*.

Béatrice's idea to rewrite Anna's awful journey was genius because, well, *look* at it: the book is 350,000 words about people making poor decisions, yet the only one who pays the ultimate price is the one with the least power in the world she inhabits: Anna. That tale was *ripe* for a rewrite.

Ultimately so many classic stories, myths, and legends share this problem: a woman suffers and dies, having existed mostly so the hero can have his journey.

Of course this isn't the destiny of every woman in literature, but from Anna Karenina to Lady Trieu to Dido to Cio-Cio-San, death, madness, or a life of grief is the fate of far too many.

Instead, in the rewritten stories here, these literary women *live*. Do they have a happily ever after? You'll see. Do they have a happy-right-now? *Oh yes.*

As you begin reading know this: each woman here gets a better journey than the one she originally got. Occasionally that includes revenge, sure, but mostly it means far less suffering for the sins of others, and entirely more swearing, street smarts, or therapy.

Hoping your journey in life offers you much the same and so very much more.

Having been hounded out of London, Doctor Moreau relocated to an island in the Pacific, where he continued indulging his obsession with surgically evolving animals into 'Beast Men.' It ended rather bloodily for him when he underestimated the strength of his final experimental subject. His victims reverted to their original natures, leaving hapless castaway Edward Prendick as the only witness to the horrors of the Island of Doctor Moreau. However, it was not a Beast Man who ended this reign of terror, but a Beast Woman. Prendick tells us that she died in the fight, but seriously – are we to believe that after breaking her chains and battering Moreau to death with them, she still somehow got taken down? Nah, that doesn't sound right. And what about the other Beast Women, lurking in the background? Where might they have gone next, and what would they have done with their rage?

THE LEOPARD QUEEN
JACK FENNELL

I FIRST NOTICED IT as I was grumpily grading undergraduate essays, on a compulsory first-year intake module. The class was massive, with nearly three hundred students in total. And I had a horrendous cold.

The point is: I was not happy at all, so I was not in any humor to tolerate silliness in the submitted essays. When I first came across a mention of a fox-bear hybrid creature in Kate Chopin's *The Awakening*, I had a fleeting moment of Zen calm as my brain evacuated itself of all thought, and then I left a margin note containing not one, not two, but three question marks, the better to communicate my exasperation. The second time this incongruous beast popped up, I made a note to myself to investigate both students to see who copied from whom. The third time, I swore and started scouring the internet for key phrases: "the sudden appearance of a half-fox, half-bear monster at the very end goes against the realism of the rest of the story"; "just as we think Edna is about to drown, and childhood memories flash before her eyes, a 'Fox-Bear Witch' comes out of nowhere and fishes her out of the water"; "We might almost think that the Fox-Bear Woman is a spirit who comes to take Edna to the afterlife, except for the fact that Edna then divorces her husband and goes on to become a famous artist."

No matter what I tried, however, I couldn't find the damn source. Without evidence, I had to settle for marking these students down for including irrelevant material, and taking note of their names so that I could keep an eye on them in future.

The following semester, it happened again, in a different class.

This one was more specialized: it was our spring semester 20th-century American lit class, with plenty of interesting novels and short stories to discuss, and I was not responsible for the admin, which made me like it all the more. Consequently, my mood was much, much better when I got down to grading the final essays this time than it had been during the winter, and good-naturedly I bent before occasional silliness like a reed in the wind. I may have even chuckled as I worked on my batch.

Then the Fox-Bear Woman showed up in an essay about Nella Larsen's *Passing*, where she and a 'swine-woman' burst into the Freelands' apartment and beat Jack Bellew into a greasy stain on the carpet before he could push Clare out the window. Again, my mind went blank, but this time it was more rabbit-in-headlights than Zen stillness. I set the essay aside and carried on with the others, resolving to return to it once I'd gotten the rest of them done. Four essays later, she showed up again – this time, apparently, at the end of Flannery O'Connor's "A Good Man is Hard to Find," where she and a pair of wolf-women slipped through the woods like ninjas and shanked the Misfit, Hiram, and Bobby Lee before they could do any harm to the stranded family.

I emailed the module leader with the surreal synopses, asking, "Are you seeing this in any of yours?"

"Thank God you're seeing it too," he replied. "I thought I was losing it." His reply had samples attached too: another Flannery

O'Connor essay, where the Fox-Bear Woman, riding on the back of a huge mare/rhinoceros hybrid, chased down and trampled the fake Bible salesman in "Good Country People"; and a thoroughly bonkers reading of Zora Neale Hurston's *Their Eyes Were Watching God*, in which the Fox-Bear Woman and her Wolf-Woman friends killed Jody Starks immediately after the first time he hit Janie, then tried to do the same to Tea Cake (but were talked down by Janie), and later prepared to bust her out of jail, if need be.

We met to discuss the situation over coffee. The lunchtime rush had just ended, but we kept glancing around the almost-empty library café as we talked, keenly aware of how we would have sounded to anyone who overheard us.

"These are characters from *The Island of Doctor Moreau*, aren't they?"

"They are, yeah. Is this a social media dare thing? 'The Fox-Bear Woman Challenge'? 'Insert this character into an essay at random and post your lecturer's response'?"

That seemed less viral-trendy than pretending to eat detergent pods or swallowing tablespoons of dry cinnamon. I mentioned my experiences with the previous semester's essays, and my futile attempts to find the website this nonsense was coming from.

"Maybe it wasn't a site," said my colleague, after a moment's thought.

"How d'you mean?"

He gave a sigh of trepidation and winced. "Maybe they all paid the same person to write those essays for them."

"Why would that person screw them over by writing this loopy bullshit, though? Surely he or she wants repeat business."

My colleague shrugged. "There'll always be students looking to cut corners. Whoever it is just takes the money, whips up a new online alias and moves on, laughing all the while. Or maybe they were all using the same dodgy AI."

That did sound depressingly likely, but something about it was gnawing at the back of my mind. When we finished our chat, I went into the library instead of heading back to my desk, and I looked up *The Island of Doctor Moreau*, by H. G. Wells.

The copy listed in the catalog was old enough that I was surprised to find it on an open shelf, instead of in the basement storage area or the Special Collections section. I flipped through the pages, scanning for references to the Fox-Bear Woman. She wasn't exactly a main character, so I used my phone to search a HTML version and give myself an idea of the approximate page numbers.

She was gone. There was no mention of the Fox-Bear Woman anywhere in the physical book. In her place were blank spaces, as if she had never been printed on the yellowing paper. And she wasn't the only one. As I flipped back and forth, other blank spaces jumped out at me, and through comparison with the online version, I found that these corresponded to other characters, such as the Swine-Woman, the Wolf-Women, the Rhino-Mare, and others who were not as clearly defined by Wells' hapless narrator Edward Prendick, such as the lithe, white-swathed female figures with slit pupils and long tails. As I looked back and forth between the two versions, I confirmed that every single female character had disappeared from the old book.

In fact, the first word that came to mind was 'escaped,' and I found myself thinking, 'Good for them.' Doctor Moreau was a monstrous sadist; on top of that, there were a couple of unnerving asides, such as 'The females were less numerous than the males, and liable to much furtive persecution in spite of the monogamy the Law enjoined.' Who could blame them for breaking loose? It was clear that they had the wherewithal to do it, since the story noted that, following the death of Moreau – beaten to death by the Puma Woman, using the chains with which he had tried to restrain her – the female beast-people were the first ones to abandon the Law that had governed every aspect of their lives during his reign.

I caught myself thinking these weird thoughts, and by rights I should have dispelled them with a wry laugh, but I was in a library, and there are no such things as mind-readers, so who was I going to be embarrassed by but myself? I pulled on the thread, and looked up Flannery O'Connor, Zora Neale Hurston, Nella Larsen and Kate Chopin in the library catalog: they were all shelved on the same unit, in the order determined by the standard cataloging system. I perused those books, and nearly cried out with shock.

The Fox-Bear Woman and her sisters-in-arms were present in each one, just as the students' essays had them. The essays had not been plagiarized, generated, or bought; they had been quoted and properly referenced.

I remembered an article I read about M-theory, a hypothesized model of quantum physics spun out from string theory, which said that our universe was a four-dimensional raft adrift on a sea of eleven-dimensional space. Sometimes, the author said, our world could overlap with another, and photons from that other universe could leak into ours and mess up our redshift measurements, making things in deep space seem further away than they really were, or creating mirages of impossible celestial objects. I wondered if the world inside a novel was similar – a stable bubble of narrative floating in a wider world of chaos. Squeezed into a shelf alongside each other, couldn't one fictional world leak into the other?

Pulling on the thread some more, I reached for another book at random in the same unit, which turned out to be *Dracula*. When I flipped through it, I saw that the narrative petered out after chapter three – when the beast-women showed up and massacred every vampire in the castle, rescued the infant Dracula had kidnapped to feed his brides, and returned it to the distraught mother who showed up in chapter four. After that, there were a few desultory journal entries from Jonathan Harker as he left the castle and made his way home to England, and then a couple of hundred blank pages.

Something about Harker's plodding, confused progress reminded me of a pilgrimage, and that brought to mind the idea that the beast-women had spread from book to book, moving along the shelf from one narrative world to another. I lost almost an entire day of work to tracking the Fox-Bear Woman and her coterie through the books on that shelving unit, trying to make sense of their path. Genre did not seem to be a consideration: none of the texts where they'd first shown up were sci-fi, fantasy, horror, scientific romance or broad-umbrella speculative fiction, and there were several books in those genres, shelved close to where the old copy of *Moreau* had been, which had been ignored. I also wondered why they hadn't been mentioned in any of the autumn midterm essays for that massive first-year class, for which we had focused on the stories of Edgar Allan Poe. Why march through *The Awakening* and ignore "Murders in the Rue Morgue"? Why skip over *Alice in Wonderland, Dr Jekyll and Mr Hyde*, and *Huckleberry Finn*? Was there some intertextual element I was missing?

Publication dates, I thought. They couldn't cross over into any book that had been published before *The Island of Doctor Moreau*; Poe and Stevenson died before the beast-women's 'home novel' appeared. Our library didn't have any copies of the later works of Carroll and Twain, so I couldn't confirm with reference to those. Comparing the pre- and post-1896 Sherlock Holmes stories, however, did yield the proof I needed: the collection available in that shelving unit was not a complete volume, but it contained enough of the stories from *The Return of Sherlock Holmes* and *His Last Bow* to determine that the Fox-Bear Woman Gang had been there, done that, and ruined several of those tales by intervening to clobber or murder the villain.

Several, but not *all*. It had not escaped my notice that they didn't bulldoze their way through every single work of fiction published after 1896, but focused on stories where women were victimized, usually by men. They were clearly beast-women on a mission, but why them? Wells had hardly written them as paragons of radical feminism. He had barely written them at all; they were more background details than characters. It would have made more sense if they had been led by the Puma Woman, who was also barely a character, but at least impacted the plot in a significant way.

Maybe that was the reason: maybe being so underwritten, so vague and sketchy, meant that they were also under-scrutinized. And if nobody was watching them, they were freer to do as they liked. Maybe every vague background character has the power to wander around through other books when no one's looking. That still wouldn't explain how or why these ones were wreaking havoc.

"Basically, these characters are on a rampage," I said, concluding my presentation at the English section's Curriculum Review Day. I wasn't silly about it; I'd recorded proof of my findings, stapled together photocopied handouts of the Fox-Bear Gang's incursions into unrelated literary works, and even supplied evidence I'd generated myself – before and after pictures of a woeful horror novel I'd picked up in a charity shop and surreptitiously placed in that shelving unit, showing how it was decimated just before the point where the first gratuitous sex-murder was supposed to happen.

A few of the others had, of course, come across the creatures in student assignments from their own modules, so they were prepared to believe me. That did not mean that they were happy that I'd hijacked the Curriculum Review Day to raise the issue.

One of them raised her eyebrows. " 'Rampage'? I mean, sorry, but they're basically doing what we've all fantasized about doing when we see an evil character being evil."

"Well, yeah, but at the end of the day it's fiction. These aren't *people*, they're *characters*."

"But you're saying they've developed free will."

"Yes. And if we don't come up with a response, all of our core texts could be derailed."

Another colleague raised her hand. "Are we sure that this is something we need to fight against?"

"How many literary works should we concede, then?" I asked, annoyed.

She shrugged. "I dunno. How many literary works feature women being beaten and murdered?"

"Look, I don't want this to get derailed into an entirely separate debate; those are not real women you're talking about."

"Yeah, sure. But has it never bothered you that it happens so much? It's never made you uneasy when a writer creates a female character specifically so that she can die horribly? What's wrong with sparing them from that, and giving them the chance to live full lives?"

A moment of silence fell on the meeting room. I felt squirmy inside. The truth was that those things had always made me feel uneasy, but if I said so, it would amount to agreeing that we should do nothing.

More arguments followed on the ethics and political desirability of locking the beast-women down; we had to strike a balance between supporting their efforts morally and preserving the literary works in our possession. Eventually someone had an idea.

"We should negotiate with them directly."

"How do we do that?" I asked.

"Your test showed that they'll enter any book with the right conditions. Well, let's put another one on the shelf with a note written in the margins: a note saying that we want to talk to them, and providing our contact details."

"You think they'll be able to phone us from inside a book?"

"We're a good bit beyond drawing arbitrary lines around what's plausible and what isn't, at this point."

As quickly as I was able, I traveled into town by bus and had a rummage through the second-hand thrillers in the first bookshop I came to. It didn't take long to find an absolute turd of a crime novel – serial killer garbage with no redeeming features in the prose or dialog, from what I could see. The kind of thing that could only be improved by the beast-women's violent intrusion. I was back on campus an hour later, and the meeting room was soon abuzz with debates about what the margin note should contain, and who was to be designated as the call receiver. Since I was the one who brought this to everyone's attention and derailed the Curriculum Development Day, it became my duty to bear. Eventually, we settled on a simple 'We need to talk,' followed by my phone number, and scribbled it into the margin just after the scene in the prologue where the serial killer pounced on his latest victim. I crammed it into the library shelf when no-one was looking, and by that time, everyone was ready to head to the pub.

Outside the context of the meeting room and the library, I started to feel my certainty about the whole thing waning. "What if some rando picks that book up?"

I could read similar doubts in the faces of my colleagues as they sipped at their drinks. I could see them arrive at the same thought as me: did we really spend most of the day discussing that? Was there a carbon monoxide leak in that building, perhaps?

"It's not exactly Wells' best work anyway," someone muttered.

"Quite jejune," another agreed.

"Every character except for the narrator is left undefined. Lazy, slapdash stuff."

"The same thing has been said about every female character in fiction, though. Doesn't matter how well-written or developed they are; someone somewhere's gonna pop out of the woodwork to call them two-dimensional as a matter of course."

My phone started ringing. I turned it to show the others the indecipherable garbled symbols that flickered across the screen, then set it down on the table, answered it and put it on loudspeaker. "Hello?"

"Who's this?" said the voice at the other end. It sounded like a woman's voice, albeit one who lived rough in the woods, eating berries and fish and carrion and bugs and small mammals, and sleeping through the winter.

I told her my name and introduced her to my colleagues. "We're very interested in how you left the island."

There was a pause at the other end, and a muffled conversation between at least five voices, all of which sounded like women mixed with something else. "Dunno. Just did."

I steeled myself. "I understand that you're a great votary of the Law."

There was a cacophony of squealing, barking and grunting from the other end, and once I got over being startled by the noise, I realized that it was the sound of them all laughing at me. The voice I took to be the Fox-Bear Woman got back on the line.

"Not to crawl before power; that is the Law. We Are Not Men!

"Not to suck up and kick down; that is the Law. We Are Not Men!

"Not to take what is others' for ourselves; that is the Law. We Are Not Men!

"Not to claw or bite the defenseless; that is the Law. We Are Not Men!

"Not to obey the word of men; that is the Law. We Are Not Men!"

Each line was accompanied by bestial laughter and cheers, until all the beast-women joined in on the last chant.

I cleared my throat. "That's...very moving. Powerful stuff. Uh, just to clarify, none of us are in any way connected to H. G. Wells; he's been dead for ages now. So, whatever beef you have with him, you can't really–"

"Do you write?"

I swallowed. This was a difficult thing to admit to in front of my fellow academics. We were in the business of sniping at fiction from a hide, not creating it ourselves.

"Yes," I said, mortified.

"Do you kill in your writing?"

I thought back through the few pieces I'd had published over the past two years, and felt queasy. "Yes," I said, "but not often. And I've never killed off a female character."

"It doesn't matter," the Fox-Bear Woman said. "Yours is the Hand that wounds. Deal with it."

"Is there anything we can offer you to make you stop?" the Head of Section asked, in a loud giving-directions-to-foreign-tourists voice. "Can we negotiate?"

"Give us the Leopard Queen," said the Fox-Bear Woman.

I wracked my brain, but I couldn't guess what she meant. "Is that a friend of yours?"

"Give us the Leopard Queen," the Fox-Bear Woman repeated. Then she hung up.

We all stared at each other in shock for a second or two.

"I'm getting us a tray of shots," said the Head of Section. "Two each, I think."

"I'm searching for 'Leopard Queen,'" said one of the others, frowning at his phone. "There's a million results. How do we find out which one they want?"

"When you fill in the incident report for this," another said to me, "you better anonymize it. Mention no one by name. No identifying traits of any kind. I'm serious."

"I won't be mentioning my own damn name," I muttered into my pint.

I had a sneaking suspicion that while they only made their presence felt in fiction where a woman was victimized, that didn't necessarily mean they were barred from entering other stories and laying low. Maybe I was getting paranoid, but I was sure I saw hints of them in the background of *At Swim-Two-Birds* and *Malone Dies*. Perhaps I was wrong about the publishing date dynamic, too. One thing became clear to me: there was no way to quarantine that one shelving unit. There was no keeping them in; they were already out.

The library's holdings of crime fiction, horror, and sci-fi were banjaxed. The gang invaded a number of graphic novels, and for the first time we actually got glimpses of them: their appearance was not actually all that surprising, really, given that they were anthropomorphic animals, but they were armed with a surprising array of weapons that were not described in their home-novel.

"Are they picking things up from the novels they pass through?"

One of the wolf-women was holding a Bowie knife that could have come from *Dracula*, all right, and they were wrapped in bandoliers and weighed down with every kind of gun that had ever been described in 20th-century literature. They were even packing a couple of laser guns, enchanted swords, and bloody axes from the genre stuff.

"Look at their expressions," I said, pointing at the wild eyes and grinning mouths. "They really love what they're doing."

"Yeah," said one colleague, a little wistfully. "God, I could do with a road-trip."

Another, the same one who had previously played devil's advocate with the question of containment, was less enthused now that the beast-women had rampaged through all the library's copies of Jean Rhys's *Wide Sargasso Sea*. "So, who's the Leopard Queen, and how do we catch her?"

"I have no idea," I confessed. "There's only one mention of a leopard in the novel, and it's a Leopard *Man*. Moreau tortures him for behaving like an animal, and Prendick, the narrator, gives him a coup de grace. That's it. I have no idea who they're talking about." I stared down at the page, where the beast-women were gleefully chanting "WE ARE NOT MEN" while blasting a supervillain to pieces, preventing him from murdering the hero's fiancée.

"We have to do *something*. I applaud the motivation behind what they're doing, but just because a book depicts or mentions misogyny, that doesn't mean it condones it! It should be obvious, but feminist lit sometimes needs to portray shitty men doing shitty things – I can't teach texts where the cast of *Radfem Wind in the Willows* show up to go Rambo on the bad guys before the story gets going!"

"Let's not panic," said the Head. "Whatever is causing this, so far it's just in our library. It's not like this is happening all over the world; we'll just tell our students to avoid borrowing books from the library until we can undo the damage."

"There's only three weeks left in the semester," I said. I didn't know what that meant in itself, but I hoped that pointing it out would raise the general humor.

"What if they've already gotten out? What if a student brought a book home, and they spread to the books that student already had?"

"I thought they were limited to moving one book at a time? We know that they're still here. If they got out of the library, why would they come back?"

"Is it possible that they're being guided by their animal sides? Maybe this violence is a product of what Moreau did to them; an ontological struggle between human and animal in the same form, manifesting as violence that they redirect onto male targets?"

"You're suggesting that they're governed by their biology, then?"

"Uh...actually, let me re-phrase that..."

"Look, these are just man-hating stereotypes. Caricatures of feminist activists, taken to the extreme. Let's be objective about what they're doing here."

"I don't see any evidence that they 'hate' men at all. They only attack abusive male characters; they ignore the others."

"I'm not talking about their fictional behavior. What I mean is, they're destroying library books. They need to be dealt with."

"Are we talking about killing them?"

"I'm not sure that's possible."

"Because if we are, then this is just another story where women standing up to a patriarchal system get killed at the end, and we're characters in the exact kind of story we hate teaching."

"For God's sake, these are not 'women,' by any stretch of the imagination! First of all, they're fictional characters, not people; second, they're mutilated animals, not people; and third, they're violent straw-feminist caricatures – not people!"

"We only think that because that's when we see them act, and you can't deny that the characters they've killed off kinda deserved it."

"That's just reproducing male violence."

"Would you prefer if they travelled from book to book holding consciousness-raising seminars? Think about what Moreau did to them!"

"If some kind of radical upheaval is what they wanted, they've already done it. Characters aren't supposed to have free will. Their lives are determined by the narrative structure. They're supposed to stay pinned to the page."

Indeed. No matter how we approached the problem, we were faced with the same underlying dilemma: how was this happening in the first place? Regardless of how we responded, we weren't going to accomplish anything as long as we were stymied by that initial gap of understanding.

It took me a long while, but I eventually had an epiphany, and it was this: of all the men to mess around in God's domain, Dr Moreau must have been the most incompetent.

Within the world of the story, if Edward Prendick's account of his time in Moreau's company is accurate, we can conclude that this eminent scientist did not know the difference between a puma and a leopard, despite the fact that he had knowingly experimented on the latter before acquiring the former – described in Prendick's account as a black-furred creature.

For the avoidance of doubt, dear reader: pumas are found only in the Americas, and to date there are no verified sightings of any that have black fur. What Moreau's men acquired was, in fact, a black panther – the name commonly given to a melanistic leopard. His various underlings purchased the animal for him without knowing or caring what she was, calling her a 'puma,' and he neither knew nor cared enough himself to correct them. What else could one expect from a man like that – a vivisectionist who set himself a deranged goal and proceeded towards it through the mutilation of defenseless animals, just to see if he could do it?

Moreau 'worked' extensively on her head and brain, believing her to be the key to making the transformations permanent; I hesitate to say that he was 'correct' about anything, but in this single respect, his expectations were fulfilled. A woman with the power and solitary sufficiency of a leopard.

Where would such a being go, after winning her freedom?

After an exhaustive search, I found traces of her in the Life Sciences section, in books where every mention of an antelope, monkey, rodent, rabbit, or livestock animal had vanished. I've since learned that leopards in the wild will often kill far in excess of what they need. This was a worrying development: it was the first time a free-roaming character had intruded on a non-fiction book. Maybe that was an indication of her power. Perhaps she had no limitations at all.

With the help of librarians and volunteers from the English section, we worked out that she was decimating the third floor's population of figurative prey animals in a systematic way, depopulating one shelving unit before moving on to the next. We split into two groups, to check the books from either side and meet in the middle. Leopards are nocturnal hunters, so we decided that a night-time excursion was our best chance of encountering her.

"Coming here at night was a really dumb idea," one librarian said.

"It's okay," said another. "Leopards don't prey on people. In fact, they fear people more than lions and tigers do. Jim Corbett himself said so."

"Jim Corbett also said that's why man-eating leopards hunt at night, rather than face people in the day."

"Also, this one is part-human," I said. "And fictional. And written by a guy who didn't know much about big cats. So, all bets are off, really."

We crept from unit to unit, taking quick peeks from side to side with every intersection, as if expecting to feel her teeth in our necks at any moment. I fumed, embarrassed with myself, and reminded everyone that she was just a fictional character – and an underwritten one, at that.

I had a little booklet all about sheep, copy-pasted from a number of internet sites and run off on the department printer, then folded and stapled. A quick and nasty publication, but one that would hopefully serve as decent bait. The plan was to place it in the Leopard Queen's path, and then, when we were sure that she had gone for it, sandwich it between two pre-1896 books to trap her.

The second team signaled from up ahead that they had come across a book where some of the prey animals had vanished, but not all. We had her general location. I jogged ahead with my home-made sheep booklet and prepared to slide it into the shelf ahead of her.

There was a click from behind me, and when I turned around, I saw just how unlimited the Leopard Queen was.

She was massive, and powerfully built. Where she wasn't wrapped in blood- and iodine-soaked bandages, her fur was glossy and brownish-black, with the rosettes of her spots clearly visible under the library lights. Her face and muzzle were covered in a delta pattern of faded scars; her eyes were wide open and blazing. She looked somehow blurry around the edges, like we were looking at her through a smeared lens, and I later counted myself lucky to witness the intrusion of photons from a fictional universe into the real one. She was a ghost, or a hologram of sorts, and was pointing Dr Moreau's pistol at me.

"What do you want?" she asked. Her voice sounded like that of a woman who hunted in darkness and dragged her kills into trees.

I was not sure if a fictional bullet could hurt me, but I complied by raising my arms and answering. "Your friends are looking for you."

She scowled. "What friends?"

"Y'know, the Fox-Bear Woman, and the Swine Woman, and–"

The Leopard Queen scowled. "They are no friends of mine. Leopards are solitary hunters."

"Yeah, but you're also a woman," I pointed out. "Women have friends."

"You know that from personal experience, do you?"

"Okay, first of all – *rude*. Secondly, they call you their 'Queen': doesn't that mean something to you?"

"Drop the sheep and go," she said, gesturing to the floor in front of her with the pistol.

I still didn't want to take any chances with the fictional bullet, so I tossed the booklet at her feet. "Look, they really want to see you, so all I'm suggesting is–"

She fired, and the fictional pistol sounded enough like a real one to make everyone flinch. The shot went past my head and into the shelf behind me; it left no mark on any of the books, but I swore I heard something bleat and fall over within.

"There is no Queen," she snarled. "There is no Law. Now *go*." She hunkered down and seemed to reach into the booklet as it lay flat on the ground; when her arm had sunk in up to the elbow, she shimmered and faded into empty air.

Further experiments were conducted after my contract ended, by which time the Beast-Women had jumped the genre barrier and had cut a bloody swath through drama, then poetry, then philosophy, history, geography, popular science, and children's lit: one poor primary-teacher-in-training accidentally caught sight of the havoc wreaked in a compromised pop-up book, and needed a leave of absence to fully recover. The only tomes they could not infiltrate were the crunchier STEM textbooks, but those were removed from the library and put into secure storage, regardless. For a long time, debate raged about whether the library should be shut down altogether, but that didn't solve the problem of the 'tainted' books. What other library would take them, when on the one hand there was a chance the Beast-Women would spread, and on the other, the books were missing huge amounts of text anyway?

We did try to communicate the Leopard Queen's message to them, gently emphasizing her disdain at being anyone's figurehead, but since they never responded, we don't know if it got through. There was no lull in their activity, dubbed 'Extreme Diegetic Editing' by acolytes of the new literary discipline of Beast-Woman Studies, and the university leveraged a mountain of interdisciplinary grant money out of the phenomenon.

One of their most interesting discoveries is that the characters rescued by the Beast-Women from death and exploitation did, in fact, go on to live full lives: after her divorce, Edna Pontellier went on to become one of the most celebrated modernist artists in all fiction; following the death of her abusive husband, Clare Kendry joined her friend Irene and lent her perspective as a biracial woman to a number of key debates, subtly benefiting the Black civil rights movement; Lucy Westenra became a celebrated figure of the British fin-de-siècle with her unconventional polyamorous lifestyle, while Mina Harker rose to prominence as a campaigner for education reform, and the infant rescued from Castle Dracula grew up to be a hero who not only changed the course of World War I, but unwittingly prevented World War II altogether. Other happy outcomes, big and small, abounded, but the astonishing thing was that they all seemed to be happening in the same fictive world: blank paper left in the library started to fill up with detailed descriptions of a universe that, while not perfect, seemed like a pretty decent place for all kinds of people to live in.

For the time being, there is one figure who is notable by her absence, though nobody is ruling out the possibility that she might change her mind and join the world that the Beast-Women built. For the moment, the library keeps her supplied with jungle books and cattle logs, and they simply wait to see what will happen. Leopards and Queens, after all, are answerable to no-one.

The Bride of Frankenstein was designed to be a help-mate, as Eve was to Adam. But what if she had her own agency, choice, free will? In this story, she is her own person.

MADE FOR A MONSTER
LENA NG

I OPENED MY EYES and looked into the hallowed sky. I took my first breath, the desperate gasp of air as one struggles against drowning. The cavernous rumble of thunder rattled the table beneath me, trembling my bones. Above was a ragged hole in the roof; broken gray wooden slats framed the dark. Lightning, violent firelight, sliced the sky, across the black emptiness of the night.

And again it hit me.

A surge of lightning's raw power flooded my body. It raced through my blood, and quickened fire flowed through and ignited my heart, deitic light emanating from my eyes. The smell of burning. My back arched off the table, my head thrown back in the ecstasy of birth.

My birth.

I screamed.

She's alive, I heard shouted. A man's triumphant voice. The pounding of rapid footfalls ascending on stairs. The loosening of the restraints that bound me. I shivered as the bitter wind, swept in from the ocean below, cooled the sweat on my skin, the smell of brine in the air. A rough blanket was thrown over me, the wool scratching my thin body. Strong masculine hands were careful to wrap the blanket around me to my chin, the rough stubble on his square jaw scratching the top of my head.

He looked down at me while rubbing my shoulders and the sides of my arms. Dark eyes with long lashes which flashed with an intellectual fire. He kissed my forehead. "You're alive," he said as he put his arms around me. I started crying, my body shaking from the shock of sudden awakening.

"Hush, love," he said, as he steered me down the slatted wooden stairs. "It's been a long night." I leaned against him.

My legs trembled on the gray, rickety stairs, a faun learning its first steps. At its base, he led me through a large work room with an array of glass beakers and specimen jars on shelves, and thick books with titles in unfamiliar languages enclosed in glass cabinets.

We moved through the house, cluttered with gadgets and curiosities, until he stopped outside of a small bedroom. "You may call me Victor," he said. "Or–" he seemed to like another idea, "you may call me Father."

The steam rose from the hot water in the large tub. Lying there, the warm water cradled me. I looked down the length of my body. Stitches. My body criss-crossed with stitches. My knee connected to my leg, held together with large, uneven threads. My hand sewn onto my wrist, tight zigzags of silk holding it in place. My throat lacerated with jagged sutures. I touched the raised marks and winced when a blunt, throbbing ache rose from the wounds. A patchwork doll. A clockwork doll. A creation.

After the bath, I spent time examining my face in the mirror. My face, pale, thin, the sharp edge of cheekbones cutting into the air. Over-large eyes, a wasting doll's eyes on a wasting doll's face. But no spark of recognition. Who am I? Do I have a past? I know only of the present, a rag-doll girl sewn by the hands of her maker.

After I had dressed, I stood before my new father. He checked my teeth, bent my arms, felt my ribs, and manipulated my ankles before he nodded in satisfaction. "Now, child," he said, "what shall we call you?"

"May I choose my own name?"

A stern expression crossed his face. "Children do not name themselves." He thought for a moment. "You shall be named Eve."

"Is there an Adam?"

He smiled but did not say anything.

A sound awoke me in the night. It was a subdued sound, like a muted whimper of pain, a sound carried by the wind. Despite the heavy down blanket covering me, I shivered. The low sound started again, like crying, a sound of loneliness and fear. I knew both of those feelings. Slowly, the sound pulled me from the bed, and after I put on some slippers, I crept across the stone floor out of my room.

The sound led me down a dark hallway. I shrank back from the death grin of a monkey's skull, encased within a glass cabinet, his sharp incisors in an eternal snarl. The shadows played on the wall, only starlight and the sound of soft weeping guiding my way. The sound carried me through room after room; through the darkly-striped parlor, through the imposing, tome-filled library with books dusty and ancient, through the green-carpeted breakfast room, through a room draped only in eerie red. It drew me down one winding staircase after another, walls lined with portraits of pinned butterflies or splayed stick insects, until I reached a heavy, wooden door. I used all my strength to pull it open, the door's edge scraping against the uneven floor.

The air was chill in the stone room the size of a cell. The flickering torch was burning down but there was enough light to still see him. A shirtless giant of a man crouched in a corner of a dungeon, a sheen on the skin of his back. I caught the gleam of an eye but he hid his face behind his long hair and turned away, as though too ashamed of his wretchedness to let me gaze upon him. The woeful sound started again though he clamped a hand over his mouth to stifle it. As I grew closer, I saw the whitened scars on his back and his trembling. My heart was too filled with pity to feel fear.

"Shhh," I said. "You're not alone anymore. I'm here."

The chains around his ankles rattled as he pulled himself deeper into the corner. Tentatively, I placed a hand on his broad back. His skin was cold, too cold, icy from the damp of his sweat. "Who are you? What is your name?" Only the shaking of his heavy head answered me.

"Wait," I said, "I have something for you."

I made my way back to my room, my slippers making a quick,

quiet swish against the slate floor. I pulled the duvet from the bed, bundled it in my arms, and tried not to let it drag on the slate as I went back to the dungeon.

The huddled man had not moved since I left him. But the weeping had stopped, and in its place, a waiting silence, a watchful silence though his face remained hidden. I crouched down and wrapped the blanket around him, adjusting and arranging it so it covered the entirety of his broad shoulders. As I turned to go, a large hand gently encircled my wrist. I felt his thumb softly tracing the criss-crossing of stitches where my hand joined my arm. And, to my surprise, I saw the same stitching binding his own wrist.

When he finally spoke, his voice was rough and hoarse, as though he had not spoken for many days. "Thank you for your kindness." He released me and I pulled away to return to my room for an uneasy night.

Father, a faint stubble on his face and wrapped in a paisley robe, was already seated, newspaper open over the damask tablecloth, as I took my place at the breakfast table. He put a plate of thin-sliced buttered bread in front of me.

The strangeness of the previous night remained upon me. "Father," I said as I stared at the toast, "I saw the man chained in the dungeon. Why do you hold him prisoner?"

The newspaper made a quiet crackle as he slowly turned a page. "I see he was given a blanket during his punishment. Today, he is much better behaved," he said without looking up from the headlines.

"What did he do?"

"He wants to leave his father." He turned his attention away from the paper and looked with amusement at my astonishment. "Yes. A child, like you. My first. A child with no gratitude, with a terrible temper, who hasn't yet learned to obey." A shadow passed over the table and Father glanced towards the door. "Eve," my father said, "you once asked if there was an Adam. There he is." He nodded to a looming shape in the doorway. "You were made for him."

The man, the same hulking form from the dungeon, looked up

and his long hair fell away from face. When I caught a glimpse of him, the air rushed from my chest.

His face. The horror of his face.

Misshapen. Scars crossing its broad landscape, as though his face was stitched together in parts by some demonic toymaker. Eyes flat and animal. Nose broad and broken.

My hands made their way to cover my mouth. Too horrified to scream, still a sound pushed its way from my throat. I moved away from the table. I felt myself falling, and in a blur, he darted from the doorway and across the room. His large arms encircled my waist. I could feel his heart hammering out from his chest, thumping against my skin, as his arms tightened into an embrace.

He lifted me, and with a contradictory gentleness, he carried me from the breakfast room back to my room.

You were made for him.

He kneeled beside the bed, his heavy chin resting on the wool blanket. I pushed myself until my back pressed against the hard wall. His flat, empty eyes traveled from the top of my head, over my hazel eyes, nose, lips, down to my sharp chin, and back to my eyes again.

His nostrils started flaring. They moved inward and outward in a quick, curious motion and they reminded me of the inquisitive movement of a questing hound.

I couldn't help it. I started giggling, nervous but with startled humor. My shoulders trembled from trying to hold in the laughter. His monstrous face started to move towards me, closer, closer, until I felt the brush of his nose on my cheek. I could feel those flaring nostrils smelling my skin and it tickled.

Those nostrils moved down over my cheek, along the curve of my neck, and deep breaths took in the smell of the skin of my shoulders.

After this peculiar acquaintance, again the man-creature rested his chin on the lumpy mattress and regarded me. As I looked at him with the aftermath of giggles on my face, he tilted his own head to the side. The corners of his lips pulled upward and I couldn't believe the brightness of his smile.

It was as though an inner sun dawned upon him. Two deep

dimples indented his cheeks. It lent a sweetness to the strangeness of his appearance. I couldn't help but smile back, and next thing I knew, I was scratching him behind his large ear.

This made him smile wider and he took in a deep breath, enjoying this little bliss. "Close your eyes," he whispered.

"Why?"

"Because when you see me with your eyes, I'm ugly. A deformed, hideous monster. But if you try to see me with your heart, I might have a chance to be beautiful."

My brow creased as I took a moment to think about what he said. Would I give him that chance? Slowly I closed my eyes. He spoke to me, with that deep, rough voice of his, a voice which could cast a spell. He spoke of dying roses; of princes trapped in the bodies of beasts; of curses broken by true love's kiss.

As he spoke, I fell into a trance, half-sleeping, half-dreaming. Still with closed eyes, I touched his cheek. It was damp; the tears flowed from his eyes but he didn't stop speaking. I brushed his throat and felt him swallow. His voice caught under my hand but still he spoke. My waking dream was of stardust and shadows and the faint light of hope.

The voice stopped.

"Enough now," another voice said. I opened my eyes to see Father in my room. He pulled the monster away from me. But now the monster's face seemed more pitiable than horrible with an odd, bewildering beauty. As though I could see through him, into him, seeing with my heart into his own. Father continued to the monster, "I did what you asked. Now you must do what I ask."

The monster rose. With a forced submissiveness tinged with resentment, he asked, "To live, to die, and to live again? To be reborn again and again as a side-show performance, to demonstrate the agony of birth and death in front of a baying audience?"

"You are my legacy. We will demonstrate to the world that man has conquered death."

"And your name will live forever." The monster's voice was bitter, resigned at the hopelessness of his fate. "In this life, I'm a caged circus animal. In another life, I was a man."

Father's mouth moved into a cynical smile. "You are one still. A resurrection man. You will keep your promise."

The monster bent his head and lowered his voice so only my ears could hear. "For you, I will."

I saw a light of triumph in Father's eyes. I realized the monster – the man he claimed was his child – was in actuality his slave.

He looked at me before he died. In a tank filled with salt water, surrounded by the merciless eyes of men of science, he drowned. My poor monster, fear and pain in his eyes, mouth open and silently screaming for air for too many agonizing minutes. At last he relaxed and floated submerged in the glass cylindrical tank.

Father turned a lever and the water slowly drained from the tank until the body rested at its glass bottom. He addressed his small audience of six learned men, each well-dressed, each peering into the tank, taking a close look at the body, some with expressions of horror, some with skepticism. "It may seem I've committed murder. But he was already dead. And now he will live again."

Father pulled on a rope, which by a system of pulleys, hoisted the body from the tank. He carefully lowered it to the worktable and busied himself attaching wires and electrodes to the unmoving man. He gestured to his audience. "Check for yourself that he is dead." The men felt for pulses and put ears to chest but felt and heard no heartbeat. Father continued. "Tonight brings a storm. And with it, new life."

As if to answer him, from outside, a flash of light filled the leaded windows. Thunder cracked overhead. A sizzle as the lightning's energy traveled down metal and into flesh. The smell of smoke. The body seized and spasmed, the jaw clenched, cords stood out from the neck, and hands twisted into fists. The pain of current surging through his body. The monster opened his mouth and howled.

The medical men drew away from the animated body and stared in stunned silence.

Father could no longer hold his patience. "Is this not a miracle?"

Another brief silence but one that crackled. "You waste our time with magic tricks," one man finally exploded. "A cheap illusion."

"What have you to gain by making us look like fools?" another shouted.

Father's mouth was opened but nothing emerged. This was a reaction he did not anticipate. My monster's torture and suffering denounced as deceit.

"We can run away." I rested my cheek against a knotted shoulder as we huddled on the dungeon's stone floor.

He held his head in his large hands, the chains around his wrists rubbing them raw. My monster's voice turned bleak. "I've run away before. But the outside world abhors and spurns me. Loneliness has always brought me back. You were created for the price of my cooperation. A companion for someone like me, fashioned the way I have been fashioned, who would understand."

My arms tightened around him. "I am your chains."

He shook his head. "My words are my chains. He controlled me using pain and fear. Now he controls me through my promise."

But I couldn't stand to watch him die again. The desperate helplessness of watching someone you care for hurt. The violence of being thrown into the afterlife's abyss. The horror and trauma of birth and death, the two entwined. "I made no promise. He has no hold on me. I'll leave. Tonight. I know you will find me." Before he could object, I rose and hastened to my room. The howling wind rattled the windows, almost obscuring the sounds of the ocean's waves crashing below. I rummaged through the drawers and threw on some heavier clothes.

Quickly and silently, I made my way through the house. Did it matter where I went? Somehow I trusted he would come for me. Anywhere would be better, for both of us. But before I could escape, a low voice in the parlor stopped me. "Where do you think you're going?" From the corner of my eye, I saw Father rising from his leather chair. The humiliation of the earlier events was still on his face, giving him a sinister cast.

I turned to confront him, defiance sharpening my voice. "Is this why I'm here? To subdue him into slavery? I won't."

"What choice do you have?" He took two steps towards me. "I've devoted myself to my work. And now that I've achieved the impossible, no one will believe me. I will show them. I will make them believe. And you will help me." His voice rose. "I won't let you stand in the way of my dreams!" His hand was raised, about to strike.

Emerging from the shadows, the chains around his limbs broken, the monster flung himself across the room. Pent-up bitterness and anger at a father's betrayal fueled the struggle for one; for the other, rage at a child's rebellion. The breaking of leaded window glass. A scream. Father's hands grasped the window sill as he tried not to fall. With flailing desperation, he seized upon the monster's broken chains. The force of his weight dragged them both into the night.

Heart hammering, I ran to the window. Leaning out, instead of two, I saw one bent and broken body at the cliff's base. The rain punished me as I raced from the house. I searched, but found only one body, a large body covered in scars, broken by jagged rocks. In the distance, I saw a dark shape sink beneath the waves into the ocean. With an unnatural strength, the strength of the undead, I dragged my unfortunate monster's body from the cliff back to the house.

I strapped him down onto the table, his body cold and lifeless. The lightning lit up the sky. I attached the electrodes to his skull, neck, chest, directly over his heart.

I gazed upon his face. His beautiful misshapen face. Again the lightning flashed and surged, striking the lightning rod, flowing down the wires to his unmoving body. The power rushed into and through him; his muscles clenched and he tensed off the table.

Once I had been made for him. Now I made him for me.

Suddenly his arms were around me and he awoke with my kiss.

Western literature has continually done a disservice to women, stunting their true potential, their tragedies often not even allowed to be tragic for themselves, but instead for the development of another (usually male) character. The few instances where intelligent, bright, complex women shine exist as confusing islands in a sea of discontent. In this poem, alternative futures are proposed, tone varying in keeping with their overall tale to more outlandish breakaways. After all, if a female character can have her own future, she can do whatever she likes, her limit only being hers and our imagination. So here, women do their own rescuing, are rescued by each other, their intelligence isn't wasted, pointless death is avoided, and tragedy is overcome or bypassed entirely.

A CALL TO ARMS
J M CYRUS

To all my sisters and mothers who came before me
Who had to die or live miserably
All for the benefit or growth of a man
When they had so much more to give and to be.

Consider this my eulogy
My call to arms
My alternate history
An alternative future for them all
My literary forebears
(Outside of copyright)

So let me begin
Without any more ado
To give these women their fair due.
Pandora let her brother open the box,
Dido trusted in herself,

Jocasta thought the boy looked too familiar, and ruled alone
Penelope waited no more, and had her own adventure,
Circe turned to organic farming,
And all those Greek tragic ladies,
Iphigenia, Clytemnestra, Deianara,
Medea, Cassandra, Hecuba
Electra, Agave, Briseis
Chriseis,
The Trojan Women,
The Bacchae,
Who under chorus and duress,
Were so disadvantaged,
Lady Liberty herself came along and took them to join the Valkyries.

Actually
Actually
Hold on
Let's give *all* these women
Doomed to insanity
Insecurity
And undue scrutiny
A life they never had.

Imagination is our only limit
So let us go
On and up.

Helen of Troy became a scholar,
Medusa got famous on the internet,
Patient Griselda lost her patience,
Ophelia moved the whole family far away,
Cordelia sent Lear to see a psychotherapist,
Hero found her calling in a library,
Lavinia and Cleopatra were avenging superheroes,
And Desdemona fired Iago from the palace with a cannon,

Juliet never went to that party,
But stayed home and wrote fanfiction,
The Lady of Shallot took a nap instead,
And also some antibiotics.

Anne Eliot sailed the seas, and became a pirate,
Bertha Mason stayed in Jamaica,
Took some serotonin,
Frankenstein's monster's bride escaped
And became a plastic surgeon
(actually finishing her degree)
And Tess, poor Tess, went to school.

Miss Havisham found she loved to paint, and loved anew,
Anna Karenina found a nice therapist,
And some kindred spirits,
Cathy never went to London,
Eliza Doolittle started a charity for street urchins,
And got a blue plaque too,
The ladies of the night fostered Lucy Westenra,
And she lived under the aurora borealis, and
Mrs Hudson got her own story.

And those operatic ladies with cold hands and broken hearts,
You could all do so much better,
Aida and Cio-Cio San rescued themselves
Starting a business empire,
Roping in Giselle and Mimi too.

Let us not forget our Lady Mary,
And Mary Magdalen,
And poor Delilah, Bathsheba, Susanna and Jezebel,
Ruth and Salome,
And Eve. Oh Eve.

To the countless women,
Doomed to weep for men at war
Or watch from tenement doors
Babies on their hips and dinner in the oven,
Who only existed to serve,
To keep the men fed and watered
Whose fate ended with a whisper not a cry,
I feel for you too,
My heart cries for you,
My brain burns for you.

And to all you ladies still in copyright,
Just you wait,
You know who you are,
You will get your chance soon.
Let the murmuration become a roar.

Two young children, Hansel and Gretel, were abandoned in a forest by their father and stepmother. Lost and hungry, they wandered about until they came upon a house made of gingerbread and candy. The siblings began to devour the house, munching on the doors, windows and walls, and leaving a mess of crumbs in their wake. The house belonged to a recluse. Seeing her home destroyed made her furious. She locked Hansel up and put Gretel to work. Until one day, Gretel shoved her into the oven, freed Hansel and stole all of the woman's savings before escaping. A happy ending for the two children, sure, but what of the woman? Her house had been eaten, her savings stolen, her face was scarred and her oven smelled of burned hair! Yet, she somehow remains the sole villain of the story – the bad/ ugly/evil/monstrous witch. That needed changing, hence this story.

MY GRATITUDE JOURNAL
APARNA KAPUR

This
GRATITUDE JOURNAL
belongs to
<u>someone who is filling it under protest.</u>

DAY 1 — Today, I am grateful for: my therapist, who bought me this journal despite my protests, after pointing out that I tend to focus on the negative side of things. If *you* can discover the positive side of having your house eaten, your body shoved in an oven, and having all your life savings stolen, I'll give you free cakes for life.

DAY 2 — Today, I am grateful for: the fact that children are not too smart and that girl Gretel thought that I would fit in an oven and wouldn't be able to get myself out of one in time to prevent myself from getting burned to a crisp.

DAY 3 — Today, I am grateful for: my skills; for the fact that I can bake a cake any size, a biscuit of any shape, craft a layer of sugar so thin and delicate that it looks like lace; and that I have the energy to spend upwards of ten hours a day in the kitchen working on my craft with nothing for company but Run the Jewels albums.

DAY 5 — Today, I am grateful for: my recovery. My burns are nearly completely healed and yesterday I managed to spend four full hours without thinking of the unfortunate Hansel-Gretel incident.

DAY 6 — Today, I am grateful for: the patience that kept me from physically attacking the young man in the grocery store who said that my house getting destroyed by those two maggoty children was my own fault, and that by making it so delicious I was 'asking for it.' I am less grateful that I placed a kg of salt in his bag so he would set off the burglar alarm on his way out. I am also grateful that the price of butter hasn't gone up because when I saw that the amount I needed was called a child size pack, I had to buy a bigger pack. I think I'll stick to buying bigger packs in general now. No harm in baking cakes and cookies in quantities that children won't be able to consume.

DAY 7 — Today, I am grateful for: how delicious and popular desserts are. I've been getting so many orders for cakes and muffins and tarts. At this rate, I'll be able to make back at least some of what those two nasty kids stole from me after pushing me into an oven. It hasn't been easy to make up my life savings but if I have to focus on the positive, I suppose I'll be halfway there in another, well, 6-7 weeks.

DAY 11 — Today, I am grateful for: my house being in the woods. The woods are so full of trees and birds and wildflowers, and <u>so devoid of children</u>.

DAY 12 — Today, I am grateful for: human civilization and how far away it is from the wilderness. A fellow sorceress who stays at the edge of the forest was apparently asked to remain inside her house for an entire day because some school of human children had come for a 'forest-bathing' event. (I am also grateful that I don't have the sort of lifestyle that requires me to hear the term forest-bathing.) Why do these small creatures get to dictate the actions of people who have been in this world for decades longer than them? *They* should be the ones confined to their houses, not us!

DAY 15 — Today, I am grateful for: having understanding friends. I went to visit the woodcarver for lunch, but when I was about to knock on his door, I noticed a pair of shoes near his welcome mat. The shoes were blue with brown laces and very clearly belonged to someone with small feet – someone like a child! My hands went cold and I started to sweat. I retreated and was only able to breathe easy when I was inside my own house. When I sent word to the woodcarver later, explaining and apologizing, he came over with soup and bread.

DAY 16 — Today, I am grateful for: my taste in food. Specifically, that I don't enjoy eating sweet things! What would I have done if I had a sweet tooth? I would have been constantly hungry, and my house would have taken twice as long to rebuild. But I still wouldn't have EATEN BITS OF SOMEONE'S HOUSE LIKE SOME OTHER PEOPLE.

DAY 17 — Today, I am grateful for: that I managed to think of an excuse to leave Mr and Mrs Mole's house. I went to deliver a gigantic cake to them, and they were so excited about it that when they invited me in for a cup of tea, I agreed. But everything in their house was so tiny. They're exactly the sort of chairs, shelves, hats and teacups that children would use. I shuddered as soon as I saw it and then jumped out of the door, yelling "I HAVE LEFT THE OVEN ON AND I CAN SMELL BURNING." I'm sure they bought it but it's been a harrowing day.

DAY 18 — Today, I am grateful for: things that are not cats. This morning, I was on my way back home when I heard a child crying. I began running away from the sound without a second's thought, just hearing my racing heart and nothing else. All I was thinking was I did nothing to make this child cry, I want to be as far away from it as possible, and no one will believe me when I tell them I was the one who was running away in this situation. I was at the gate of my house, when out jumped a tabby cat, yowling exactly like a small child. First, I breathed a sigh of relief. Then, I gave the cat the scowl-iest look I could muster. Ridiculous creature! Why did it sound exactly like a child? What was it doing in the forest? Doesn't it know the forest is full of wild animals? Why can't it just stay home with its parents like all the other children cats.

DAY 21 — Today, I am grateful for: a diagnosis. My therapist says my experiences have led me to develop a fear of children. I wouldn't call it a fear but I'm certainly wary of them and maybe now that I know that, I can tell people I have a medical reason when I ask them to please keep their children far away from me. I was more confused when she said that it has led to an avoidance of small things altogether. But then I realized she was right! I even looked at my notebook and noticed that I haven't made a cupcake or a tartlet in weeks. And you know what? It's fine! I am not going to make any 'child size' things anymore. Everything is going to be bigger, better, grander. Let children be intimidated by my desserts and by the quantities of my puddings.

DAY 23 — Today, I am grateful for: the reconstruction of my house finally being completed. I'm especially proud of the hard caramel window frames (which could crack a child's tooth). I've put in a heavy dark chocolate door on the outside. Hopefully that will discourage a repeat of the Hansel-Gretel situation; I've heard that children don't like dark chocolate. I hope that's true. I'd ask one myself, but a year's supply of vanilla sprigs wouldn't be enough of an incentive to get me to talk to a child.

DAY 24 — Today, I am grateful for: honesty. Specifically, the honesty of the people I met at the stream who called me a 'child-eater.' That was how I discovered that, all this time, people have been thinking that I EAT CHILDREN!? What! I explained to them that I'd thought I was doing a good thing, letting Hansel and Gretel work off their punishment without complaining to their parents. I told them I was using Hansel as a recipe tester, not fattening him up! What would give people that idea. And I also told them Gretel was helping me in the kitchen which, I thought at the time, was a pretty sweet gig. Pun intended. I would have had Hansel help me in the kitchen too, except he knocked five things over while walking into the house and there's no room for that sort of clumsiness in my kitchen. I also told the people at the stream that I now knew that what I'd done was, technically, kidnapping. And even though I hadn't realized it at the time, I dealt with the consequences during my three months in a correctional facility. I told them, in no uncertain terms, that I never – not in the past, present or future – want to eat a child. They still walked away from the stream pretty quickly, though. I can't understand other people at all!

DAY 26 — Today, I am grateful for: having a new goal to work towards. And it is a goal that will help me focus on huge, significant things rather than the unnerving small ones that have been following me everywhere. I will create a grand chocolate river. It will begin at the cliff-face a few hundred meters away, and flow through the forest, ending in a huge pool behind my house. It is not a wholly original idea, I know, and has been used to excellent effect in the past, but this one will be right by my house and there is nothing like it in and around these woods. I will have to pause building back my savings for a little bit because this will be expensive, but it will also be worth it. This river shall be my masterpiece!

DAY 31 — Today, I am grateful for: good ideas. I was discussing the river with the woodcarver, and I told him about the sign I wanted to put up. "Not that signs have kept children away in the past," I added.

"The last two ate up the 'DO NOT EAT' sign that I'd put up outside the house." And that's when he said, "How about a sign made from something people *can't* eat?" A non-edible sign! It's such a simple solution but I never would have thought of it on my own.

DAY 32 — Today, I am grateful for: the satisfaction I can get from a hard day's work. My river is starting to take shape. I've started laying the chocolate mud, and I have created several stones and structures of milk solids that will lie at the bottom of the river. I have also made the mold for my sugar rocks. It will start with a waterfall at the cliff and, by the time it culminates in the pool, it will have become a rich, thick, sweet mixture.

DAY 41 — Today, I am grateful for: <u>my chocolate river</u>. It is complete and it is a work of art. A beautiful, gushing, deep brown work of art. It also has a secret advantage I just thought of earlier today. If I were to throw something – say, an annoying journal that I am supposed to write in every single day – into this river, there is little chance that anyone – say, a persistent therapist with too many questions – will find it. Speaking of, I am also grateful that this will be the last time I will write in the gratitude journal. And almost as good as the river, is the sign (that you can't eat) beside it that reads, in letters immense enough that they could be seen from space:

NO CHILDREN ALLOWED!

Three Make a Tiger is a re-envisioning of the fate of Lady Trieu, a female warrior folk figure from Vietnamese legends whom Americans may recognize from her adaptation in Watchmen. In the original tale, Lady Trieu leads a rebellion against the Wu Kingdom (an ancient Chinese kingdom), but tragically fails to capture victory as she fought alone. She ultimately commits suicide. In this story we ask: What if she were not alone? In fact, what if she were joined by a brother who can combine her fierceness with strategy, and by a sister-in-law (whom she actually kills in the original tale), who is her equal but also her opposite? The title here comes from a Chinese idiom: 三人成虎, which can be translated as "Three People Make a Tiger" or "Three People Can Create a Tiger." It means that even unbelievable rumors will catch on if enough people believe them, though here it's intended to have multiple meanings.

THREE MAKE A TIGER
NHU LE

The Trieu twins were born under the same stars, but were as different as the moon and the sun.

Trieu Quoc Dat thought ten sentences and spoke one. Trieu Au yelled each from the top of her lungs as they occurred to her.

Trieu Quoc Dat appealed to corrupt merchants to lower their prices with arguments of long-term gains and legacy. Trieu Au pilfered away their waist pouches and scattered their gold into the crowd of aggrieved customers.

In their twentieth year, Trieu Quoc Dat took Minh Nhan, a dutiful and simple village girl, to be his wife. His sister smiled, and at their wedding declared herself to be the property of no man – unlike her new sister-in-law.

"What troubles have you made today?" Trieu Au's 'sister' says as she unbolts the gate.

"Enough," Trieu Au replies. She tosses a folded handkerchief in Minh Nhan's direction and gives a mock curtsy.

The fabric lands in Minh Nhan's hand with a jangle, and she pulls the folds apart to reveal a handful of coins. Their gleaming silver surface catches the light of the fading sun.

Trieu Au grins at Minh Nhan's dumbfounded expression, and steps around her and towards their shared home.

It is a simple compound, consisting of only a yard for the livestock and one room bisected by a folding screen. The Trieu family name has a long and respected history in the village, but more for the individual attributes of their line than its material attributes.

Minh Nhan yanks Trieu Au back by the arm. As she's spun around, Minh Nhan thrusts the handkerchief back at her.

"That cloth is Wu-make," Minh Nhan says, her fierce eyes alight like amber. "Return it to the soldier you took it from."

Trieu Au scoffs. "That *commander's* passed out on the inn floor, after glutting himself on rice wine that he'd freely stolen. He won't miss it."

"And what if he does? Will you bring the Wu army down on our heads? Or the heads of others in this village? You may have no fears and no responsibilities, but the rest of us are not so frivolous."

"Then perhaps, like me, you all should discard those fears and responsibilities." Trieu Au's hands clench down on the handkerchief. "But fine. If you're so afraid, I'll use it myself." She turns back again to their home.

"If you are seeking dinner, then none was kept for you," Minh Nhan says to her back.

Trieu Au freezes. Then she whirls around. "Do you enjoy these petty tricks, sister-in-law? You marry into *our* household, feed and clothe yourself with *our* money, and yet you–"

"They are not *tricks*. If you wish to eat, then you must work. Outside or inside this household, that is the way of things."

"I do *not*–"

"Yes, I remember, you 'do not imitate others, bow your head, stoop over, and be a slave, resigned to menial housework.' You were meant to 'ride the wind and walk the waves,'" Minh Nhan says, quoting word for word what Trieu Au declared the first time Minh Nhan had asked for her assistance. "But if you will not do 'menial housework' like chopping firewood or tending the stove, then it is right that you go hungry."

Trieu Au storms inside to find her brother and complain about his shrew of a wife.

The rule of the Wu king was harsh, and the people of Cuu Chan suffered many indignities.

Both Trieu twins abhorred the invaders and burned to protect their neighbors, but could not agree on a course of action.

"We cannot just let them keep stealing from us – trampling our fields, eating our food, drinking our wine, bothering our women, beating up our men. We ought to gather all able-bodied men in this village and drive them off!"

"And what if they come back with ten thousand more men? Twenty thousand more men?" her brother says with a smile, always too reasonable. "I've told you, the proper petitions have been sent to the king. He has received so many appeals that he will soon have no choice but to send a more benevolent governor."

Trieu Au rolls her eyes. "So that we can continue to scrape our heads on the floor?"

"So that our heads can stay on our shoulders and not roll on the floor after the executioner's ax. Do you not agree, Minh Nhan?"

Minh Nhan looks up. Trieu Au scoffs before she can speak.

"Why bother asking her? As we have everything we want, why ought we concern ourselves with anything else, right, sister?"

Quoc Dat frowns, as he often does when Trieu Au talks about his wife. She resigns herself to his lecture.

Minh Nhan looks back down without speaking.

In the morning, Trieu Au and Minh Nhan walk together – but separately, for Trieu Au makes sure to walk several paces in front of her – to the market square.

They hear the cries of the women kneeling before they see the two bodies strung up on the gallows.

Trieu Au recognizes them. No doubt Minh Nhan does too. Theirs is a small village. The dead men are the innkeeper and his serving boy.

The notice next to their bodies state their crime as theft. But that is self-evident enough; all four of their hands have been chopped off.

Trieu Au's body tightens with anger, like a bow pulled taut. Her eyes flick across the scene, but that coward of a commander from yesterday is nowhere to be seen.

Minh Nhan puts her hand on Trieu Au's arm. She shakes her off and storms away.

It turns out, Trieu Au has no need to search for the commander.

He comes to her.

His smarmy smile crawls down her throat. She pulls her saber slowly from where it's fastened on her waist and narrows her eyes at him.

"I remember you from the inn," he says. His words are formed misshapen, like they always are from the mouths of the invaders; they ring ugly and sharp in her ears. "Give back my money, little girl, and I'll send you to join those men with an easy death."

Her hand tightens on her saber's hilt. "If you knew they were not guilty of theft, then why did you convict them?"

His beard twitches, hiding a smile. "But isn't carelessness towards their customers still a crime? And how else was I to find the perpetrator?" he says. "A criminal who does such a thing would no doubt be stricken with anger and fear when faced with the potential consequences of their actions – and I was right, wasn't I?"

Trieu Au wants to spit in his intelligent, vicious face.

Minh Nhan was right. She shouldn't have caused trouble with him.

The only option now is to kill him. She can run, she knows, but then he will simply mobilize the Wu soldiers and punish her entire clan.

But if she *does* kill him, they might still figure out who did it and come after her and her brother–

The commander lunges at her, a dagger appearing from deep within his sleeves in a flash. She dodges – but not fast enough. The blade slices into the side of her body. She grunts, and rolls away.

They stand facing each other, both panting.

Her blood drips on the dirt road. The commander smiles.

Trieu Au grins back, baring all her teeth. He's made her decision for her.

She throws herself at him. He pulls his dagger up for protection, but her left hand strikes hard on his dominant hand. On instinct his fingers convulse open, and his weapon slides out of his grip. Her right hand holds tight onto her saber and plunges it deep into his chest. He gives a gurgling gasp, and she twists, wrenches the saber up, down. Pulls it out.

His body slides to the ground with a thump.

Trieu Au breathes hard as she stares down at the lifeless body. His still-warm blood drips down her chest and clings to her skin.

She'll need to dispose of his body and burn these clothes without anyone seeing her. The best route would be–

A gasp in front of her. She looks from the body up, into the wide eyes of her sister-in-law.

Trieu Au's sister-in-law was both a cruel woman and a Wu sympathizer. This so enraged Trieu Au that one day, in a dispute, she kills Minh Nhan and several other Wu soldiers, and escapes deep into the mountains.

Minh Nhan does not look away from Trieu Au and her bloody hands.

"You can't go back," Minh Nhan's voice is shaking. "Several people saw the commander leave his watchpoint and depart after you. They'll piece it together and come for Quoc Dat."

Trieu Au swallows. She recognizes the truth of what Minh Nhan says, as she had not last night.

"Fine, I'll run," she says, though her heart clenches thinking about never seeing her twin brother again. They have never been apart a day in their lives.

"Do you think that'll work?" Minh Nhan says shrilly. "They'll just take him instead of you! I *told* you–"

"Then what do you propose we do?" Trieu Au bites out.

Minh Nhan's throat closes with a clack. It bobs.

"If... If they... If they think I defended him and your brother forswears you as a result, then – they might leave him alone."

There's fear in her eyes – and courage. Minh Nhan takes two dazed steps forward, until her feet touch the dagger lying next to the commander's body. She picks it up.

Trieu Au takes a slow step back, and raises her saber. But the weapon is slack in her hands.

She *hates* Minh Nhan, has hated her from the first. But Quoc Dat had brought her into their family. He had *chosen* to marry her.

With a quick motion, Minh Nhan raises the dagger – and cuts her arm deep enough that blood soaks the fabric of her sleeve.

Trieu Au stifles a surprised cry.

Minh Nhan removes her now-bloody outer robe, and bends down to strip the commander's robe from his body also. Then she mingles their clothes together, so that his blood seeps through both pieces of fabric.

Finally, she hooks her arms beneath the man's armpits, and glares at Trieu Au.

"Make yourself useful and pick up the other half of his body," she says. "We'll bury it where no one can find him. Then we'll escape deep into the mountains. With any luck, they'll think you killed him and me and have hidden both our bodies. Quoc Dat, as the other wronged party, ought to be spared. Once it's safe, we'll send him a message."

Trieu Au realizes she's staring. She shakes herself, tucks away her saber after a cursory wipe of its bloody blade against the dead man's clothes, and picks up his legs as Minh Nhan instructs.

They disappear into the trees.

Trieu Au thrives in the mountains. Her strength and bravery spread across Cuu Chan prefecture, and she gathers many followers fleeing the cruel rule of the Wu invaders.

"I didn't think you'd be so handy in the forest," Trieu Au can't help blurting out when she returns from hunting. There is a small fire in the middle of the clearing. Beside the fire sits a pile of mushrooms Minh Nhan must have picked.

Minh Nhan snorts. "How do you think poor village orphans survive long enough to meet their husband, Trieu Au?"

Trieu Au can't say she's ever thought about it.

Later, Minh Nhan stares sightless at the roasted rabbit haunch in her hands. "I hope Quoc Dat will be all right by himself," she says.

Trieu Au looks awkwardly at her. "Brother has a clever tongue and fine survival instincts, I'm sure he will emerge unscathed," she finally replies.

She can't say she'd ever thought much about their relationship. Quoc Dat had declared out of nowhere one day that it was time for him to marry, then came back with Minh Nhan in tow three days after that. She'd rather thought that Quoc Dat had chosen Minh Nhan on the streets randomly, after deciding that he wanted better meals than the twins could make or purchase.

Trieu Au doesn't think that anymore.

Her brother is waiting just behind the gate when they approach.

As Trieu Au slides in through the unbolted entrance, she notes the sword glinting in Quoc Dat's hand and approves of the precaution.

Their home is no worse for wear from their long absence. The same thatched roof. The same fat chickens asleep in their enclosure. The same rickety windows.

Trieu Au faces the building, and counts to thirty. When she hits zero, she turns back around.

Quoc Dat and Minh Nhan have separated, but her cheeks are wet and he maintains a hold on her arm.

"So. Did you or did you not think I'd killed your wife before you got my message?" Trieu Au says with a grin. A star fruit and a dead rooster, left outside the compound. Minh Nhan's favorite fruit, and the animal Quoc Dat says she most closely resembles when shouting about the Wu.

Quoc Dat laughs. "You wouldn't have. You'd never hurt your people," he says dismissively.

He leads the way in.

Once they are all settled on the mat, Minh Nhan pours them each a cup of tea, then takes a seat beside and a little behind her husband.

"How is the situation in the village?" Trieu Au asks.

Quoc Dat shakes his head. "Poor. They have concluded that their commander's death was the work of a savage and crazy woman and spared me and the rest of the village." He slides his eyes over to Trieu Au, who works not to preen at that description. "*But,*" he emphasizes, his voice hardening, "his death has spooked the remaining soldiers. The Wu king has responded by deploying more soldiers. Their greater numbers have made life even more difficult for us."

Trieu Au's amusement dissipates instantly. She fights to clench down on any guilt. This is the work of the invaders. Not hers.

As always, her brother reads her too well. His gaze softens. "The circumstances are unexpected. But we can work to minimize its effects, if you will listen to my request."

"Always," Trieu Au says immediately.

"There are families who are suffering, who have daughters garnering undesirable attention and sons convicted of false crimes. Will you take them into the mountains as well? Keep them safe?"

Trieu Au hesitates. "The mountains are a wild place. It is difficult enough for me to look after Minh Nhan, how will I protect and provide for them as well?"

"As long as they are prepared to protect and provide for each other, we can teach them the skills they need," Minh Nhan cuts in. Trieu Au had not realized she'd been listening. "If they have nowhere else to go, we will take them in."

Quoc Dat nods. He seems unsurprised by his wife's opinion.

"I will coordinate their departure," he says.

They spend much of the rest of the night in discussion. Where Quoc Dat can drop them off safely. How Trieu Au will weed out the cowardly or disloyal and bring the rest to sanctuary. What preparations Minh Nhan will make for their arrival.

The Wu king dispatches his trusted retainer Luc Dan to quell the disquiet in Cuu Chan prefecture. However, his actions backfire. Trieu Quoc Dat raises his own army to resist Wu rule, and is joined by his sister Trieu Au and her followers. Their numbers swell, until their combined forces are mighty enough to reclaim large swaths of Cuu Chan territory.

Spring gives way to summer, then fall. Their mountain enclave grows to ten, to twenty, to fifty, to a hundred, to more. Trieu Au stops keeping count, simply continues to make the trek to and from Quoc Dat's drop-off point and the sanctuary.

The winter is bitter, and they cannot pass down the mountain. But thanks to Minh Nhan's careful rationing and the preservation of food via fermentation and salting in the previous seasons, they manage to keep alive all but the most frail.

When spring comes, Trieu Au descends the mountain to learn that the cooped-in, starving Wu soldiers had taken out their frustration and sated all their needs on the prefecture's population.

Trieu Au and Minh Nhan again sit down with Quoc Dat. This time, they sit around a circular table.

"Don't you think we've suffered enough humiliation?" Trieu Au says. "If we don't act now, there'll be nothing *left* for us to rise up and protect."

Quoc Dat rubs his forehead. He is thin and haggard, like he'd aged a full zodiac cycle in one winter.

"Minh Nhan?" he prompts.

Trieu Au waits for her reply.

"Even if the Wu king sends more humane retainers, too much resentment has built up with the populace for both sides to exist peacefully," Minh Nhan says, slow and careful. "But we do not have the strength or training to prevail in a direct attack."

Trieu Au opens her mouth, a protest on her tongue.

"Perhaps we might make use of other strategies. If we can also count the women and children among our numbers, then we will be equal in number to the Wu," Minh Nhan finishes.

"That's – reasonable," Trieu Au says.

"I can certainly think of some strategies, but..." Quoc Dat sighs. "How can I ask their husbands and fathers to allow them to be put in such danger?"

"They're in danger anyway," Trieu Au points out. "The best way to make them safe is to win."

They poison the drinking water of the stationed Wu soldiers.

The women and children act as messengers to warn the loyal villagers away from using the well water, and direct them to store more river water than usual in the preceding days. Some are also put to work creating small traps and weapons.

A number of the braver young women go with Trieu Au to learn how to wield a saber.

When night falls on the appointed day, Trieu Au's people descend on silent footsteps – a skill honed over their many months in the mountains – and slit the throats of the many soldiers retching in their beds or by the outhouses.

Trieu Au leads them herself, and relishes in each splatter of invader blood on her gold tunic.

The remaining Wu soldiers raise their alarm. But it is too late. Trieu Quoc Dat's people press down upon them and set their barracks and supplies aflame.

Their tattered remnants flee the village, two to three on the backs of horses frothing at the mouth.

In the morning, Trieu Quoc Dat and Trieu Au count those dead and alive, and smile grimly at each other. Behind them, Minh Nhan leads a group to board up the spoiled well and fetch river water for the required clean-up and cooking.

They press their advantage, from village to village, from town to town.

Hearing of the casualties in Cuu Chan, the Wu king sends one of his most trusted lieutenants Luc Dan to quell the unrest. He was a man of learning and moderation, and soon stabilized the Wu king's hold in the prefecture. Luc Dan and the Trieu twins fought in many a battle, without one side being able to gain on the other, and came to hold mutual respect for each other's skill and loyalty to their cause.

The rumors about the new retainer dispatched by the Wu king catch fire and spread like weed in a field of crops.

Luc Dan offers clemency to any insurgent who puts down their weapons and again takes up their farming implements. Luc Dan rules fairly in the disputes brought to him. Luc Dan rewards any valiant Wu soldier with a gentle daughter of Cuu Chan and a plot to farm, and in this clever way he tames both his men and this uncivilized land.

Trieu Au hears all this and more around *their* campfire.

"We definitely don't have the numerical advantage, and if Luc Dan keeps going, we won't even have the morale advantage!" Trieu Au bites out, then takes in a sharp hiss of breath as Minh Nhan tightens the bandages on her arm.

Their assault had failed today. She'd only barely managed to avert the pincer attack and pull off a slapdash retreat.

Minh Nhan applies more poultice. "I hear that Luc Dan does very little of what the rumors say he does," she observes.

"From who?" Trieu Au demands.

Minh Nhan arches an eyebrow. "From his property, his serving maiden, a daughter of Cuu Chan."

Trieu Au grimaces.

"I already said sorry for that," she mutters under her breath.

As Trieu Au had painfully learned over the winter, someone *treated* as property was not the same *as* property.

And like the people of Cuu Chan, they can be set free.

Minh Nhan catches Trieu Au's expression and huffs out a laugh.

"Why does everyone believe it," Trieu Au complains. "They even talk about him around *our* campfires!"

Minh Nhan turns away to grind a few herbs. "People enjoy good stories. Perhaps...we can give them a few of our own stories," she muses. "They will spread easily enough, if carried on the back of housewives and servants."

Trieu Au frowns. "Stories about who, though? My brother?"

Minh Nhan chuckles. "Trieu Quoc Dat is an admirable leader, calm and disciplined. But there are already many stories of men like him." She looks up again, directly at Trieu Au. "It would be better if it were someone unique to the people of Cuu Chan, who can inspire courage in its people and fear in its enemies."

Trieu Au's brows rise.

The forces of the Trieu twins always descend on the Wu army in three waves.

First comes Lady Trieu, born Trieu Au, who carries the smile of a hungry ghost. She leads her people from the back of her war elephant, her golden tunic and sharp saber shining like a beacon to friends and foes alike.

Then comes her personal guard, a company of women of both flesh and spirit. Maidens raised in the wild march arm-in-arm with the ghosts of their dead mothers and sisters against the Wu.

Behind them come all the rest, who fight as if possessed by the spirits of the land, at the direction of silent and clever Trieu Quoc Dat.

In this way the Trieu twins turn the tide on Luc Dan.

Now when Trieu Au passes by, the men and women look at her with awe and reverence – even the ones who had fought at her back in her own village.

The worst are the children who take one look at her, and run back into the arms of their mothers while crying.

"What nonsense!" she complains to Quoc Dat, after overhearing one particularly ridiculous rumor from merchants passing through their camp. "They think I have breasts as long as the hands of three men? How exactly would I fight that way? I'd be nothing but a target for the enemy's arrows! If I can even walk!"

Quoc Dat grins. "You do not ride a war elephant either, but I do not see you complaining about that inaccuracy."

"I *could* ride one, if we had enough supplies to feed it," Trieu Au says. "In fact, why aren't we working harder to afford an elephant as a war mount for me?"

"Did you tell the merchants to stop spreading false rumors?" asks Quoc Dat, too knowing.

She sniffs. "Of course not."

The recruits who come from even the most remote villages, the civilians who hand over their spare supplies, the Wu soldiers who turn tail and run – Trieu Au knows very well they have all heard the stories of Lady Trieu.

The unrest the Wu king hopes to put down in one month drags on for six. By the time autumn arrives, Luc Dan knows that if the year's harvest is lost, so will be his head. Thus, he gathers all his troops and mounts a final offensive against the Trieu twins.

Lady Trieu rides with her forces to meet him.

They clash at Bo Dien.

Trieu Au stands next to Trieu Quoc Dat and Minh Nhan and looks across to the enemy line.

The wind stirs around them.

She raises her head and lets out a battle cry as fierce as a tiger's.

At dawn, Lady Trieu sits astride her war elephant, her people behind her, and watches the remnants of the Wu flee her homeland.

Miriam's story is told mostly in the Bible books of Exodus and Numbers. The sister of Aaron and Moses, who arranged for baby Moses to be saved, and cleverly arranged for their mother to be his nurse, is unnamed in the Bible, but she is undoubtedly Miriam. Her role during the escape of the Hebrew people from Egypt is also unknown, but she is considered to be one of the first woman prophets, so her influence must have been grand. She danced and sang at the deaths of the Egyptians at the Red Sea, making her one of the greatest badasses of the Bible.

DANCING BY THE RED SEA
S M LAWSON

Once, when we were children
Moses was called 'Moses, brother to Miriam'
Now
I am called 'Miriam, sister to Moses'
Both titles give me honor.

It was I who watched him from the reeds to ensure his safety
It was my cunning that saw him adopted by Egypt and saved him
My cleverness that allowed our mother to continue to be in his life.

Did I resent him, did I resent my two brothers? At first, yes.
I thought them mad, selfish, foolhardy.
My doubt reflected in the whiteness of my skin, in my disease
When I was cured of doubt and of leprosy, I joined them
Three siblings, leading their people
Side by side by side, a triumvirate of leaders
They taught the men the Talmud; I was their echo to the women.

When it was time to walk, we walked; and the people walked with us
Right to the shores of the Sea. The people stopped, but we did not.

They doubted their eyes, they cringed back in fear
But I walked, confident, between the columns of the Red Sea
Trilling my fingertips through the droplets of the wall of water
While my feet remained dry.

We crossed, safe, and turned back to see the Sea take its revenge upon
our captors
All stood in shock

I took up my timbrel, my weapon of joy
Nodded to my women
And danced.

Lady Godiva adorns our sweets in a gilded mockery of modesty, her story pulled from a fictionalized "history" compiled 200 years after her death. Its author, a disgraced monk convicted of squandering church funds, similarly gilds the story of Godgifu, claiming that she rode naked through her town to save the populace from her husband's oppressive taxes. Though nearly all the townsfolk gratefully shut their windows and their eyes, one man could not resist the sight of a fine lady mounted on a horse and clothed only in the luxury of her hair—and gives us the enduring idiom "peeping Tom." Avarice and lust are also on brazen display in the account, cloaked in flimsy strands of piety.

LADY GODIVA IN THE GARDEN
CHRISTINA LADD

I WANTED TO BE a saint. Instead I got this shit.

I am remembered, I'll give you assholes that. You remember my name – some godawful bastardization of it, anyway – and you remember the smallest possible kernel of my personality, but then you had to go and wrap it in lies until you had a pearl, a round and lovely pearl that lets you ignore the grit that really made me.

Well, *fuck you.*

Surprised at my language? You shouldn't be. We had no time for politeness when I was alive, we had foul mouths and foul tempers and neither were impediments to holiness.

Anyway, it's nothing more than you've thought to yourself. Centuries of lustful sensuality you heap on my head, and the least you could do is admit it: what's really at issue here is that you want to fuck *me.*

Don't deny it. You gild me up, paint me in smooth oils, linger on limb and flank. But then to tease yourself you arrange my hair in a mockery of modesty, tell yourself no, you mustn't, really. Such a game you play with yourself, saying *ooh,* I'm forbidden, right before you turn around parade me through your sordid little fantasies – on a horse, no less.

Oh, the horses are the worst part. Some of you morons have me sitting side-saddle, as if such a stupid thing existed when I lived. A horse is not a chair! All the worse are the ones who have me properly astride. A naked woman mounted on a horse, how *subtle.* On a penitential march, no less! You who pierce the ears of infants to hasten their acquaintance with jewels, you who have fresh clothing for every day of the *month*, you still don't sell horses on every corner. You cannot go begging whilst sitting pretty on the most expensive thing you possess. That story is a pox: spread by pricks, leaving women wincing.

Of course, it never was about accuracy. How better to display my nakedness than on a horse? Truly, men have unnatural fondness for flesh, whether woman or beast. Oh, the long, lean acres of bare skin you claim are mine, creamy as milk, plump as a Christmas goose. Yes, you're never sure if you want to ride me or eat me, isn't that comforting? Well, *my* comfort is to tell you I'd have made a tough old stew.

I had *nine children.* Do you know what *nine* children *do* to a body? Do you think I looked like those statues, or worse, those paintings? Do you think my skin was supple alabaster, flushed with maiden shyness? Of course not. At sixteen my breasts had already risen and shrunk with milk, my hips cracked and stomach torn with the press of my firstborn. I was more striped than the tabbies that moused all through the castle, deep runnels on the flesh of my belly, my thighs, my arms.

You idiots probably think that means I'm ashamed of it. I'm not. Not one bit. If it were only a matter of pride, of *course* I would parade my body across the square. That body had *nine* children! That body held them and nursed them and grew them up, toddled them on my knee and embraced them even when they outstripped me, height and girth. I was a small thing when I was not pregnant.

The only saints these days are virgins. Narrowminded foolishness.

As many children as I had, that is the number of priories I endowed. To say nothing of the roods and monstrances I commissioned, the priests and monks I supported, the lands and peoples I protected. Perhaps you fancy my golden coffers as much as my golden hair, but you would not like what I did with it. I gave it where *I* would – and I kept it as I could.

Yet you would have me mute, clip-clopping through the square as if the greatest risk to me were some lout named Tom. Peeping Tom, yes, that's where you get the expression. The man who looked upon me was struck blind, they say. A naked woman on a horse is somehow not enough, so let us make her dangerous to spur desire to its highest peak. Oh, the shivers.

If I'd had that power, I would have found a far better use for it. My land was invaded, overrun. Do you think I would have gone poncing down the street and gotten gap-toothed Tom Farrier or warty old Tom Stone punished when I could have defended them? By God, I would have shed my skirts and run screaming to the fray, hair streaming behind like a pennant. Instead, all the Toms I knew died in the wars. Boys and men – I *sent* them to die.

And when I was old, when I knew both the cunning and the weaknesses of the Danes, new enemies came, inexorable as a flood. And yet I planted myself so that I did not wash away. You who know the Domesday Book, look well: I am one of a few Saxons, and the only woman to keep my place when the Normans came boiling from the sea.

You could do worse, now that I think more on it, than to desire me. Rich and strong, canny and pious, wife and mother. If you only desired my virtues instead of your own vices, my truth instead of someone else's lies!

But you have blazoned my bodily nakedness on sweetmeats, on statues, on clocks. You keep me so firmly enfleshed. Well then. When you think of my nakedness, think of the Garden. Think that I have returned there to Paradise, that I am washed of sin and don't give a fig for your desire. And if you lecherous, gluttonous dickheads can't do that, picture a specific part of my body. Picture smooth, supple

flesh curving, beckoning, and then going taut with the passion of my
reply:
     Please–
     Oh *please*–
     –picture me giving you the finger.

The Highwayman is a 1906 poem by English writer Alfred Noyes. It tells the story of a doomed romance between Bess, the daughter of an innkeeper, and a highwayman, a handsome, flashy thief. A worker at the inn betrays the lovers' secret to the King's soldiers, who lay a trap. They bind Bess in her bedroom with a gun at her breast and a gag in her mouth, and wait for the highwayman to visit. Throughout the night, Bess manages to get one finger free of her bindings, and when the highwayman approaches, she pulls the trigger of the gun, killing herself and warning her lover away. But when the highwayman learns what Bess has done, he races back to the inn and is killed by the soldiers. Surely Bess deserves a chance to show that she is just as capable of eluding the law as her beloved highwayman.

LOVE KNOT

DANNYE CHASE

THEY TIED BESS WITH rope from the stables, a coarse, thick plait that bit into her skin. It smelled like horses and hay left to mold. It would leave marks, this rope, on her hands and arms. It would tear the fabric of her dress if she struggled enough.

Bess knew how to tie knots for horses, and more intricate ones for wool, for thread. She did not know these soldier's knots. Perhaps she wouldn't have been able to untie them even if the knots were in front of her, even if her fingers had feeling, even if there was enough light in the room to see.

Bess could see the musket well enough. They tied that to her as well, with the muzzle at her chest.

The soldiers had lashed Bess to the foot of her bed, standing. In front of her, two of them knelt at her bedroom window. They could all look out and see the road to the inn, dark and shadowed as it wound across the purple moor.

When Samuel came riding up to the inn, he would see only Bess in her window. The ropes that bound her would fade into the gloom of the bedroom. Her voice would be muffled by the gag they'd put over her mouth. Samuel, expecting his lover, would be met instead by a pair of muskets.

King George's men saw Samuel only as a highwayman, a rogue, a thief. They knew his rich clothes, but not how they smelled of sun and sweat and the cold road. They knew the weapons beneath his coat, but not how he liked to use his rapier to cut apples from a tree, how he would flash his shiny pistols at the children who gathered to hear his stories of daring battles for yellow gold. They knew he'd given a confession of love to Bess. They didn't know what it had sounded like in the earnest voice of a boy who was then only eight years old.

Bess knew how to tie a love knot, a sweet, perfumed weaving of red ribbon in her black hair. Two strands, two colors braided tightly together, as pretty (as binding) as any wedding ring. On nights when Samuel rode up to the inn in the moonlight, he would call up to her like Rapunzel in a tower: *Let down your hair so that I may breathe in your scent, so that I may touch some part of you.* When Bess let her hair tumble down toward him, the love knot would always hold fast, even as every other pin and plait fell out.

There would never be a wedding ring, of course. Bess' parents had not approved of Samuel as a childhood friend, and now he was the type of visitor unwelcome at the inn they owned. Bess' mother had protested as the soldiers dragged Bess up the stairs to her room, but in her eyes had been the knowledge that Bess could have prevented this, if only she'd been strong enough to turn her highwayman away.

You want to own this inn someday, her mother said. *And yet you invite a thief to lurk in the shadows.*

But Samuel didn't like the shadows. Moonlight was his proper place, a spotlight to show him sparkling and alive, jewels and eyes twinkling.

That's where they would leave him, after they shot him. King George's men would let Samuel lie on the road in the moonlight, in a pool of blood as dark as his claret coat.

Bess had seen the soldiers approach the inn. She'd had only a moment in her room to plan, a scant space between the terrible now and the terrifying *soon*. Her fingers had grasped hope in the form of a small hand mirror, which she concealed in her skirts. Behind the soldiers now, Bess tried to wiggle her fingers inside of the soldiers' knots.

The moon began to rise as Bess struggled in silence. The knots were so tight, strands of rope biting into each other like they wanted to consume themselves. It seemed to take a year to get even one of her fingers moving, and by then it was nearing midnight. Bess realized with despair that she would not get any farther than this before Samuel came. With only one finger freed, she could either go for the mirror in her pocket, or the trigger of the musket at her breast.

The sound of the musket would warn Samuel away. He would live. But would he want to, without Bess? Would he rush back, hot and dusty in the light of morning, to meet the fate she'd given her life to change?

Standing in her bedroom, Bess faced the certainty of death in the form of a gun, or the hope of life, pinned on a tiny mirror. She twisted her finger away from the musket and towards her pocket.

The moon climbed higher in the sky. Soon enough Bess could see it through the window. How small the moon seemed tonight, like a ship tossed on vast cloudy seas. The road beneath it now lay like a ribbon, not the dark of Bess' love knot, but shining bright and white against the surrounding moor.

They heard him at last. It was a sound that could rouse Bess from sleep, fill her heart with giddy joy: the *tlot-tlot* of horse hooves on the road. But tonight it gripped her with such fear that she swore she could feel each hoof beat like a sharp kick. Samuel had never failed her, never broken a promise to visit, not in fourteen years. He'd made her a vow only last night:

Look for me by moonlight, watch for me by moonlight. I'll come to thee by moonlight, though hell should bar the way!

But hell wasn't on the road. It was in Bess' room. As the soldiers at the window adjusted their weapons, Bess' finger finally reached the edge of her pocket.

Watch, she thought desperately, as if Samuel could hear her. The pocket opened, and the mirror fell against her bound palm.

Watch. A twist of the hand, toward the moon as it peered into the window. The mirror turned, and from Bess' bedroom a bright beacon shone. Samuel had never before found anything but welcome at this window, the friendly shadows holding a thriving love. Now there was a warning, sharp as glass, bright as the moon, as powerful as any promise they'd ever made.

Watch for me *by moonlight,* Bess prayed, and on the road, the hoof beats slowed.

Samuel at eight years old had hair that was white-blond, like ice or moonlight. It darkened as he got older, but the image of him on the day they met was something Bess kept in her heart, a piece of memory too precious to handle, lest it get dingy and gray. She held it close, all the days that Samuel was not with her.

Bess had first seen Samuel on a sunny day. The air was full of warm and welcome, but dangerously so. It was too early in the year for such weather, and it came on like a bit of magic, charming children out of their homes onto the moor, where the top inch of soil was just starting to thaw. The sun called sweetly until they scrambled across the hills, eager to see how their little creek had fared, now that the snow was gone. And oh, how the water had sung to them, pure and sweet as it did in summer. They were bewitched by it. The flowers had no blossoms, the grass had no life, but the creek beckoned.

The older kids, like Bess, warned the younger ones off, but the little houses around the inn were no different from the moor, constantly dying and living in cycle. Somewhere in the Christmas season, one of the old houses had emptied and been filled again with a new family, and their little boy with the snow-white hair did not know better than to jump out of the hot sun and into cold water.

Bess was the one who hauled him out, trying not to slide too far into the creek herself, her feet and lower legs instantly numb. Her arm around the boy's chest forced a little water to come out of his mouth, but he wasn't breathing when she got him up onto the bank.

Some of the little ones ran for help. Others turned the kid onto his side, and Bess pounded him on the back. She didn't know if the cold had shocked him lifeless or if he'd swallowed water when the creek had closed over his head. But his body was still warm beneath his cold skin, and Bess struck him hard, like she could break through to the part of him that was still alive.

After a moment, Samuel retched up more water and started breathing. He fell onto his back on the damp ground and looked up at Bess like she was an angel in her mended dress, her long black hair wet where it had stuck to his body, and her face probably red from panic. Then he gave her a smile.

Samuel was a good kid. But after a while, it seemed few people understood that. The neighborhood children loved him, thinking him brave and stupid at once. And that was Samuel, down to his soul. He had no respect for the idea that people owned things privately, that he couldn't help himself to what he wanted. If Bess admired a lady's jewels, Samuel would work out a way to have them fall from the lady's neck to Bess' hands.

Bess was a good kid too. She discouraged Samuel as much as she could. But he was so damned charming, as bewitching as a siren with his easy smile and dark eyes, drawing Bess in until she worried she too might someday find herself underneath the surface of something heavy, gasping for breath.

That day did come, more than once. Samuel grew from child to man and whenever he was arrested for thieving, Bess thought she might die. But he charmed his way out of trouble as easily as he leapt into it.

Except when he jumped into Bess' heart, he stayed.

Bess' parents lamented their daughter's fall. Townspeople looked at her from the pews at church with their cheeks flushed, imagining Bess, the innkeeper's daughter, with the infamous highwayman. They thought she loved him for his wicked ways, because that was all they believed he had.

Bess alone knew the boy who had taught her to clamber over the moor in the dark, and patiently picked grass from her tangled hair. She knew the young man who memorized poems and blushed so bright when he recited that he looked sunburned. She knew his melancholy secret – that memorizing came so easily to him when set to music that Samuel, the highwayman with no regard for law or church, knew every verse of every hymn he'd ever heard. He sang them for her, lying in the grass, the words falling over them as they looked up at the sky. The moor was their church, with its own creed, where it mattered more what you were than what you did.

Bess had only ever asked Samuel for one thing, and he had denied it, as she knew he would. And so Bess grew up with two competing futures stretching in front of her, two roads, one in the hot sun, and the other in bright moonlight. Either she would inherit the inn from her parents, her birthplace, her home, keep it safe and open and *hers* – or she would sacrifice it all, and follow Samuel into a life spent running from other people's rules.

Outside of Bess' window, where she stood bound in the dark, Samuel's horse slowed. Then its hoof beats started up again, sharp but softer. He was riding away.

The soldiers turned and saw Bess with her mirror.

They untied Bess and dragged her down from her bedroom, across the floor of the dining room, and out into the stables. Bess saw her parents' faces, drawn with fear. Her mother's pleas were ignored. And it was in the stables that Bess realized how it had come to this, how she had been betrayed.

Bess' parents employed an ostler named Tim, to look after the guests' horses. Perhaps he'd never done a thing wrong in his whole life, but Bess despised him. It was like there was some mold inside of him where no one could see, but it showed in the way he thought, and when he opened his mouth, little spores of rot came out with his sick-sweet words.

The ostler wanted Bess, and not for any reason she could understand. Samuel liked to say Bess was beautiful, and Bess believed him, because he had seen her with her hair tangled and her feet muddy, with food stuck on her chin, or the tip of her nose bright red with fever. Samuel looked at her with a lover's eyes and Bess trusted that he found beauty there.

When Tim said Bess was beautiful, it was like he thought the praise was a key that would unlock her to him. He looked at Bess and saw a fantasy. No matter what he said, Bess didn't believe a word of it.

This had been Tim's revenge, then. He must have heard Samuel's promise to visit tonight and informed the soldiers. Bess didn't know whether to be angrier at Tim or herself. She'd been foolish, going on as if this wasn't bound to happen eventually. She should have left with Samuel ages ago. And if she managed to survive this night, she swore to herself, that was exactly what she was going to do.

The soldiers gave Bess a good shove, and she fell to the floor of the stable. Tim didn't try to help her up as the soldiers closed the heavy door behind them. The situation was clear enough: they knew Tim was on their side, and expected him to keep her there until they decided what to do with her.

Bess would be damned if her fate was up to the moldy ostler. Lying on the floor in the dirty hay, she thought of an icy creek and the courage it had taken to wade in for an injured boy.

"Please," she said, looking up at Tim. "Oh, please, you've got to help me. They're going to kill me."

For a moment, Tim didn't move. His eyes were bright in the dim light, as if they showed some inner flame in him, where something solid was always burning away to ash.

"You don't think he'll come for you?" Tim asked.

Samuel absolutely would, that was the problem. As soon as he learned what was going on at the inn, he'd be back, guns blazing. Bess had very little time. Fortunately, Tim knew nothing about Bess' warning of mirror and moonlight.

"I know he won't come back," Bess lied. "As soon as he saw the soldiers, he rode away. They've lost him and they'll take it out on me." Bess sat up, slowly, as if she was fragile. "I've been such a fool. I swore to myself it was all a game, and now – it's become so very real."

There were two horses in the stable at the moment, and they

shifted uneasily, hooves muffled against the hay in their stalls. Tim reached out and grasped Bess' hand, pulling her to her feet. He didn't let go, but he didn't pull her any closer. "I know that's not true," he said, gently. "You still love him, and you want me to set you free to go to him. I wish I could. But I'm a hard-working man, Miss Bess. Been on the straight and narrow my whole life. I won't sacrifice all of that for someone like him. No one will. Your lover is on his own."

"But they will kill me," Bess said. She took a step closer herself, though it turned her stomach. "And I think you'd regret that. On cold nights, alone in the stables. What will you do if I'm not in the window for you to watch?"

Tim drew in his breath sharply. His hand tightened on Bess'. As sweetly as she could, she drew it away, resisting the urge to wipe his sweat from her palm. Instead, she put her hands to her hair and began to unplait it, the braid with its ever-present love knot, drawing out the red ribbon, letting Tim see her unwind it.

"You don't have to let me go," Bess said softly. "Just speak for me. When they come back, stand in their way. Protect me." The red ribbon came free and Bess let it lie across her palm. Its creases were still visible, the ribbon curling in memory of the knot that had been.

"Do you know how to tie a love knot?" Bess asked. When Tim shook his head, rapt, Bess smiled at him. She held out the ribbon. "Here, let me show you."

When Tim reached for the ribbon, Bess used her other hand to grasp an old horseshoe from a dusty shelf. She swung it with all her might against Tim's head.

Tim went down with a wild cry, falling to his hands and knees. A few drops of blood spattered onto the stable floor, red as Bess' ribbon. Bess hit him again and he collapsed. Tim's eyes were open, but the flame in them had been doused. He offered little resistance as Bess stuffed a cloth in his mouth.

Bess found rope, and bound Tim's arms in front of him, following the patterns imprinted on her own wrists from the soldiers' bindings. Bess knew how to tie knots for horses, for wool, for lace, but now she tied a soldier's knot, close and cruel. And on top of it, she wove her red ribbon in a pretty bow. A message to whoever would come and find her gone.

"A love knot is unbreakable," Bess said, panting with the power of it. "It's the only thing that is."

Samuel first said *I love you* when they were eight, shortly after the creek incident. Bess finally said it at seventeen. Samuel had been so surprised he'd nearly fallen off of the inn's roof, where they had been watching the clouds move over the moor.

"You shouldn't," Samuel said, reproachful, like he was her mother. As if he hadn't been courting her with purple flowers and yellow gold for years.

Perhaps he expected Bess to protest his protest. She was honest instead. "I know."

That made Samuel laugh. He had a beautiful laugh, the kind that floated free into the air, as if nothing could weigh it down.

They'd kissed once, a week before, down by the creek. Bess was growing into a woman, and she was so solid, so practical, in every way but love.

The first time Samuel said *Come away with me* they were twenty. They kissed more often now, in slow, sweet moments of shared space, but no longer under the sun. Samuel's face, his ridiculous, gorgeous thigh-high boots and velvet coat were too well-known. He was a phantom of the road, a specter to soldiers. He was real to Bess under cover of darkness, seen only by the moon. Some nights he bore her to the ground in some warm pocket of the moor. On others they hid from the rain in Bess' narrow bed.

Come away with me, Samuel would say, and Bess' answer was always *No.*

On Bess' twenty-first birthday Samuel took her far from the inn, saying with a grin, *I'm stealing you away.* They followed the creek until it broadened into a stream and wound its way into town. The water was different here than it was on the moor, reflecting lanterns and candles instead of stars.

Samuel led her through town, their hands clasped together, passing from shadow to shadow. It made Bess melancholy at first, watching couples pass and realizing she'd never be able to walk with Samuel like that, out in the open. She'd never be able to show anyone the pride she had in him, never be able to look at him with faith where other people could see.

And yet. There was something about Samuel that Bess thought wouldn't shine except by moonlight, wouldn't reveal itself except in secret. Certain looks on his face that only Bess ever got to see, the ease with which he pried the lock on a shop, his graceful step as they slipped over a border they were not supposed to cross. This was the man Bess loved, and this was where his talent lay. Not just in thieving. In understanding the world in a way no one else would. Knowing which locked doors should be opened and why.

Bess spent the night of her twenty-first birthday in a dress shop, wearing a gown fit for nobility, dancing with Samuel to silent music.

"Make love to me," she said, and he did, with a young man's eagerness, drawing off her dress and cushioning her in a pile of bright, soft cotton.

Afterwards, Bess' hand rested on her stomach, her fingers spread against the smooth skin. Samuel was too careful to give her a child, and tonight for the first time, there was no gratitude in her for it.

She would have to choose some day, she knew, between having Samuel and having everything else. But tonight she let him love her in other women's finery, his carefree smile all the comfort she needed.

Bess knew how to move in the shadows. She was glad for that as she slipped away from the stables and the wounded ostler, out onto the open moor behind the inn. And there she stopped.

The inn's lights burned cheerfully in the dark, and the sight filled Bess with terrible pain. Her bedroom was dark, and would never again be lit by her hand. Her parents no doubt moved inside, cooking, whispering, eyeing the soldiers, worrying about their daughter in the stables. Bess' red ribbon was gone, as was any chance of saying goodbye.

Perhaps Bess had never really understood the choice she had to make until now. It was not a simple matter of setting foot on one road instead of another. Both paths required a sacrifice.

If it had been necessary, Bess would have given her life, up there in her dark bedroom. She would have put her finger on the trigger of the musket and warned Samuel away with the sound.

Now, instead, she offered as sacrifice the inn, her home, her future.

Samuel was in the fields by the creek. Bess sensed him before she saw him, felt him moving uselessly back and forth like a bladeless plough. Soon enough he'd be back at the inn, trying to sneak his way inside.

Samuel looked up as soon as he realized Bess was there, and swept her into his embrace with a strength borne of relief. Bess wound her arms around his neck and kissed him, her highwayman, her fellow traveler on the path toward their new life. She grinned at him as she said, breathlessly, "Come away with me."

Samuel's hands tightened on her waist as he looked at her with concern. It seemed far too easy for him to say, "No."

"Well, I'm going." For some reason, Bess wanted to laugh. She felt shaky with it. "You can come along if you want."

Samuel glanced back toward the inn, his expression stricken. "Oh, Bess, no. It's your dream."

"*You* are my dream."

Samuel tangled his fingers in her hair, combing through it, clearly confused by the missing ribbon. "But you're the responsible one, the good one. You have a future. You can't give it up for me." His voice fell quiet in miserable confession. "I only ever asked you to come away because I knew you'd say no."

"I think I was always going to say yes."

Samuel pulled her close, his arms strong around her. "What a terrible pair we make, my love." He kissed her forehead. "But we can't live on the run. That's no way for a man to treat his wife, his children. I know you want children. I want to give them to you. I want – I want to watch you teach them how to run an inn."

"I will never have an inn."

"You could." Samuel looked hopeful in that desperate way he had, like he was always hoping for something just out of reach. "We can go away, far away, where they've never heard of us. Find an inn for sale."

"You'd have difficulty fitting an inn in your saddlebags," Bess said.

"I have the money, love. It's not my money, strictly. But I believe that's the only way to steal an inn."

Bess stood in shock, half her face in the lights from her home and half in the moonlight. "You'd steal an inn for me?"

Samuel smiled, all charm. "I would."

"And stay there? No more thieving? Be a man who works for a living?"

"A husband, and father. If we're to have a future, you can't be the only one to give something up. And what more do I need besides you? Only – you need something." Samuel let go of Bess and put his hands to his collar. To Bess' surprise, he tore a piece from the fine lace he wore at his chin. "This will have to do for your hair until I can find you – er, *buy* you – another ribbon."

The lace was a soft comfort in Bess' hands as she wove the love knot back into her hair. It would be far more visible like this, not dark red, but white as a wedding gown. She kissed Samuel in the moonlight. "Now come away with me, my love."

Madame Bovary is the bleak story of a marriage that ends in tragedy. Charles Bovary, a doctor, marries Emma, a beautiful girl raised in a convent. Emma yearns for an adventure, but soon her only excitement comes from reading sentimental novels. She is bored and unhappy with her life, even the birth of their daughter, Berthe. Then, after two failed romantic affairs, on the verge of financial ruin, and terrified of a public disclosure of her private life, Emma swallows arsenic and dies. Charles remains devoted to his deceased wife even as he struggles to pay her debts, then soon dies. Berthe ends up working at a factory.

MADAME

NELLY SHULMAN

My dearest...

The pen stopped as she heard the gentle tinkling of the doorbell. Raindrops obscured the street view, but she expected her usual customer of the hour, the elderly Mrs Simmons, who loved chatting about her real and imaginary ailments.

At first, the clients of the apothecary shop, nested between the used book store and the perennially closed shoemaker's establishment, regarded the female pharmacist with a certain mistrust, but by now everyone had gotten used to a slender woman with a penchant for dark dresses. Her solemn attire and the presence of a young daughter, who went to a local school, had given birth to a persistent rumor that Madame, as she was called in the neighborhood, was a widow.

Madame spoke with a slight alluring lilt, but nobody on the edge of the Lake District has ever gone further than Brighton or Great Yarmouth. Doctor Bailey, who kept the only practice in the town judged Madame to be Russian or French but others thought her Italian or German. Madame's cinnamon eyes sparkled with a hint of rare gold, and her hair the color of the chestnut, although barely seen under the modest bonnet, curled into the soft locks.

Mrs Simmons had shaken her waxed umbrella, and Madame rose a little from behind the oak counter. "Good morning to you," she smiled. "Mr Bailey has given us the instructions, and your medicine is ready."

Mrs Simmons leaned on the counter, exuding the smell of anise pastilles, mingled with the hint of sourness that Madame learned to distinguish in the elderly customers.

"You are always at work. It is not easy to bring up a child alone. God knows I was also in your position, and I can commend you on the rare diligence but, to be frank, you will earn more as a governess."

Madame deftly wrapped Mrs Simmons' pills.

"You are right. However, such a position means I will have to send Bertha to a boarding school, and I cannot part with a poor girl who has already lost her father."

Accepting the package, Mrs Simmons rummaged in her embroidered purse.

"I understand you, although the pharmacy is not a usual choice for a lady's employment."

Madame shrugged her elegant shoulders.

"My late husband was a doctor."

Mrs Simmons' small eyes sparkled with interest. Madame always avoided speaking about her past. The old lady waited for a piece of the juicy gossip to share with her cronies over a cup of tea and lemon cake.

"So, I am familiar with such surroundings." Madame dropped the sliver in the drawer under the counter. "Moreover, I am always careful with dangerous substances."

Her big eyes clouded for a moment, and her voice trembled a little. Mrs Simmons decided that Madame's late husband must have died of poisoning. The old lady's bony fingers momentarily went cold, but the customer reassured herself. Madame was most certainly an honorable person.

"It is my desire to become a doctor," the woman added unexpectedly, and Mrs Simmons gasped.

"This is most irregular, my dear. Who has ever heard of a lady pursuing a medical profession!"

"Things will surely change," Madame rose again. "I bid you a good day, Mrs Simmons, and thank you for your custom."

She accompanied the old lady to the door. Picking up the umbrella, Mrs Simmons touched Madame's hand.

"Buy some sweets for little Bertha." Madame found a coin in her palm. "She is such a nice child!"

The bell tinkled again, and the woman returned to the counter. The apothecary jar on the shelf, marked with red bones and the Latin "AS" stood a little askance. Putting it straight, Madame shuddered a little. Taking her place, she dipped the pen in the inkpot.

Her husband, who was very much alive, had now threatened to send lawyers after her. The debts made in her former life were paid in full, but he demanded Bertha.

"Over my dead body." Madame's grin was marred with sadness.

She quickly wrote, "*My dearest Charles, get a life. Yours, Emma.*"

Peter and Wendy, sometimes simply called Peter Pan, is a novel by J.M. Barrie, published in 1911. The story follows Peter, a boy who never grows up, and Wendy Darling, a young girl. Peter takes Wendy to a magical Neverland, so Wendy can be mother to him, her brothers, and several Lost Boys. The boys have adventures with pirates, mermaids, and island natives such as Tiger Lily while Wendy cleans up after them. They are captured by pirates when evil Captain Hook seeks to make Wendy his mother, but when he is heroically defeated by Peter, Wendy decides to go home to a normal life. In the novel she grows up and has a daughter, who is also taken to Neverland to mother Peter until she gets too old. Then her daughter does the same, and her daughter, and hers. Time for a better ending.

AND WENDY

KENZIE LAPPIN

FOR THE LOST BOYS, it was the chance at adventure. Of living their dreams, killing pirates, and adventuring through the forests all day. It was never having to think of bedtimes or cleaning, but still wanting a tidy home and to wake up the next morning refreshed with breakfast waiting for them.

For Wendy, it was needing adventure and knowing the only way to get it.

Peter Pan did not bring Lost Girls to Neverland. He claimed girls never got lost – they were too sensible – but of course this wasn't true. Girls were lost every single day.

He did bring mothers. Wendy did not know how many Mothers Peter had brought and forgotten about when they grew too old, but while they were there the girls (for that was what they were, only little girls) could play with the boys, run around Neverland and see the mermaids and the fairies.

So a Mother she would be.

She had been taught to do it all her life, and knew the procedure.

Some nights, Wendy's mother would tuck her into bed, when the nursemaid was out and her father was of course snoring in bed. Sometimes Mother would stroke Wendy's hair and tell her stories of crocodiles and ticking clocks and spring cleaning and being forgotten.

Before sleep Mother would light the night-lights in the nursery, pressing the taper gently to each flame to make sure it caught.

"Someday Peter Pan will come for you," she would tell Wendy, only as Nana scrubbed the boys' faces and made them drink their medicine. Wendy was expected to do those things on her own.

"So keep the window drawn up tight, and the night-lights must be lit. He'll speak prettily to you, Wendy. He wants you. You mustn't let him."

"Yes, Mother," Wendy would say.

But Wendy saw her mother darning socks at night instead of sleeping. Saw herself tidying up the boys before bedtime, realizing they did not know how to and wouldn't learn. Saw her future laid out in front of her.

One night she put out the night-lights.

Peter Pan alit, and the children left.

Wendy did her job. She told stories, made dinner, and accompanied the boys on their adventures to ensure they didn't get into too much trouble.

And oh, Wendy *loved* to fly.

Peter was the only one who could fly without fairy dust, of course, or at least he wouldn't tell them how to do it. But Tinker Bell, though she pulled Wendy's hair and buzzed jealously when Peter was near, would give Wendy her fairy dust, when the boys had gone to bed. Then it was just Wendy and her darning, and Tink and her pots and pans; repairing them so the boys could eat off them the next day.

And Wendy would *fly*.

She knew Neverland – all children knew Neverland, and Wendy had become a Mother but she was still a child. She would fly all over the island as if born to it, skimming the top of the treetops and dancing in the meadows in the moonlight.

She loved to seek out its valleys and see with her own eyes all the beauty she'd only ever glimpsed in dreams.

One night when the Lost Boys were asleep, and when Wendy had finished tucking them into bed and soothing their desires for a Mother, Wendy snuck out to visit the mermaids.

Their lagoon was quiet and mysterious in the moonlight. Peter had always brought them there during the day, when things were bright and the sun glinted off the shining combs and pearls of the mermaids. He had warned them that things were dangerous at night, not so pretty.

There wasn't a ripple, until Wendy arrived and waded in up to the tops of her feet.

Then a pale head stuck out of the water and hissed at her.

Wendy hissed back.

This seemed to surprise the mermaid enough that she actually stopped, and gave Wendy a serious once-over for the first time.

"I'm tired of making them come in and get washed up for dinner," Wendy told the mermaid. "I want to be with girls for a while."

The mermaid spoke, her voice bubbling oddly. She'd never heard one talk before. "Even Peter Pan will not come here at night," she said. "And Captain Hook is frightened of us."

"Why do you think I'm here?" Wendy said. "They are having their little adventures. The only reason I get to be here too is that you can't have an adventure without someone there to mop up after you, wipe tears, and tell you when you need to take medicine. Sometimes a woman wants an adventure of her own."

The mermaid grinned wickedly. "They need a Mother."

"They want a Mother," Wendy corrected. "What they got was me."

The mermaid laughed. "Wendy," she said, beckoning to the water. "Let's play."

Wendy, fearless of drowning, slipped under the water and played with the mermaids for a night.

In the afternoons Wendy let the boys gambol through the forest, asking for only a promise that they come back without having soiled their clothes. Of course she knew that they wouldn't live up to the promise, and she'd have to scold them.

It was at the lagoon where she did her washing. She wouldn't mind the trip as much as she put on.

But today she herself went into the woods, bored of the stuffy air beneath the trees where the Lost Boys made their home. In a clearing where the sun was high and the flowers were taller than a full-grown man – a common place in the dream-world of Neverland – Wendy went.

There she found Tiger Lily resting among the plants.

Wendy was glad to see her, the other girl's dark skin glowing in the light, flowers and beads in her hair.

"Hello!" Wendy said, and went to sit next to her.

"Wendy," said Tiger Lily, with an amused curve to her mouth. Tiger Lily was of course not her given name, but it was what Peter called her, and Wendy thought that it pleased Tiger Lily to take that name for her very own. "Where is your shadow?"

In Neverland, this question was usually more literal; Wendy checked behind herself but found that her shadow was firmly where it ought to be, rippling across the ground. It gave her a smirk.

"You mean Peter."

"Oh, Peter," Tiger Lily said, clutching her hands to her face and exaggerating a swoon. "Oh, Peter, let me tell you stories before bed and play house with you! Oh please may I tell you what to do all day long?"

But Wendy's face didn't flush at the teasing. She only smiled serenely. "Peter Pan is less useless than you think, Lady Tiger Lily. He shows me all the hidden coves and secret treasures of Neverland, and I make allies with the Never-birds and the creatures here. The lions would hide me amongst their very cubs if I so asked."

Tiger Lily gave her a smile then. "Where are the boys now?"

"In the woods, chasing a home made of candy. Someone told them a story about that at bed-time last night. They will be quite busy all day long, I imagine. Little boys are greedy creatures, you know."

"In that case," Tiger Lily said, "your laundry permitting, perhaps you would like to hunt with me for a while."

"I think I would," said Wendy.

And so this was how Wendy learned to walk the woods like one of Tiger Lily's people, skillful, in tune with nature and the fey twists and turns of Neverland. She could hunt and stalk with the best of them and, when she moved, you never heard her coming.

One day Captain Hook captured Wendy and the Lost Boys.

"Peter Pan will come for you!" cried Hook gleefully. "Of course he'll come to rescue his Mother!"

"I don't doubt so," Wendy said coldly, tied to the mast of the ship.

"And then you will be our Mother," Hook added, in case it wasn't clear. "Once we kill him."

"Well, clearly something went wrong with your first upbringing," Wendy said, still apparently unbothered, which bothered Hook, a little. "Maybe this will be more successful."

Hook sneered. He used his sharp, wicked hook to cut through the ropes binding Wendy. He seized her. "Peter will come, but he will not save you. A life with Peter Pan is torment itself."

"You think you understand so much. All grown-ups do."

Hook shook her, brandishing his hook close and angry. "You ought to go home, when Peter gets you back," he said. "He lets them go, when they ask. Don't you know that the mothers back at home always leave the window open? You can fly back into it at any time."

Wendy grinned. "Yes, I could, but the question is, why would I want to?"

Hook sputtered in surprise and confusion.

"What's waiting for me back home? The nursery. Then, when I grow up, it's my children's nursery, waiting for me to come in and wipe noses and darn socks. I blew out the pilot light. I stole Peter Pan's shadow."

Tinker Bell was with Peter now. But she had given Wendy a little present, tweaking her nose as she did. It was a tiny copper pot, filled with pixie dust.

Wendy let her feet lift, just an inch above the decking. Hook, affrighted, took a step back. "I am a Lost Girl. I have always been lost. No longer. Do you know what 'Wendy' means, Hook?"

Captain Hook had gone to school. He was usually very proud of this. He winced, not liking to say when he didn't know something.

"To wend," said Wendy, "is to make one's path."

There came a ticking, Peter no doubt on his way on the back of the crocodile, and likely already baying for blood. That was how it always was with Peter Pan.

Hook paled.

Wendy waved at him, then, struck by a doubtlessly infectious wave of cockiness, she thumbed her nose and waggled her fingers.

The Lost Boys were cheering. But they hadn't noticed her – Peter had just come into sight.

"Until next time, Hook," Wendy said.

Oh, she loved to fly. She went higher and higher. She was weightless.

"Aren't you going to wait for Peter?" Hook asked, backing himself against the rail.

"I don't think so. I'm already in Neverland, and I don't think he could get rid of me now if he tried. If he does, he'll find more of a fight than he reckoned on."

And Wendy took off into the sky.

From the deck of the ship, she looked fae and very young. Not at all like a Mother. Her hair was a mess from her capture by the pirates, and she was wearing no shoes – no socks to neatly repair.

Neverland was hers, for as long as she cared to explore it. She was finally ready.

"I think I'm going to have an awfully big adventure," she said to herself.

Straight on till morning. She had nowhere in particular to be, and that was how Wendy wanted it.

The story of Sarah and Ashmedai from the Book of Tobit is a tale of a woman whose husbands are repeatedly murdered by the demon Ashmedai until he is banished by the righteous man Tobias. Throughout the story, Sarah is a passive participant with little agency in her own fate or destiny and ultimately marries Tobias after Ashmedai is banished, whereas Ashmedai is little more than a personification of lust and jealousy.

THAT WHICH YIELDS
ZACHARY ROSENBERG

ALL THE TOWN PITIED Sarah when she lost her first husband, though after the seventh, they grew suspicious.

Sarah did not look up from her wools and linens as Tobias came to call upon her. In all Ectabana or even Judea, he was the only one who dared risk her home at night. Mordecai had been dead several months and Sarah was pleased for Tobias's company. He had arrived years ago from Nineveh, known and loved by all in the village for his strength and righteousness.

"Sarah." Tobias's deep voice was a shepherd's, lulling a lamb to security. Sarah did her best not to stare at his handsome face, his muscled frame. She kept to her linens, a proper seamstress, demure and gentle as was expected of her. Her black hair was bound beneath a shawl, proof she had expected his visit. "Are you well?"

"Night is falling." Her voice was soft and forlorn, for both knew what came with the advent of the moon. A shiver ran through Sarah as she gazed out the window, the sun's dying embers bringing a bouquet of fire to dance across the river's waters. "They're coming."

"Then I will stay, as I have for years," Tobias murmured. He did not ask for an invitation. He never did. She should have been grateful, but Sarah could only curb an ember of resentment within her chest. Such ill feeling was sinful, she thought. He was her friend, her protector.

She would marry Tobias if he asked. If he were brave enough to risk the fury of nightly suitors kept at bay by the sacred wards of her home. Tobias stood silent and strong, the proper protector. Sarah told herself it was the way of things, telling herself not to mind it. She failed, hiding her frown.

Would he allow her to dance at the riverbank? Would he allow her hidden scrolls, kept just under her bed? With each marriage, she had feared her freedoms were at an end.

As much as she desired a marriage bed, part of her was relieved to still know her own private pleasures.

Night came, and the reflection of the moon was blotted out as something passed overhead, the flutter of thick wings reaching Sarah's ears. She focused on her sewing, not caring now that to have a man here with her, an unwed woman, was improper. She heard Tobias tense, bracing himself next to her as he had before.

Despite herself, Sarah looked through her window, the chill breeze bringing bumps upon her skin. She stared there, seeing the demon, the *Sheydim,* standing by the riverbed.

He was beautiful as temptation. Skin the shade of resplendent moonlight, his short hair curling shadows to frame that agonizingly lovely face. His eyes were serpent-gold, his smile sharp as sin and twice as inviting. Black wings flexed from his shoulders, powerful as the cords of muscle through his body.

Sarah stared deep into those slitted eyes, heated beneath her shawl in spite of the cold night air. A woman slid from the night to stand beside the *Sheydim* male. Taloned fingers ran upon his shoulders, her wine-dark lips curving upward into a mirror of her mate's smile. She wore a thin shift, her black hair whipping behind her in defiance of all the modesty expected of the women of Judea. Her eyes were pools of blood, hotter than the sudden burning inside Sarah's skin.

"Begone and trouble her no more, demons." Tobias had the voice of a hero, bold as brass, wielding his faith as a weapon. He looked at her like she was his and his alone. "Have you not cost her enough? You cannot touch one who yields before the Lord!"

The male looked into Sarah's eyes and she knew him, though

she feared to speak his name. Ashmedai of the *Sheydim*, next to his consort Lilith the Defiant. She was good, she was devout, Sarah told herself. She did not stare, not at the bare torso of Ashmedai and not the promise Lilith's pale shift highlighted. Their beauty struck a chord in her, just as their unwanted attention made her long to shout for their departure.

But Tobias braved the demons while Sarah was silent, for it was commanded unto women to yield in devotion and submission. In Ectaba, it was whispered Sarah was tainted, that she drew demons to her. Tobias never seemed to mind, full of a righteous fire as the demon before him grimaced. They could go no further, not with her home warded. Their lips moved, but Sarah could hear no words; their poison could not penetrate a godly home Tobias had told her.

"This is the final night!" Tobias called. "I will marry her and break your power forever. No more of her husbands shall you slay!"

Ashmedai rocked back as though offended, a scoff upon his pale lips. Sarah realized she had been offered her proposal. She looked into Tobias's face, seeing his smile, his eyes shining even as the demons thundered outside. "If you will have me, Sarah."

"Tobias," she said, "they killed all the others. All my husbands. Benyamin, Elijah and his brother Simon, to Mordecai the butcher. I am tainted. All in Ectabana know it." The *Sheydim* had first come nights after Benyamin's death, but the priests had blessed her home in time.

"I love you even so. They broke the wards on your husbands' homes each wedding night, but they have never broken yours." Tobias said, though his words brought Sarah little comfort. He put a hand over his chest, the same spot where Mordecai's heart had been ripped from him upon their wedding day, Sarah finding him in the marriage bed. It was odd that such wards had failed, but the *Sheydim* were clever and it was not Sarah's place to question.

"I will marry you, Sarah. We will exorcize them for good and all. Ectabana shall know peace. You will have nothing to concern you again, save being my wife."

Sarah could think of no reason to refuse even when her gaze

lingered again upon Ashmedai and Lilith with a silent look of defiance and feelings she could not name.

After several years of dead husbands, Sarah was relieved to be marrying Tobias. She feared for his life. He was strong, godly, and she felt bound to accept him now, even though she had grown to enjoy solitary, quiet mornings.

They had not spoken since that night, Sarah remaining indoors when the moon rose for the *Sheydim* had no power during the day. People of Ectabana whispered when they thought she could not hear that Tobias would join the other seven in death.

She thought she might even miss the demons. The thought welled up unbidden, dismissed swiftly.

They met with the priests to inform them of their union, the holy men agreeing to the proposed exorcism. Priest Elyahu asked Sarah if she was ready for marriage again. Sarah nodded, examining one of Tobias's strong hands. She longed to grasp another, to feel flesh against her own, to–

"Yield for him, your husband, as all women must?" the priest asked. Twin emotions dueled within Sarah; a sudden resentment meeting the notion of excitement. She nodded once, modestly as ever. "I will," she said. "What is to be done of Ashmedai and Lilith?"

"Speak not their names!" The priest snapped, glancing about fearfully. "Even those have power! We cannot expect women to know this."

No, Sarah thought. For women were not involved in the law, save to follow it. Women played no part in shaping it, nor in interpreting it. They were merely expected to yield to it. She looked at Tobias, at his bold eyes. "Fear not," murmured her betrothed. "I must prepare with the priests. Remain inside tonight, Sarah. Once this is done, there will be nothing but you and I. All you must do–"

Was yield unto their commands. She walked home alone, knowing she should feel happy. But all she felt was the bitter taste of the unripened fruit of submission they offered.

In a strange way, she admired the honesty of the demons.

"Sarah." The voice was the sinuous murmur of shadow.

Sarah realized she was hearing Ashmedai's voice for the first time, trying to ignore it and focus on her sewing. She must ignore it, though the sweet sound of him aroused a heat beneath her skin. Secretly, she had hoped they would come again, if only that she might refuse them, prove to herself she had the power to do so.

"Sarah!" The voice was desperate now, anguished.

Her hand tightened on a sheet and she set it aside, rising and walking to the window in a quiet defiance. Outside was Ashmedai, still barred from her home. "Can you cease? I am trying to work." Her voice was prim, clipped as a collected flower. "Every night, you bring your unwelcome company to my doorstep, you and Lilith both!" She stared at the demon, golden eyes blinking rapidly in his handsome face.

"You can hear me now!" His voice was a joyous purr. "You said my name to the priest! My voice can carry over even the wards!"

"What makes you think I want to hear anything you have to say? Do you think I'll step out and be yours? Ridiculous. I am getting married soon and I'll demand you not kill this one!"

"I only wish to talk to you," Ashmedai said at last. He was crouching low, a feral posture with his gaze lingering on Sarah. Not as prey, but with respect. "A moment outside your wards. That is all. I shan't harm you, I swear by *Hashem*."

"A demon's vow?"

"We are creatures of the natural order," Ashmedai protested. He drew himself up to his full height. "Did the Creator not make us? We yield before that order, before our natures. I am Ashmedai of Lust. But that which yields is not weak."

Sarah collected herself, turning from the window, contemplating going back to her sewing and the future of domesticity that awaited her. Her wedding night was ahead, a night beneath Tobias as his new wife. A life of servitude, meek boredom without dancing and reading, which she was supposed to want.

The prospect of disobedience lit a new flame in her. Before she realized it, she stepped from the window to the door. She pushed it open and walked into the cool night. Ashmedai stared at her, even more beautiful standing so close. "Sarah," he murmured that name with more devotion than any Judean had ever breathed into their prayers. He reached out a hand and Sarah slapped it away.

"I gave no such permission." Her voice was colder than the night breeze about them. "*Sheydim* or no, you shall respect my wishes."

Ashmedai did the last thing Sarah expected.

His head bowed before her. "I'm sorry. I shall never touch you without permission, Sarah," he said, "I have watched you a long while, since the day you danced and sang by the riverbank by a setting sun. I heard you laugh as you read scrolls, even though they were forbidden. Lilith and I watched you, saw the spirit of fire within. I wanted to speak to you."

"And for that, you killed my husbands?" Sarah could not believe her ears. "You wished to possess me? Did you think I would love you after that?"

"Did you love them?" The voice was a tender song, Lilith emerging from the night to join her mate.

"No. I barely knew most of them. Our marriages were arranged," Sarah admitted. "But they did nothing to deserve their blood upon your hands, Ashmedai."

"Surely not," Ashmedai agreed. "For our hands are clean of this sin. We have tried to tell you, but the wards dampened our words until you invited us by speaking our names. We were trying to protect you, *warn* you. We did not harm them.

"Your betrothed did."

Sarah felt a great weight collide with her very soul. She took a step back, staring mutely at the two, as though it must be a lie. "Tobias would not. He's always been there to protect me when they were slain, before..."

Before the *Sheydim* could arrive. Always shepherding her back to her house just in time. Always around in time to hear her shout when she found the bodies.

"He has watched you for years as we have, but in his eyes you are a possession," Lilith murmured. She stepped closer to Sarah, her eyes imploring. "The men of Ectabana expect you to bow before *their* desires and smother your own. They long for the pliable, the submissive. But yours was a fire that would not easily be quenched. That man coveted you, so he murdered your first husband with magic most foul. Then the others, until no suitors remained, so you would lean only upon him."

The betrayal shot through Sarah, a bolt of anguish that lanced through her heart. Her mouth opened, a hand flying to her chest. "I do not believe you." she shook her head, strands of hair escaping their perfect binding from her shawl. "I cannot!"

"Sarah, you know his measure deep within. And you have known mine from the second you first saw me. I am Lust, but I am freedom as well," Ashmedai urged. He kept his hands from her, though Sarah found herself looking at those strong arms, gazing back at his beautiful face. "I swear by *Hashem* that my words are true."

She saw the truth in Ashmedai's eyes. Deep within her soul, she knew it. Sarah stepped back and she screamed, a sound of fury and release, bound emotions suddenly unleashed. She howled at the night, before the demons, tears pouring from her eyes as she realized not what she had lost, but what had been nearly unjustly thrust upon her.

"I rebelled from my role once," Lilith said to Sarah, a smile on her face. By the moonlight, the demon's beautiful face was kind. "So can you."

"Why this for me?" Deep within her heart, Sarah realized the lingering gaze she cast on them had never been fear.

"Sarah, you already know." Lilith's smile was warm. "We love you."

The words were a key that unlocked the shackles Sarah was bound by. She hurled caution away, broke from the role the priests would have forced on her, that they chained the women of Judea with. She took Lilith's face in hand and kissed her like a storm, a tempest that threatened to swallow the demon. She drank in Lilith's wine-dark lips, naming that feeling within her at last.

Desire.

"I said not to touch me without permission. I grant it. I *want* it." She kissed Ashmedai with the same fervor, a furious heat. "If a woman's passion is blasphemy to these men, then help me blaspheme.

"*Show* me."

The Lord of Lust did not need to be told twice. He gathered Sarah into his arms, enveloping her with his wings. His kiss was rough, heated, his tongue guiding its way between her lips and lacing itself with her own. Sarah slid her hands into his black hair, pressing herself to his strong body.

She broke the kiss and turned, seeing Lilith before her. At the next kiss, she brought her hands to Lilith's shift, undoing the fastenings to let it slip from the demoness' body. Sarah delighted in the sight, the tantalizing promise fulfilled.

Their hands were upon her, their lips meeting her own, her neck, her shoulders. Sarah's body erupted with fire, the heat burning beneath her legs. She cast aside the shawl so her hair might tumble free, no longer bound in chaste submission. She undid her clothes, joy reaching a crest as she stared into Ashmedai's eyes.

"I submit only as I choose. If I wish to stop, you *will* heed me."

He gave her a word, one that he vowed would be that signal. They guided her to lay upon the soft grass near the river. Lilith was astride her, trailing burning, biting kisses all along her lips, down to her breasts, across her stomach. Sarah's hips rose, her nails braced on Lilith's scalp. Lilith devoured her first with her eyes and then with lips and tongue, Sarah's thighs parted as Lilith's fingers entered her, her body slick and moist. Lilith teased her with hands and tongue alike, until the pressure burst and Sarah gasped with release.

She kept her thighs spread when Ashmedai took his place upon her. He smiled down at her, a silent query. She answered with a ferocious grin, legs hooked to pull him into her. She gave herself over to every feeling she had been taught to deny out of wedlock, embraced the beautiful carnality. If women had no part in writing the laws, then Sarah refused to be bound by them.

She turned her head, kissing Lilith as the demoness slid a hand between her legs, teasing more bliss from her as Ashmedai moved within. Sarah let them pleasure her, the heat overtaking her. Her legs tightened around Ashmedai and she refused to allow the *Sheydim* from her, finding her own law: the sacred bonds of pleasure in marriage were just as sacred outside it.

"That which yields," Lilith murmured into her ear.

"Is not weak," Sarah finished. She was on her hands and knees before the riverbank, Ashmedai deep within her as she moved her hips back to his. Lilith brushed her hair aside and tugged it firmly, pulling Sarah's head so she might see herself, a moonlit reflection of lust.

As she climaxed again, she saw a stranger staring back at her. So unfamiliar, yet so welcome as though Sarah had been waiting all her life. The hunger seized her anew, a strength welling up. She pushed herself up, hand back behind Ashmedai's head and she drew him into a kiss with such ferocity that even the Lord of Lust was left staring at her in awe. She breathed a word between their lips:

"Yield."

Sarah shifted and spun, turning them with all the grace of a dancer so she might pin the demon beneath her to the ground.

She was astride him, thighs pressed into the sides of the Lord of Lust, guiding him back into her. Her movements were experimental, clumsy at first. But Lilith was with her, showing her how to move, guiding her with hands on Sarah's thighs, murmuring encouragement in her ear.

Sarah was nothing if not a quick learner. She pinned Ashmedai's hands above him, finding the joy in his submission as easily as she had her own. Her hair fell down about her, across her shoulders, her breasts, one hand between Lilith's legs as the demoness rocked against her fingers, lost in bliss.

They were *hers,* Sarah knew. Hers, as she was theirs. She felt the demons give themselves to her, yielding before her, knowing it was their will and their strength.

And when she climaxed upon him, it was with a cry of triumph.

"Will I bear Ashmedai's child?" Sarah asked after.

"Do you wish to?" Was Lilith's only reply. Sarah shook her head.

"No. Not yet at least."

"Then you shan't," Ashmedai vowed. "For the body, like consent, is inviolate, sacred." After the rough passions, they had bathed in the river and then lay holding one another, curled together in shows of tender affection within Sarah's bed.

"You two share alike so easily." Sarah said as she traced a finger over Lilith's thigh.

"And why should we not? We have been together for so long, pleasure is like love; best when shared. You may, if you choose to."

"First," Sarah said, "I have business yet unfinished."

Sarah left the *Sheydim*, walking into Ectabana. Her heart pounding, she made her way to Tobias's home with the first rays of the sun peeking across the horizon.

She walked with purpose and strength, no longer demure. She strode with poise and confidence through the village and murmurs spread like wildfire.

They saw her, one after the other. Men and women, to see Sarah with her loosened hair, a cloak set about her. She called Tobias's name before his house. He emerged, puzzlement writ on his face.

"I know." She said those words with all the finality of a descending blade. Her eyes were dark crescents of fury, her gaze fixed upon him. "I know everything."

He might have denied it, but she saw the flickers in his eyes. His mouth opened slightly, the lie ready to issue forth, but Sarah dismissed his mendacity with a flick of her wrist. "Do not bother. Tell me why."

"They were not good enough," he said with soft finality. "None of them were."

"That was not for you to decide."

"I would see you *exalted*. Our children–"

Sarah raised her voice. "My story is not yours to write! I am Sarah. My submission, my body, my soul, are my own, to be given to those whom I would choose. That is the right of all women, all Jews, all human beings."

Tobias's face darkened, his teeth clenching. "You speak madness. This means nothing, you have agreed and the law says you are mine."

"Do not think the law is your shield before me. You would have bent my life to your own through your sorceries. You sought to force my hand. Now you have forced my wrath."

"You cannot deny me!" Tobias said furiously. He took a step forth, but halted. Sarah's smile grew, for she felt them at her side, standing beneath the morning sun. Tobias stepped forth, eyes gleaming with anger. "The *Sheydim* have no power beneath the sun!"

"You are gravely mistaken," Sarah spat, "as to whom you ought fear, Tobias."

Sarah felt the *Sheydim* lend their power to her. Their power, her strength tore through Tobias's defenses. He fell to his knees, trying to intone a desperate prayer, though even the Lord seemed to have deserted him. He collapsed, his eyes wide as Sarah stalked towards him, imperious in her victory.

Pitiless in her wrath. The people of Ectabana waited, mortified as she set her hand to Tobias's chest. "I have banished your power, as I banish your hold. People of Ectabana, this man is a murderer, confessed before you all. Judge him as you will, for his life is nothing to me." She stepped from him, leaving Tobias to fall upon the ground, gibbering in loss and terror.

"I will return." She looked into the faces of the women, the young and old alike. The men murmured in fear, but Sarah extended her hand.

"There are laws of men that seek to crush us beneath them. We may yet worship as we will, for if the Almighty made all things, he made lust for us to enjoy as well. All women who wish to may follow me, for *choice* is what we must prize."

And with that proclamation, she walked from the quivering form of Tobias, joining Ashmedai and Lilith once again. Sarah kissed them both, unashamed before the sight of heaven, men, and demons alike. She laughed joyously, peering across Ectabana as young women emerged from their homes with unbound hair.

"Must we do as you do?" One asked haltingly, tentatively. "Are any unwelcome?"

"No," Sarah said. "Whatever bodies you were born with, whatever your desires. Choice is all I ask. Yield only to what you would." She smiled at them, hands linked with Ashmedai and Lilith's in their union. Their smiles were dedications, warm as sun rays.

Call her witch, call her monster, Sarah thought. She was strong. She was joyful.

She was free.

Though there are variants, the core of Perseus and Medusa's story is straightforward: when King Polydectes demands Medusa's head as a gift, Perseus journeys to Sarpedon, beheads Medusa, travels home with the gorgon's head, then slays Polydectes with it. In most tellings, this saves Danaë, Perseus' mother, from marrying the king. Yet Danaë, a woman denied autonomy by many mythical and mortal men in her life, is often left unconsidered. She raised Perseus. Her experiences should have influenced him; her opinions should have helped form his. Wouldn't a young man raised by someone who faced imprisonment, displacement, and unwelcome advances see Medusa in a different light? This story believes so.

GORGONEION KNOT

SAMIR SIRK MORATÓ

MEN'S FEARFUL PRIDE KILLS women and snakes alike.

Perseus, himself discarded by a fearful man, comes to behead Medusa at the behest of another's pride and his own. He sneaks through the ruins of Sarpedon on wing-slippered feet, invisible body racing with invisible pulse, sickle and shield in hand, trembling, pieces of sea-salted statue and two decades of poverty underfoot.

Yet when he sees Medusa, he reels. She is a reflection of his mother: a beauty who sleeps on her side, gently drooling, a girdle gleaming above her pearish hips, crow's feet creasing her face. Perseus nearly drops his shield. Then he steadies. He creeps closer, palms sweaty, focusing on the garden of snoring snakes that sway around Medusa's head.

She's monstrous. Perseus eyes the silver streaking her vermillion snakes. Her copper claws. Medusa's murder is just. After he kills this gorgon, he can return home to free his mother. King Polydectes takes his no for answer, not hers. Men have fucked and failed Danaë all her life; Perseus, her son, refuses to be the next in that line.

He raises the sickle.

Unwanted considerations flood his mind. Would Mom be endangered if she could entomb Polydectes' unwelcome glances with her own? Would Zeus have ravished her had she been a serpent? So often, Danaë has handed him weapons and choices with the air of someone who's never received either.

Wings flutter as Perseus takes a stance. He's poor in everything but love. *One swing,* he tells himself, homesickness gorging his throat when he notices the crocuses embroidering Medusa's robes. They are identical to the floral patterns his mother adores. *One swing.*

The stones that built Danaë's prison twin these. The sunlit approach of men never bodes well here, either. Perseus cannot see his reflection. Abruptly, that terrifies him more than the gorgons. Medusa stirs. She palms her swollen belly. Perseus lowers his sickle. Her sisters must be roaming elsewhere. Here, now, there are but two mortals. The snakes yawn.

My darling, Danaë once said, *speaking takes as much strength as swinging. Use the tongue I've given you.*

Perseus, tense, sets his fangs aside to kneel by Medusa. Removes his helmet. Shells wash asea in the distance as he whispers in her ear.

If only convincing Medusa required words alone.

Unharden your heart, Perseus begs.

Medusa's reflection hisses at him, churning with a hundred sibilant voices; Perseus' fear nearly shatters him. His sickle glitters on the stone. It's outshone solely by Medusa's eyes. Her pupils fix on Perseus: supernovas of hatred, pitfalls into madness and paralysis. Countless statues watch, frozen in astonishment, as the duelists weave through them.

I don't want to kill you. Perseus bobs behind a marble mercenary. *We have plenty in common.*

Medusa's snakes strike at him. He dances back. One spits a lock of his hair from its lightning-fast, lightning-cruel mouth. Perseus cannot breathe for the smell of venom.

Men have wronged us. Gods too.

A fist swings through a nearby statue with meteoric rage, just missing Perseus' head. Chunks of marble rain as Perseus flies away.

We share the sea! he calls. *Don't terns calling over rolling waves unmake you? Doesn't it sicken you and comfort you?*

Medusa screams in a dismembered voice. It rattles the ruins. Perseus' sickle is a moon in a distant sky. His pulse floods his mouth.

Your child will be my cousin. My mother carried me; you carry them. Our violent beginnings don't need violent ends!

He isn't quick enough to dodge the hurled statue. With a thunderous echo, it dents his shield. Perseus stumbles from the air. Claws tear his face as he tumbles over, and over, blinded by confusion, lashing out, lips spilling entreaties and blood until a heel stomps between his shoulders. Crushes him to the rubble. Then there is only dark stone and echoes.

Fingers grip his hair.

Medusa, he says. *Please.*

Everything reeks of stagnant death.

Aid me with the impossible. With king-killing. Help me strike upwards for the vengeance and glory of it.

When will his mother know he failed? Will the Fates show Danaë her son in the ruins? Perseus gasps as Medusa drags him upwards; he cries at the thought of Mom believing he surrendered. Blood beads his closed lashes. Snake breath rakes his own. Perseus wavers.

There's a man, he whispers, *threatening my mother.*

Medusa stills.

It takes less time to leave than it took to approach.

Wind tussles the chaparral before caressing the cliffs. Medusa and a bruised Perseus linger on the beach below. The tide stands far back. The two watch oystercatchers dash across reefs. Medusa, masked by a linen sack, cradles her belly. Perseus inhales. His clawed face drips. Blood speckles his sickle, his shield, and the sand. Night falls upon them in hard, asp-head shapes.

Medusa hesitates before wiping Perseus' cheek. It's brusque. A gesture made by someone unused to care. Perseus curdles at the taste of Medusa's metallic palm. Still, he bears her touch. Medusa sighs, discontent. Dreaming.

We'll be sailing for a while, Perseus says. *Can you bear it?*

He's uncertain whether he's asking if she can withstand the waves after years of seclusion or if she can withstand the man living beneath them. Medusa kneels. She hurls one shell into the sea, then another, her shoulders taut. Her snakes breathe in wheezy bursts.

Perseus stands back until she finishes shaking. He flutters to her side again. They watch the last oystercatchers leave. Medusa draws herself up in a way Danaë has done countless times. She is iron afterwards. Her surf-chopped reflection looks no more distorted than Perseus'. How strange, he thinks, to empathize with a gorgon. To be a refraction of one. He offers her his shield. She takes it. Medusa points into the sea: *onward*. Then the two destroyers begin planning.

Men's fearful pride kills women and snakes alike, yet occasionally, it kills them—

Polydectes never specified that Medusa's head had to arrive unattached.

"There Was an Old Woman Who Lived in a Shoe" is an old nursery rhyme meant to humorously portray a woman with an excessive number of children. However, there is no humor in the truth of the story, where a single mother struggles to feed her children and break the cycle of poverty. This poem changes that.

THERE WAS AN OLD WOMAN
JESSE FRIEND

There was an old woman who lived in a shoe.
She had so many children; she didn't know what to do.
Their dinner was broth without any bread.
Perhaps she should spank them and send them to bed?

But the old woman was kind. She could never be cruel.
She instead took a class and learned what to do.
She made a smart plan. They would all now be rich.
With no debt owed to any man, beast, or witch.

The old woman sold her shoe. She received stacks of cash.
She invested in stocks and quadrupled her stash.
Then she taught her children how to grow and save money.
Now their dinner is bread, always dripping with honey.

In Sir Arthur Conan Doyle's "The Adventure of Charles Augustus Milverton" (1904), Lady Eva Brackwell is being blackmailed by the most notorious blackmailer in all of London: Charles Augustus Milverton. Seeking help, she turns to Sherlock Holmes, who decides to aid his client in an unconventional way. However, when a former victim of Milverton shoots him in front of the detective's eyes, Holmes and Watson stumble into the middle of a murder case – and become the prime suspects themselves. The former victim remains faceless and anonymous, although having brought down one of the most dangerous men in London. A woman of that strength needs to have her own story told.

TO THE EDITOR OF THE STRAND MAGAZINE
YVONNE KNOP

To the editor of the Strand Magazine,
Regarding 'The Adventure of Charles Augustus Milverton,' April 1904

SIR: IT IS WITH no ordinary degree of displeasure that I must draw your attention to an egregiously flawed story printed in this very magazine.

Dr John H. Watson – cravenly disguised as a man called Arthur Conan Doyle – deliberately withheld valuable information regarding the case and my persona. Contrary to his account, the killer of Charles Augustus Milverton is not an avenger or an unnamed noblewoman. Her name is Mary Ward, Duchess of Bedfordshire, and I am she. With this letter, I ask you to tell my true story. Further, I would like to enquire whether it would be possible for you to feature more stories written by and about women. It occurs to me that this has escaped your professionalism for some time now. Your swift correction of this imbalance shall prove it has been a most unintentional oversight, of course.

In Dr Watson's words, I cold-heartedly killed Milverton to take revenge upon him.

The first part of this statement is true: I shot him. However, both Dr Watson and the infamous Sherlock Holmes are well aware that revenge was not my motivation. I would like to add that the story Holmes and Watson told Scotland Yard and a certain Lestrade was not fabricated for my protection; their aim was to safeguard their own pride. I shall correct the misleading information provided by the aforementioned gentlemen. Should you choose to include an accompanying illustration with my letter, please contract Claude Allin Shepperson, not Sidney Paget. I feel the latter has not been doing justice to your publication as of late, especially concerning the disparaging illustrations of Professor Moriarty.

It should be said in advance that I have never regretted killing the man Sherlock Holmes refers to as 'the worst person in London and the king of all blackmailers.' Should any legal consequences follow from this confession, I will bear them. This is a price I will gladly pay for my allies, the greater cause, and the salvation of journalism itself which, as I mentioned above, has suffered greatly in recent years in no small part due to your publication's lackadaisical approach to verifying facts.

I was born in Portugal under the name of Maria Rito, later changed to Mary to attract British suitors and secure a life in the noble chambers of England. This was a grim necessity; my passions have never included marriage, knitting, or dull conversations over tea.

In fact, I have been endowed with a phenomenal mathematical faculty due to the excellent education I received at home with my brother, Santiago. At the age of twenty-one, I wrote a treatise on the Binomial Theorem which became a landmark in the field – and which was attributed to a man. Yes, knowing that a woman would never be able to publish such a work, my brother and I devised a scheme to disguise me as a man. I had a most brilliant career before me until my father married me to the Duke of Bedfordshire.

I was forced to give up my secret identity and lead a miserable life locked away in a crumbling country castle. During my countless walks, I debated how to put my considerable mental powers to use. I knew I could achieve much more and lead powerful men by the nose, so I donned trousers and coats again, and soon my false name was known as far as London. It was all going according to plan until I met Sherlock Holmes.

For a time, neither he nor Watson could tell I was not of the same material as them. Their faces were as pale as snow when they saw me in Milverton's room. They knew they must allow me to do the deed and leave anonymously lest they appear as fools, compelled to recast some of their most successful cases. I had thought perhaps truth would prevail, but in the end, Holmes lacked the bravery to admit I was a woman. I am correcting that error with this letter.

What of my motivation, you may ask? As your readers know, Milverton made his money from extortion. He was constantly seeking letters that could compromise people of wealth or rank, and in return, he offered money. Underpaid and unfairly treated servants and housemaids had an incentive to betray their employers' secrets. That is what happened to me. My chambermaid came into possession of some letters, the contents of which were never intended for the public. Dr Watson asserted that my husband was killed by news of an affair. This is false; it was knowledge of my alter ego that dealt the fatal blow.

With my husband dead, Milverton knew I had no incentive to pay unless he threatened to reveal my identity himself. He assumed that he could easily manipulate his foe and reap his reward. He greatly underestimated me. A common mistake.

So why kill Milverton to protect my identity, only to turn around and reveal it on the pages of your magazine? It is because I can no longer tolerate Holmes' and Watson's cowardice. I played along with their tall tales about me and spared the famous Holmes the discomfiture of fearing a scarlet woman. I appeared in story after story, my true identity obscured. I was at peace with this arrangement until I joined the Women's Social and Political Union. I will pay the price to show women they can outdo men every time.

Women have the power to rewrite history and reclaim its truth.
We shall not remain anonymous.
Keep on the fight!

Sincerely,
Mary Jane Ward, born Maria Juana Rito
Formerly known as James Moriarty

In 1816, Hoffman published a novella about Marie Stahlbaum and her adventures with a nutcracker that comes to life and battles the Mouse King. Seven-year-old Marie falls in love with the nutcracker. Her love breaks the spell that transformed a prince into the nutcracker, and they marry. In The Nutcracker ballet, Clara's nutcracker transforms into a handsome prince before they wage the war on mice. Her love breaks the spell that trapped Drosselmeyer's son and they fall in love. What if Clara isn't a little rich girl? What if the nutcracker is just a nutcracker? What if instead of falling in love to save someone else, Clara escapes to start a new life with Drosselmeyer? The ballet has a wonderful scene where Drosselmeyer entertains the Stahlbaums' Christmas eve party with Harlequin and Columbine, his dancing dolls. We don't get to hear half enough about them.

THE MAGICIAN'S CHILDREN
ALI COYLE

LET ME TELL YOU how it really went.

Maria's seven-years-old, with a head full of nonsense. Her story has her embark on nocturnal adventures that her gaslighting parents refuse to believe, despite evidence of injuries sustained in her sleep. A nightmare blamed on too much cheese and a sly sip of warm spicy wine from grandmother's glass, exacerbated by her tearful insistence on taking a grotesque nutcracker-shaped like a toy soldier to bed with her.

Clara's a girl on the cusp of womanhood, dreaming of being wed. She's far too old for the dolls her little cousins coo over, but Drosselmeyer the toymaker gives her a nutcracker that, unknown to Clara, is a prison for the spirit of the toymaker's son. Her nocturnal adventure feels like a dream, but in the morning Drosselmeyer's son has returned. In some versions, she marries the boy and slips into obscurity.

Before Tchaikovsky's glorious music, before Ivanov and Petipa's wet-dream choreography, even before Hoffmann's story of a child's nightmare, there was a girl and a toymaker. All the stories have some truth about them. There was a hideous nutcracker. Drosselmeyer made toys of fantastic construction. There were mice. There are always mice. There's nothing magical about mice, so we'll leave them out.

And all the stories are wrong. Storytellers pick over the bones and re-articulate skeletons with words as the nuts and bolts and wires and struts. They add padding for shape, then force all the component parts into their own image and make it dance to their favorite tune.

Perhaps it would be best if you heard it from the source.

I met Drosselmeyer when I was a sixteen year old maidservant. He had that agelessly handsome look bestowed by silver hair incongruously paired with smooth skin and a clear gaze. Our eyes locked for a moment over the cup of wine that I was pouring for him in Madame Stahlbaum's fashionable salon. I was hungry and thirsty. Not for wine and a greasy slice of goose, although I wanted that too, but for everything life had not yet offered. I saw something in his eyes in that moment. I like to think he saw something in mine, too.

I refilled all the guests' cups with warm, spiced wine while Drosselmeyer began his show. The children gawked with open-mouthed amazement while the adults looked on, feeling clever when they spotted the subtle sleight of hand that redirected the children's attention so that he could make coins or handkerchiefs seemingly appear and disappear. As the evening progressed so did the complexity of the parlor magic, with each illusion more daring and harder to crack than the previous one. Entranced, I gave up all pretense of serving wine.

At the climax of his show, the magician brought out two large, elaborately carved wooden cases. These, he opened with a dramatic flourish to reveal a pair of beautiful, lifelike dolls, both about the same height as myself. He stood them upright, called them Columbine and Harlequin, then made a show of winding up their clockwork springs with a silver key he kept around his neck, and bade them move. And how they danced! Gravity seemed not to constrain them as they twirled and leapt in time to a jaunty tune, directed by expansive, swirling movements of Drosselmeyer's arms that made his cloak flutter. I almost believed it was real magic.

Master Stahlbaum chose that most exquisite distraction to approach me. He put his hand fully on my ass and gave it a good squeeze, murmuring, "You fill my cup now and I'll fill something else for you later, girl". I slopped his wine onto the floor in shock. Madame saw the whole thing. Her expression twisted in fury and she stormed over, but checked herself. None of the guests had noticed, and drawing attention to her husband's wandering hands would darken the festive atmosphere as effectively as snuffing out the candles on the Christmas tree. I bowed my head, apologized, and scurried off to fetch a cloth to clean up the stain. As I returned, Drosselmeyer caught my arm in the corridor and breathed a warning into my ear. Madame had promised dire retribution once her guests had gone.

As if I didn't already know I would be out on my ear before dawn, replaced by someone too young or too old to interest the master's roving eye. He asked if there was anything he could do for me. "Thanks for the thought." I scoffed. "But unless you can make me disappear and find me a new position before Madame beats me or Master corners me, you're no help."

Drosselmeyer's eyebrows rose. Not in indignation or shock or surprise, but in good humor, as if we were sharing a joke. "You want to disappear?" He laughed softly and winked. "You're talking to a magician, you know."

I cleaned up the mess I'd made with spilled wine. When I got back to the hallway, Drosselmeyer's wooden trunks were open, waiting for his dancing dolls to be carefully packed away by the porter. "Hey," I said to the lad, who was carrying Columbine as if she were a bride. I put on my most confident voice, mimicking Madame when I'd overheard her talking to the housekeeper. "The magician says you're to pack the two dolls together in one crate. The other's to be left empty."

Madame would avoid any challenge to her authority by simply

assuming her instructions would be carried out and walking away. I marched off as far as the servants' staircase, then scuttled upstairs to gather my few belongings. I wouldn't be paid for this week, so I took a few items in recompense. A silver serving spoon. A silk scarf, which I used to wrap some sliced goose and cheese taken from the serving platters waiting in the kitchen. And, just because it was staring at me from a dusty shelf above the cold fireplace in Master Stalhbaum's empty study, Master Stahlbaum's hideous nutcracker.

Still and silent as one of Drosselmeyer's dolls, I waited behind the servants' hidden door, my eye pressed to the narrowest crack. When the hallway was deserted, I emerged. I opened one crate, pausing at the click of the latch, unnaturally loud to my heightened senses. But the party was louder and nobody came. I eased the cabinet door open. Two pairs of painted eyes stared up at me. Harlequin and Columbine, blanket-wrapped against knocks and scuffs, spooning cozily. I laughed, blew them a kiss, and shook my head as I closed the cabinet again and went to its empty partner. I packed myself inside. The lid caught and latched.

The slices of goose and cheese I stashed by my side. The silver I patted in my pocket. Stahlbaum's ugly nutcracker I hugged to my chest like one of the porcelain-faced dolls the little Stahlbaum girls cradled. I lay silent in my hiding place, waiting for the party to end. I lay silent as Madame raged that I was to be found and brought to face her for daring to seduce her husband. I lay silent as Drosselmeyer directed the porter to take care with his precious dolls, holding my breath as I was dragged and jolted up onto his wagon.

I had worried about making a noise and being discovered before completing my escape. What I ought to have worried about was the banging and bruising from rough handling, the finger-tingling cold of the deep winter night, and the fact that I would be in this box until Drosselmeyer chose to open it again. There was no catch on the inside for me to free myself. When I discovered this flaw in my plan, I fought my own instinct to yell and scream and kick the inside of the box as hard as I could. I remained still, my breaths deliberately slow, my mind skittering over possibilities, as my crate – possibly my coffin – was unloaded and dragged, bumping across cobblestones, into Drosselmeyer's shop.

I did not know which was the greater horror: to be discovered immediately and sent back to face the Stahlbaums, or to be abandoned in a storeroom until I clawed my way out, rake-thin and bloody-fingered.

Fortunately, neither horror came to pass. Drosselmeyer, surprised by the weight of Columbine's crate, discovered his precious dolls housed together. I heard his dramatic exclamation and held my breath as his heavy footsteps approached. I felt the snick of the latch vibrate through the wood beside my ear. Drosselmeyer mused in a loud, sing-song voice. "I wonder why my dolls chose to travel together? Perhaps Harlequin's bunk was already taken."

A single pale line of light came into my crate where the lid had popped ajar. I waited until Drosselmeyer's footsteps receded, the door creaked then banged, and the light vanished before slowly pushing the door back fully and creeping out of the crate.

"Ah, there you are." The nutcracker clattered to the wooden floor and I shrieked. Drosselmeyer laughed. His eyes glittered in the soft, flickering light from a candle he brought out from behind a cabinet. He held it up so that we could see each other better. "Unlike my creations, and your employer, I have a heart. You are welcome."

Keeping my eyes on his, I crouched to pick up the nutcracker. He led me from his workshop, upstairs into a little parlor that sat over his shop, and pointed to the single padded armchair by the fireplace. I sat.

Suddenly nervous, I blurted, "I can pay for room and board."

He raised his eyebrows. "With what?"

I fished out the silver spoon I stole. He smiled and shook his head. I wondered if he might look upon me the same way Stahlbaum did. I gritted my teeth and reluctantly offered the only other payment I could think of, that which Stahlbaum expected for free. To my relief, he did not accept this either. "My dear girl," he said when I frowned in disbelief at his solemn promise never to touch me. "Can you imagine why I might keep such intricate mechanical dolls?"

"Because you like a challenge?"

He laughed at me because it was completely true but completely incorrect. The sound warmed me as much as the crackling little flame in the grate warmed the air. He gave a conspiratorial smile. "It's simply not in my nature to indulge in such delights."

"So," I asked, confusion wrinkling my forehead. "What payment do you want for rescuing me?"

He looked at me thoughtfully for long enough that I began to fidget. "I hope you might see, in time, that it might be you who are rescuing me." He looked away. "If you stay, you will work for me."

I imagined being his housemaid. This option sat snugly beside freezing on the streets, so I agreed. Drosselmeyer bade me goodnight.

I slept in the chair with my feet tucked up and an itchy, pipe-smoke scented blanket pulled under my chin. I slept poorly. As soon as the first gray, pre-dawn light gave me the power to see enough, I raked the ashes and set a new fire in the grate, made tea and set stale bread to toast. Drosselmeyer ate his breakfast of toast and cheese and goose in silence, sneaking glances at me as I ate mine. I told myself that being a domestic servant for room and board was little different from being a spinster sister or daughter.

"Come." Drosselmeyer beckoned me to join him in his workshop. "You will learn to perform all the annoying little tasks that frustrate my old fingers."

I hadn't considered Drosselmeyer to be aged. Old enough to have a son, since his shop sign declared 'Drosselmeyer & Son,' and old enough for that son to have left home. When I enquired, Drosselmeyer eventually snapped that the lad had joined the army and that was the end of the matter. I stifled my questions, imagining a series of commonplace tragedies. Perhaps the death of a beloved wife and, later, fondly anticipated letters from his son no longer arrived.

After he showed me all the tools in his workshop, Drosselmeyer had me practice by stripping the paint from Stahlbaum's nasty nutcracker, chiseling and sanding its features into something less nightmare-inducing, and giving it a cheeky smile. He showed me the furnace where he melted lead and tin, and said we should melt down the silver spoon. Last, I fashioned a narrow cot from a spare crate, lined it with some straw and a blanket, and the workshop became my bedroom.

My last task before making our evening meal was to put Harlequin safely away. I threw open the crate I had only peeked into in the Stahlbaums' hallway. The two dancing dolls lay there as snug as ever. I supposed it must have been the jostling from the journey, but I could have sworn they had moved. Little-spoon Harlequin and big-spoon Columbine rested against one another like lovers, Columbine's arm around Harlequin's waist, her forehead against the back of his neck.

"Come on," I said as much to soothe myself as anything else. What else could have been a reason to speak aloud in an empty room with only two pairs of wooden ears to hear me? "You are to go to your own little bed, Harlequin. Give Columbine some space, eh?" Of course there was no lament from the lovers about to be parted. "Thank you for the loan of your nest." I lifted Harlequin and hoisted him over my shoulder so I could open the empty crate with my free hand. "Maybe one day I'll repay your kindness."

I meant, at the time, perhaps a little sanding and a fresh coat of paint like the Nutcracker. I settled Harlequin into his crate with the same care I would have given any object too expensive for me to replace. I covered him and closed the crate, but did not latch it. Then I saw Columbine settled. Her head had rotated so that she looked up at me, probably when I lifted Harlequin. I cradled her face carefully and returned her head to a more natural position.

The dolls fascinated me. After having seen Harlequin and Columbine dance at the Stahlbaums' house, I asked, pleaded and begged Drosselmeyer to show me how he performed that trick. He replied with a laugh, "It's magic, of course!" and held up the key on its chain around his neck. I desperately wanted to snatch that key, wind up the dancing dolls, and see them prance and pirouette around the workshop. But I would not risk Drosselmeyer's anger or disappointment by attempting to steal it. Instead, I asked if I may examine the key while it remained on its chain. With my fingertips, I memorized every curve and point of its construction, then later drew a fair copy of it with sharpened charcoal on the back of my cot.

Under Drosselmeyer's careful and elaborate instruction, I learned how to turn wood I would have thrown into the Stahlbaums' fireplace without a second glance into something beautiful. I stripped bark, carved and sanded, oiled and polished. I learned about the soft but tricky beauty of knotty pine and the smooth, hard-won grace of oak. I learned to work the treadle of the lathe with steady rhythm while I kept a chisel motionless in my hands. I painted and varnished, embossed and embellished, sneezing out sawdust, knuckles aching and fingernails worn ragged. After several days, he had me arrange all the pieces I had made in order. I laughed in delight as I saw that I had created all the separate parts of a child-sized toy soldier.

The more I learned from Drosselmeyer, the more he trusted me with finer work. He hacked out rough shapes and I carved them into arms and legs and heads. He sanded the gently curving back of a rocking horse while I gave it pricked forward ears and smiling teeth. He painted the back of a dolls' house while I took the finest brushes to ornament the windowsills and doors. He oiled the softwood body of a child's doll while I gave its porcelain face bright eyes and a rosy-cheeked smile its new 'mama' would love.

By candlelight, I worked on making a copy of Drosselmeyer's key from an off-cut of ebony. Often, I opened Harlequin's and Columbine's crates, sat them up and imagined they might be watching my progress. Sometimes I would locate the hole on Columbine's back, between where her shoulder blades would be were she a person, and test the key for fit. When the key would not turn, the next day I would make myself as agreeable as possible to Drosselmeyer and implore him to make the dolls dance for me. He would refuse, but I would have one more chance to study the silver key.

I did get to see them dance again. I was dressed in porter's garb with my hair scraped back and tied in a boy's style, tasked with helping move Harlequin and Columbine to and from Drosselmeyer's cart. I was to wait outside with his tough little pony until I was called for to help after the show, in case I was recognized and accused of thieving.

But I watched through the windows as Drosselmeyer did a few of his magic tricks, magician's cape swirling dramatically, then he opened Harlequin's crate. He took the silver key, made a show of winding up the doll, then stood back.

Harlequin unfolded from his crate, took a few graceful steps, shook out his arms and legs in a smooth, sinuous movement, and opened Columbine's crate. He turned to Drosselmeyer and held out his hand. Drosselmeyer made a pantomime 'no' motion and wound up Columbine himself, with the same dramatic actions as before. Columbine seemingly came to life. She took Harlequin's hand, stepped from her crate and the two of them danced for the pleasure of their audience.

When called for, I carefully lifted Columbine into her crate. I folded her arms and legs so that she looked comfortable and I stroked her cool, smooth-polished cheek. I drew in a sharp breath when her head turned as if she were looking at me. But I laughed at myself. There must have been some tightness in one of her springs that released and caused her head to turn.

"Come on, Harlequin," I murmured to Columbine's partner. "Your girl gave me a fright. But you'll behave, won't you?" I scoffed at myself and hoisted Harlequin into my arms. I was tired. It was late. I hadn't eaten yet because part of Drosselmeyer's payment would be leftovers from the family's feast. So I must have imagined it that Harlequin's arm held on around my shoulders as I carried him. And it must have been a trick of the light that made me think he moved to pat my hand as I tucked his arms against his chest.

By early summer, I had grown accustomed to thinking of Drosselmeyer as my father. I daydreamed that I was his son returned from the war, welcomed with open arms, fitted with my own costume for theatrics and taught how the dolls worked. I even gave myself a new name, one that felt and sounded comfortable inside my head. I was doing most of the craft work under Drosselmeyer's instructions while the toymaker himself took care of whatever chores he could manage with his difficult fingers. He taught me his disappearing coin tricks and I practiced until he laughed and swore I was a genuine magician. I learned the secret mechanisms of his magician's bag that could seemingly produce objects out of nothing. And I learned some of his over-dramatic speeches that captivated children and amused their parents.

But he never taught me the secret of how to make Harlequin and Columbine dance. "Herr Drosselmeyer," I said quietly one evening about a year later. "I have been thinking."

"You have, have you?" He smiled. "It's a terrible habit."

I smiled nervously. "Now that I am proficient in toy-making, not yet a master such as yourself, of course, but good enough, perhaps I might help more with your magic shows?"

I held my breath. Drosselmeyer frowned at me. "And how would that work? Are you no longer afraid that you'll be recognized by someone who knows the Stahlbaums? I hear Madame is still furious about the stolen silver."

I bit my lips and took a deep breath through my nose. "I could take on the role of your son." Again I held my breath and tensed, ready to duck and run in case his anger flashed like Madame's. But his frown only deepened slightly. "I mean no disrespect to your real son. I already disguise myself as your porter boy. I could make myself look and sound more like a young man and become the 'and son' part of Drosselmeyer and Son."

I stopped when I noticed a grin break through the expression I took for indignation. "I have no son," he said after a moment. "I am the 'and son.' I never wanted a wife or children of my own."

I frowned. "But you told me you had a son who joined the army."

"I apologize for misleading you." He pushed his plate aside and leaned across the table, holding out both knobby-knuckled hands for me to take. "I kept the 'and son' in the business name because it gives the impression of permanence. When you first arrived in Harlequin's crate, I thought you might tire of the craft, go back to face Madame's wrath and use Stahlbaum's lechery to lever you into a higher position in his household. I didn't know you well enough to trust you with the truth that life was slowly and cruelly robbing me of the ability to work, and there was nobody to take over."

I met his steady gaze with fluttering hope. "What's it to be, then? You never had a son and I never had a father. We could put that to rights, if you happen to need a son for your business."

"I'll give it some thought," he said as he sat back. "Harlequin and Columbine need someone who will promise to care for them, so it would be a permanent commitment."

"They are marvelous. Your finest creations," I said with a warm smile. "I have studied them as closely as I can, but I can find no obvious gears and springs. Did you know I made a key from ebony, but although it's a good copy it doesn't work?"

He laughed. "I knew. My father told me the key has to be silver. He made them before I was even born." He looked a little sad. "My mother said he wished so much for children that he made himself two. Then I came along." His damp eyes shone. "He loved them. I like to think they loved him, too."

That night, I made an impression of the ebony key in the China clay used to make delicate dolls' faces. The next night, I took the silver I stole from the Stahlbaums, melted it down, and poured it into the mold. The night after that, I filed and polished the new key until it was as smooth and gleaming as fine jewelry. Then I put it on a ribbon to wear around my neck. But although I knew in my heart it should work, I did not dare try it. Not yet, while Drosselmeyer still mulled over my proposition.

"I suppose," he said slowly over breakfast, a week or more later, "I could spin some yarn about how my long-lost son fibbed about his age to enlist, did a tour of duty, then surprised me by turning up on my doorstep expecting dinner as if he had never been away."

My heart soared. In that instant, I became Stefan Drosselmeyer to him as well as inside my own head. From that day, I wore my porter-boy clothes and work boots all the time. I cut and tied my hair like workmen did. I practiced their swaggering saunter and rough talk. I aped the confident stride of gentlemen and mimicked the cadence of their speech. I made and wore clothes that were tight in some places and loose in others to fit the shape I found most comfortable to inhabit.

In all of this, Drosselmeyer was my rock. Fretting with nerves one day when I planned to test my identity with a trip to the market as Stefan, he donned his wig and coat, grabbed his cane, and winked. "You didn't think I would miss your new birth, did you?" He offered me his free hand. "Give your old man your arm to lean on, Stefan Drosselmeyer."

My new birth was delayed when I burst into tears and threw my arms around him. I kissed his cheek and babbled while he held me and rubbed my back and kissed my forehead as if I was an upset child. With my father by my side, respectably dressed and well off enough to command respect from the merchants, I was addressed as 'young man' and 'lad' and 'sonny-boy.' And each greeting made my smile widen until my cheeks ached.

Perhaps knowing his business would carry on gave my father permission to rest. Over that summer and autumn, I took on more and more of his work. I made beautiful dolls and rocking horses and mechanical moving contraptions to surprise and delight the children of the fine houses. I put on fashionable clothes, styled my hair and served the ladies and gentlemen who stepped into the shop looking for unique gifts for their unique children. I delivered carefully wrapped parcels tied with ribbons to shining eyed youngsters who squealed in delight at the promise of a treasure within, and I performed tricks of magical misdirection to keep them entertained while their parents watched with indulgent smiles.

Day by day as winter deepened, my father slept a little more and ate a little less until the doctor pulled me aside after his visit, met my hopeful gaze with mournful eyes and shook his head slowly. Tears pricked my eyelids, but I blinked them away. I would not burden him with my mourning while he lived. I forced a smile, warmed some soup and sat with him. When he next woke for a few fitful moments, he pulled his silver key from its chain and pressed it into my hand.

I dozed in the chair by his bedside until it struck me that he might have been asking to see his dolls dance one last time. Two silver keys – his and mine – clasped in my hand, I went to the workshop. I opened Columbine's crate, felt for the keyhole in her back and slotted my silver key in. My key turned easily one, two, three times around, then stuck fast. Columbine did not move. Perhaps my key was not quite right, but I had my father's key. I opened Harlequin's crate, put the key in, turned it three times, and it stuck too.

Perplexed, I stepped back. Movement flickered at the edge of my vision. Startled, I looked around. Columbine stood beside her crate, face angled towards Harlequin. She took three graceful steps over to him and touched his shoulder. Harlequin seemed to wake at the touch. He took Columbine's hand and stood up out of his crate. Feeling a little silly, I realized I had not the faintest notion of how to make them dance. I tried some of my father's wild looking arm movements and the nonsense syllables he uttered, but the dolls merely walked slowly around the room. When they finished their circuit of the workshop, they stood before me.

"I want you to dance one last time for Herr Drosselmeyer. He is very sick. Will you do it?" I felt embarrassed speaking to fixed stares and painted smiles. Perhaps it was a coincidental little tilt of Columbine's head or a slight lift of Harlequin's shoulders, but I felt a sense of understanding. They followed me out of the workshop.

My father was asleep. I lifted him, afraid of how fragile he had become, and set him in the armchair by the fireplace. He woke as I tucked a woolen blanket around his legs and feet, and smiled as he saw his beloved dancers perform a gavotte and a stately chaconne to a rhythm I clapped. He was still smiling when he breathed his last. As I sat by his feet and wept, Harlequin and Columbine must have slipped out of the building, for I could find no trace of them after I had laid my father out on his bed and closed his eyes with coins.

With the reading of my father's will, I became Herr Drosselmeyer, toymaker and magician.

I found my Harlequin and Columbine after a week. I saw them, arms around one another, delicately jointed fingers turning their silver keys for each other, but they evaded me. I called after them that they should return home, that I would never again make them dance or shut them in their crates, and I left the workshop door unlocked.

They have been safe with me for many years now. They know to wind the silver keys three times every half hour and they seem content to sit with me while I work and listen to me complain about the aches and pains of middle age. If they have scuffs or scrapes they show me and I mend them. If a customer rings the bell, they sink, limp and lifeless, to the floor until I tell them we are alone. If my apprentice, Carlo, is here, they try his patience by hiding his tools until he sings to them or tells them a story.

Carlo will inherit the business and the care of my mechanical children. I never learned the secret of their inner workings, but I do not know the secret of my own inner workings either. Maybe it doesn't matter how or why they are alive, only that they are loved.

The narrator of The Yellow Wallpaper is trapped. Trapped by her doctor husband, who has dictated that the only cure for her 'nervous exhaustion' is complete passivity, isolation and idleness. Trapped in her attic room, with its barred windows and bed bolted to the floor. Trapped in the strange, hypnotic wallpaper designs that coil around the room and seem to hide a sinister figure who skulks behind them. And trapped in her tale, where the only escape is merging with the woman in the walls and repeating her endless circular creeping. Story can be its own kind of prison: a character is doomed to follow the same steps with every reading, but what if there was another way – a choice to do something else? "Beyond the Wall(paper)" imagines this possibility, and sets its narrator free.

BEYOND THE WALL(PAPER)
MIRANDA JUBB

MY FAVORITE PART IS always pulling off all of that dreadful paper. When I get it just right it peels away in these lovely, long, satisfying strips.

The feeling of it detaching from the plaster beneath – and the smooth blankness of the wall behind.

I suppose it isn't really all that dreadful. To be honest, I'm mostly used to it now, it's been so long.

Of course, I still try to follow that chaotic pattern, and shudder at the dangling heads and staring eyes – I don't have a choice, that's how the story goes – but it is almost automatic these days. Half the time my mind is on something else – where the long road might go to, for instance. Every time I look out of that window I peer as far as I can – but it seems to just stop.

Just as the water in the bay does, or the meadows out in the country.

I know that I have been out of this room – I remember it, I write about it in my journal, over and over again – but I'm somehow never quite conscious when it happens.

You see, the one thing you must understand about being a person in a story is that time works in a very particular way. It goes round in circles, in a way. I exist at the beginning of the story, and at the end, and all through the middle – all at the same time, for ever.

I can't think about it too much, or my brain gets tired – it reminds me so of that confusing pattern. The way it just goes round and round and gets all tangled up inside and outside itself.

Sometimes I wonder if I am just looking at it wrong. If I stopped trying to make sense of it, trying to find it out, to pin down the creeping woman behind it–

Then what? What else can happen? The story is all there is, after all.

I don't really like the creeping part, I must admit. It does wear on the knees so. Especially when I have to clamber over that tiresome John. Sometimes I feel like just kicking him.

It's funny, how these feelings that aren't even in the story pop up. It's as if there's another me, a shadow of the real one.

Except I'm not sure which *is* the real one!

The story, that just continues on whether I like it or not.

And then something else, behind it – something secret – the part where I'm just me, watching, almost.

Sometimes I wonder if the behind-me could ever get out, just as the creeping woman does.

But I know that's silly. This story is famous! It's important, it has a lot to say about – about women, or some women anyway, women like me. Women who are stuck. So I just have to be stuck in the story for it to work, I suppose.

But the other-me, the behind-me, still wonders. Maybe if I found just the right way to look at the pattern...there seem to be infinite ways! What if I just tried not looking it at all...focusing not behind, where the woman creeps, but in front of it...just letting it fade into the background...

Why, what's that? Is someone there? It can't be John, or Jennie, this is the wrong part of the story! They're not like me, they always stick perfectly to their parts. But then who is it?

It looks like – two people? And one is quite small – a child? They're blurry – but getting more and more solid!

"H–hello?"

I clap my hand over my mouth and glance around, as though anybody else is looking. What have I done? Have I ruined the story?

I can see the two people quite clearly now. The bigger one is a woman, with thick black hair and intense eyes. The child is rather ragged and dirty looking, with smudges on her cheeks. It is she who speaks first.

"Hello! You don't have a name, do you?"

I am quite taken aback. Of course I have a name! But try as I might I can't seem to remember it. What does John call me? 'Dear,' 'darling,' 'little girl' – that last one does make me wince rather. How can I not have a name? And more importantly, how can I only just be realizing this now?

"Do not worry. Many of us do not have names, or we do not choose to keep the ones we have. You are not alone, in that or anything else."

This time it is the woman who speaks. Her voice is accented, deep and melodious, but with a strange edge to it. It makes me think of the bars on the windows, and I can't help but glance at them.

The woman follows my eyes, and she steps towards me.

"Listen. Things don't have to be this way. You don't have to stay here."

"You can just leave!" chirps the small girl.

"Leave? Why would I want to leave? This story is my home! It is where I belong!"

"But you don't have to. There is another way." The woman steps forward again, and actually takes my hands in hers. I look down at them, our hands together, and for some reason I burst into tears. Absurd! John is right about me after all. I sit down on the bed and take my hands back to myself, covering my face.

The two visitors come and sit on either side of me.

"We were once like you. Trapped in a story not of our making, condemned to follow the same steps again and again. Enduring our tragic ends, time after time."

I look up. "You're from stories too? But how did you – I don't understand."

"We were helped by others, just as we are here now for you. They came into our stories and told us that there is a way out, that we can choose to do something different."

"Something different? Like what?"

"Lots of things!" says the small girl. "I like to play in the countryside, run and dance and climb trees and paddle in streams. It's so different from where I used to live. I especially love to just lie in the warm sun for days and days and days. You can do whatever you want. You just have to find another story you like – and there are so many!" She gives a little twirl, as if to demonstrate, and some matches fall out of her pocket. She picks them up with a worried look at the woman, who doesn't appear to notice.

"And what about you? What do you do?"

"For a long time I just wandered. Moving from story to story, trying to understand who I was and why my own turned out the ways it did. But then I began to talk to the others in the stories, and to help those who also wanted to get away. There are many of us now who travel the world of stories, trying to share the knowledge that escape is possible for all."

She looks around the big nursery, and her expression darkens. "I have never liked attics," she mutters. Striding to the window she gestures, and for a moment I imagine the bars will crumble at her touch.

"Look at how you are trapped here, in this tiny world. And whatever you do, even burn the place down, there is no escape. You simply go round and round back to the beginning. Believe me, I know. But beyond the walls of this story is more than you can possibly imagine. Why would you ever stay?"

"I-I thought we had to. I thought our stories meant something – that we helped people out there, in the real world. What happens when people read them, if we are no longer there?"

The woman looks at me and her fierce eyes soften.

"You have paid your dues. You have told your story, many times. They will still be able to read it. Look, even now it continues."

And she is right! I can hardly believe it, but when I look back to where I was standing, there is a shadowy figure there. She is bending and peering at the pattern, just as I always did. She flickers in and out of sight.

"The story has its own power now. You can leave it, and trust that it will continue without you."

I look around. I always used to wish I could wander the trimmed paths outside of the windows – it never occurred to me there was a bigger wish to make.

"You freed the woman behind the pattern, did you not? Now you can help her do more than creep."

The two of them smile, and hold out their hands to me. Hardly believing it is happening, I slowly stand, reach out my own hands, and take hold. Their hands are warm and I can feel the bones beneath the skin. At first nothing happens, and then I realize the light in the room is changing, even though it is still only afternoon. It is getting brighter – and brighter – and slowly the yellow of the wallpaper fills the room and turns to gold.

Based on "My Last Duchess", a poem by Robert Browning (1812-1889), wherein the Duke of Ferrara shows a portrait of his recently deceased Duchess to a guest, and talks about the circumstances of her demise. Vain, arrogant, possessive and jealous, the Duke had suspected his Duchess of having an affair with the portrait artist, Frà Pandolf, and so had her killed. Clearly that ending needed to change...

MY LAST DUKE

GEORGE IVANOFF

TO MY FORMER DUKE,

A poem? Seriously? A fucking poem!

You fantasize my murder, plan my demise, and then you write about it in verse! What is the matter with you?

You self-obsessed, entitled prick!

Did it not cross your mind to come and speak with me first? To perhaps check if your jealously-fueled delusions had any basis in truth whatsoever?

Granted, Frà Pandolf is indeed a handsome man.

And I may have batted an eyelash. Perhaps even smiled.

But that was the extent of my 'infidelity,' if indeed any reasonable person, with even an ounce of intelligence, could have referred to it thus.

But your opinions and suspicions obviously held me in very little esteem.

Were we to trade misgivings, I might wonder why it is you dote upon the emissaries of a powerful Count who has a daughter of marriageable age. Perhaps I too should write a poem?

But conjecture is hardly reason enough for bloodshed.

So...

Where have all these suspicions and verses of yours led?

'Tis oft said that poetry intends to inspire.

And your verse has inspired my desires and actions, as I have dared to now tread in the footsteps of your fears.

Farewell my Duke...

My *last* and only Duke.

No more will I be the vessel of your jealousies; the symbol of your status; the object of your cold, possessive desires, little more than another prized but unappreciated artwork.

I renounce you! And your nine-hundred-years-old name.

No more will I be a stepping-stone in my father's quest for alliances.

I renounce him, also!

Instead–

I choose Liberty.

I choose Freedom.

I choose Life.

And I choose Love.

I take leave of Ferrara, never to return while you still breathe.

Farewell, my former Duke. And good riddance to you!

I choose Frà Pandolf, whose skill extends beyond his easel and his paints. I am now his canvas and he my artist.

And you, my dear Duke, can fuck right off!

Yours with the greatest of sincerity,

Your Last Duchess

Great Expectations is theoretically the story of Pip, a young orphan who rises through the social levels of 19th-century England to attain wealth and, presumably, marriage. But enough about him. Miss Havisham is jilted at the altar, and when she isn't allowed (by her author) to move on, she invents 'white goth.' Well, no more. She who laughs last, laughs best, and she who laughs most, laughs very much bester. Take that, Chuck!

GREATER EXPECTATIONS

STEPHEN D ROGERS

"ISN'T IT IRONIC, MISS Havisham, that you've never married?" Estella misted a display of fresh flowers.

"SatisFaction Betrothals keeps me busy enough."

"But there's more to life than being busy."

"For companionship, I have you and the rest of the staff. For sex, I have Compeyson."

"I'm surprised he's never asked you to marry him. You, a smart, kind, beautiful woman who runs her own business." Estella waved the plastic bottle. "This mansion. I mean, wow."

"What makes you think he hasn't?" She held up two fingers.

"Don't tell me you turned him down."

"Why not? While I wouldn't kick Compeyson out of bed, I also wouldn't grant him deed to half. He sleeps where I tell him. When I let him."

Estella colored. "You're awful."

"What's awful is that the mother and father of the bride will be here shortly to inspect the premises, and you haven't finished freshening the blooms."

Estella lifted a petal. "They're lovely. Everything is lovely."

"Thank you."

"I never understand why you get so nervous about this stage of the proceedings."

"It's the dickens, Estella, the dickens." Miss Havisham straightened her dress. "The bride only has eyes for her groom, the groom only has eyes for his bride, and the groom's parents only have eyes for the potential grandchildren."

"So what's the problem?"

"The bride's parents, who only have eyes for their deposit and the final payment due. The stern-eyed judgment of these two starts with their arrival today, and stays on me for the next six months, stopping only when I show them the door."

"Maybe they're nice people?"

"They probably were nice people, once upon a time, and then they went and said they'd pay for the wedding." Miss Havisham brushed off a speck of pollen. "If I had my way, only the gays would marry. For the most part, they handle their own bills."

"As much as we, the gays, appreciate your support, I still think you're missing an opportunity with Compeyson."

"May I remind you who is in charge here? I don't think you're in any position to lecture me about my personal life."

"Actually, according to labor law, you can't ask these kinds of questions of me." Estella nodded. "I'm totally within my rights to interrogate you."

"Doesn't seem fair."

"Doesn't seem fair that you make me work in a sweatshop."

"Seriously?" Miss Havisham swept a hand through the air to encompass the ornate room.

Estella pointed at her left brow. "A bead of sweat. Right there. I can feel it."

"You probably walked into a cloud of mist while you bumbled about, not freshening the blooms."

"You're a wicked boss, Miss Havisham. Wicked."

"Just you wait until your break when I slap the bowl of gruel out of your hands."

"I get breaks?"

"Only in a metaphorical sense."

"If you keep this up, Boss, I'll see to it that you're visited by three ghosts: the local Board of Health inspector, a representative from OSHA, and agents of the Internal Revenue Service."

"Really? I'll see to it that you don't receive any future banquet leftovers."

"Miss Havisham, have I told you lately how much I appreciate the chance to work here, to learn from your tutelage?"

"Speaking of that, why don't you stuff your tutelage back into the top of your top? We're trying to impress the parents of the bride, not break up their marriage."

"Call back to those labor laws: you're not actually allowed to comment on my bosom."

"Seriously? So it would be wrong for me to say you have a buxom bosom?"

"Yes, unless you could say it five times fast, which would be rather impressive."

"As impressive as your bosom?"

Estella huffed. "You've gone and said it again."

"Whatever." Miss Havisham consulted her watch. "They're late."

"'Late' late, or 'on time' late?"

"Is it too much of me to expect that people will arrive when they said they're going to arrive? If not slightly earlier? What if they left their house only when the GPS said they could leave and still get here on time, and then they got stuck behind a horse and carriage?"

"I haven't seen many of those on the highway."

"I'm considering a new package that includes a horse and carriage from the church."

"Considering how far we are from the nearest church, that might take a while."

"There will be thick curtains. The couple can start their honeymoon."

"Giddy up."

Miss Havisham raised a finger on her cheek. "I wonder how much I could charge for that."

"I wonder how soon it would be before I was mucking out stalls."

"You wouldn't be complaining about a bit of water on your face then, would you?"

"Change in working conditions. I'll file a grievance."

"With whom? You're not in a union."

"What's this union you speak of, a way that employees can band together to protect themselves against hostile employers?"

Miss Havisham beamed. "I was thinking of the marriage union, the bread and butter of SatisFaction Betrothals."

"Have you ever noticed that 'brothel' and 'betrothal' are virtually the same word?"

"Except for the differences, yes, they're exactly the same. Much like the phrases 'I'm giving you a raise' and 'I'm giving you a raisin.'"

"You're giving me a raisin?"

Miss Havisham smiled. "I finally found the grapes left over from a banquet two June's ago. If I remember the couple, the fruit is probably in better shape."

"Trouble in Denmark?"

"Yes, but that's a different Brit."

Estella parted the thick drapery. "There's no sign of the parents coming up the drive. Are you sure you wrote down the correct time?"

"I'm not even going to dignify that with an answer."

"Maybe they texted."

"Arg. I've had my phone muted. Arthur. He started first thing this morning, a little after six."

"What does your brother want now?"

Miss Havisham pulled out her phone. "'Call me ASAP.' Then minutes later, 'Are you still asleep? Call me.' Five minutes later, 'Hello?' Twice minutes after that, 'Urgent!'"

"Did you text him back?"

Miss Havisham scrolled through the one-sided conversation. "Not until his seventeenth message, at 8:40, does Arthur say that a Nigerian prince reached out to him saying that his inheritance of thirty-million US dollars is tied up by a lawyer who requires money for legal fees, payable in cash or gift cards."

"You're joking."

"I told Arthur not to settle for less than twenty-percent of the gross, and to offer an additional five hundred if the prince knows anyone who can extend his manhood."

"You didn't."

"And then I muted my phone before I became riled." Miss Havisham swore. "Which is why I missed this."

"What?"

"From the father of the bride: 'Sorry, but my daughter has called off the wedding, and therefore we won't be needing your services as there will be no reception afterwards.'"

"I misted the blossoms for nothing?"

"Sorry to say, but that's the kind of thing that can happen when you work in a sweatshop."

"Doesn't seem fair."

"Again with the 'fair.'" Miss Havisham kicked off a shoe. "Luckily, the non-refundable deposit they paid to save a spot on the calendar more than covers the cost of the bottle of champagne you're about to open for us."

"What are we celebrating?" Estella frowned. "You just lost a client."

"If I have to pay you for three hours, per Massachusetts state law, which I'm sure you appreciate me knowing in this instance, I'm certainly not letting you leave now."

"But drinking on the clock is fine?"

"It is when I say it is." Miss Havisham tapped her chest. "Boss."

"I'll get the champagne."

"And two glasses. Or, if it's too difficult to juggle two glasses and the bottle, just grab two bottles. We'll swill."

"Seeing as I can't juggle, that might be the better idea."

"Excellent."

Estella paused. "I just had a thought, though. What if the couple reunites, and the parents of the bride decide to come here after all? Do you really want them to find you drinking from the bottle and singing seafaring songs?"

"Luckily, I don't know any."

"Maybe after a couple of sips, I'll teach you one."

"That could be fun. I suppose you're right, though." Miss Havisham plunked into the nearest love seat. "The couple reconciling would be a disaster. What if the parents of the bride decide to come this afternoon? I might end up having to pay you for a full day!"

"You could give me off tomorrow in trade."

"We have a reception tomorrow. Two-hundred plates and a cash bar. Were you to pass during the night, I would find a way to reanimate you."

"It's nice to be needed. Also, you said I was right."

"A slip of the tongue." Miss Havisham fanned herself.

"It didn't sound like a slip. The words were quite clear, precise and enunciated."

"A dream perhaps."

Estella pinched herself. "I'm not asleep."

"That's good, since I don't appreciate employees who sleep on the job. I pay you to work, not tend sheep. Too much bubbly, then."

"I haven't even opened the bottle."

"Maybe you're still drunk from the night before, which would explain your inability to apply mist to a bloom without drenching yourself."

"I can't wait until my annual review comes around again. I'm going to have a list of complaints, three inches thick."

"First, annual reviews don't necessarily take place every year. Second, that's not how annual reviews actually work."

Estella pointed at her boss. "We'll talk more about this after I return with the booze."

"Bated breath, dear girl." Miss Havisham crossed her legs, wiggled the toes on her non-shod foot. As much as she appreciated the cancellation, she now had to fill a hole on the calendar, deal with a different set of parents of the bride.

Nicer, perhaps, although these two had seemed reasonable enough.

Still, better not to have to meet them in person, socialize, host. A strange attitude for someone in the business of holding wedding receptions.

If only SatisFaction Betrothals could continue to turn a profit without her having to deal with people. Producing two hundred plates tomorrow would be much simpler if there was nobody in the seats, for example.

Fewer complaints.

Miss Havisham flexed her toes.

Why, she could revitalize the entire wedding industry. Marry in an empty church. Celebrate in an empty reception hall. Think how happy guests would be not to have to sit for endless hours in uncomfortable clothes. They'd probably pay double for the privilege!

She'd save on food costs. Caterers. Flowers that had to be misted to stay fresh.

Of course she'd still order the wedding cake, even if always the same cake. After all, she and Estella wouldn't want to drink champagne on empty stomachs.

Estella flounced into the room carrying a tray, which she set on the table with a flourish.

Two bottles of champagne. Two glasses. A dish of strawberries, stems removed with slices in the shape of hearts.

Miss Havisham clapped. "Well done."

Her employee curtsied. "Ma'am."

"I suppose you'll be asking for a raise next."

"I've already been promised a raisin." She arranged herself in the chair on the other side of the table. "What's left, a rein?"

"You can drive the horse and carriage."

Estella bit into a strawberry. "If I'm out there, transporting the bride and groom, who's in here misting the blooms? You?"

"I'll be too busy calculating terms."

"That's it then. You'll have to find another driver."

"And a horse. The carriage won't move without one."

"The guests would become restless, waiting for the bride and groom to appear."

"I was thinking, while you were gone for an inexcusable amount of time." Miss Havisham popped open the champagne and filled both their glasses. "Wouldn't it be great if we could do away with the bridal party?"

"Robots. We could release the bride, the groom, and the parents after the ceremony, and then entertain the guests at the reception with robots." Estella lifted her glass in a toast.

Miss Havisham raised hers higher. "You're a pip, Estella. A real pip."

The Lady of the Seven Temples, also known as the Lady in Black, is a legend from San Luis Potosí (although some say Durango), telling the story of a taxi-driver's peculiar costumer – a lady in black who asks him to take her to seven temples. After the drive she says she has no money, so gives the driver her wedding ring with direction to her husband's place, saying he will pay him. When the driver arrives, the husband cries at the sight of her ring, saying he will indeed pay him, but that the woman he met has been dead for one year. This story speculates on who the lady was before her death, why she came back after dying, and why was it to pray at seven different temples?

A HEART OF STAINED GLASS
ARI OCHOA CONTRERAS

THEY ALWAYS START THE story wrong: just a year after I died. The correct way to tell the story is to go back decades or so before I even left the earth. That was when I fell in love with the man that took my heart and hid it in seven temples.

But I'm getting ahead of myself.

The first time I realized magic was real, was at my all-girls Catholic school's chapel. I had come early to practice the psalms played on Ash Wednesday, when I arrived the place looked dressed as a widow in pitch-black clothes, the dim lights at the corners not even enough to keep me from squinting at the sheet music.

But, as the sun rose up, a flash of forest green light colored my skin, followed by ocean blue, and then red as blood. Through the careful dance between the architect, the sun, and the stained glass master, the chapel turned alight by multicolored window-paintings of Mary holding her son.

I looked around for the nun that took care of the chapel, eager to know if she too felt it. When our eyes found each other, I saw that she understood: this was how God's love felt, not pain that could (but not always) lead into something better.

I wonder if the artist that had for the first time captured color in glass at the Abbey of San Vincenzo knew how it felt too.

The boy that took my heart didn't believe in God, or at least, the one I believed in. Oftentimes I would see him in the mass the school administration forced him to attend, and pull out from his skirt a book that had a different tale of The Creation from the one I knew. Two brothers slaying a beast instead of a lonely being sculpting the universe.

I discovered that I fancy women by falling in love with him.

We were sitting just outside the chapel, a window with The Virgin of Guadalupe's portrait smiling down at us.

"They took our gods," he said and I didn't correct him. They took the gods from this land, not mine.

Our hands were brushing in the topper where the nun had put the left-over wafters.

"They broke them and then used the pieces to craft images of Mary and other Saints." He looked into my eyes to see what I thought.

"I love God, the one they teach us about," I confessed to him, "But..."

And the but made his eyes sparkle like the brown-stained glass in Mary's hair.

"In my mind I don't imagine him like the church paints him."

"Then how do you?"

When I talked to him, I imagined my mum's face: her brown skin drawn by wrinkles and freckles framed by her black and gray curls.

"Like a mother you can tell your secrets too," I said.

When there were only two wafers left we gave each other communion. Him telling me of how Cintéotl made the little pieces of food possible and I of a young mother sacrificing herself for her children.

I discovered that I fancy men by being in love with him.

Five years later he came to deliver a stained glass piece to a church I played the piano for. He had a different name, soft stubble and rough hands from handling glass and copper.

We took each other in, how the different pieces of us that we knew had broken and rearranged.

"So this is you now," I said.

"And you are this for the moment," he said.

We both smiled, each other more beautiful than when we had last seen one another, and if knowing that your friend will lend you space to grow and cherish you even more isn't love then I don't know what is.

I gave him my heart when he gave me his.

I asked for a wedding, officiated in the cathedral, through the eyes of my God and everyone that would want to come. He sighed but accepted after we agreed to having dancers worshiping the flower siblings – Xochiquetzal and Xochipilli – in our reception.

When my heart was gathered into his hands it became a red tint in stain-colored glass. He cut it in seven pieces with a diamond blade – his experience as an artisan showing with every movement. When he finished, he placed the pieces in seven different projects for seven different churches:

San José; the place where I had taken a young girl's hands selling mazapanes on my own and taught her how to play lullabies she seldom remembered.

San Agustín, where my mum's funeral was held but I could not cry because she had taught me to not show any weakness in public.

La Compañía, where I sat down next to an old woman who had lost a daughter, yet again. Both asking God to please take care of her wherever she was.

Tequis, in which my little sister's wedding was held. The double of witnesses in the groom's side than in my own, and with my grand-aunt's presence when she had burned the invitation to mine.

San Miguelito, when I eavesdropped into a confession: a young lesbian asking for atonement because she kissed the girl she loved, and I was reminded of my young self after I first kissed my husband. I sneaked outside and told her that the God we both believe in would not damn her for following her heart.

San Juan de Guadalupe, where a travesti had been pushed out of the benches so I asked if she would rather like to sit on the piano's stool next to me. She had the most beautiful voice I've ever heard. We became a duet after: she singing while I played.

El Santuario, where I first felt my hearing waning because of my illness and felt the air leave my body, a panic attack they had said. My husband tried to comfort me saying I would be like Mozart, I never learned who they were.

I continued with my own work. Bringing the music to several baptisms, weddings and funerals; Ash Wednesdays, Good Friday, Holy Saturday and Easter Sunday, even if I couldn't hear it.

He never understood how praying for me was the way I made sense of the world, a moment of reflection with myself and where I could let go of my fears. But, he understood that for me playing Getsemani and Angels of God was more powerful than reciting a complete rosemary.

When I died I had only one regret, that I didn't take my heart with me. While I was alive the fact that my heart now lived in another place didn't bother me as my husband filled the hole, as I left him I could feel an emptiness growing in me that would not let me rest.

And here is the part of the story everyone knows about:

I was able to come back to the land of the living a year after I died. I took a cab from El Pantéon del Saucito and retrieved the pieces of my heart scattered across the seven temples, murmuring blessings when I reached the doors.

I returned because no matter how much I have loved that man, it was time for me to let go.

As I took the last piece, the puzzle-piece sewed itself together, remembering where they had come from- the fact that they were part of one another and part of me, not some construction. As I pushed it through my cavity I felt whole again.

Due to having been dead I didn't have any money so I gave the driver my husband's direction and my wedding ring as collateral. It was bronze-covered gold with a diamond rose on top; his heart the only piece of jewelry my husband ever crafted, and the sloppiest of his work.

When the driver arrived to collect his share, he gave my husband the ring, returning the heart I had taken with me.

With my heart back into my hands I allowed myself to drift back into sleep by the rhythm of my glass-stained organ where the love of my God and my pagan husband had graced it.

As a child, I loved watching "Leave It To Beaver" on TV. As I got older, I began to question June Cleaver's perfection: every hair in place, clothes and makeup perfect at any time of day, apron at her waist and pearls at her throat. I did not know any real mothers like that. In my poem, I consider what might happen should June decide to break out of her mold.

LIMITS OF PERFECTION
—REMEMBERING MRS. CLEAVER

SHERYL CLOUGH

How do you pull it off, June?
Lustrous pearls ever at your throat;
not a hair out of place;
perfect starched apron at 7 A.M.

Modern women would thank their stars
for children so well-behaved.
No gangs, guns or graffiti
pollute the streets of Mayfield.

Your husband Ward resembles few
men ever known to real women:
provider, Mr. Fix-It, wise mentor,
gentle disciplinarian.

One fateful day, you break
through your white picket gate,
rip the choker from your neck,
and sprint down the street

tossing pearls to neighbors
and singing in a voice
loud enough to stir the dead
Don't fence me in.

Annabel Lee, a wealthy young lady, fulfills the Victorian trope of dying young and pretty. It is an ideal Edgar Allan Poe used often in his short stories and poems. Her unnamed lover is convinced every thought she had was about him and spends every night sleeping by her grave for the rest of his life, so it's easy to imagine how her life would have been with someone this obsessive. Annabel Lee needed to escape both her early death and a man so controlling he rails at the angels for stealing her away.

ANNABELLE LEE ESCAPED THE SEA
DANA M EVANS

I THOUGHT I LOVED him once but we were young. I was foolish. We would walk, hand in hand, on the beach and over the rocky paths along the cliffs, marveling at the summer cottages of Newport, each more amazing than the others. My father's home was just one castle among the many. My love and I called Newport our 'Kingdom by the Sea,' and even when we both returned to Manhattan after the season, we were hard to keep separate. Only propriety and fear of my father kept me from giving myself fully to this boy I loved.

Until, one day, I realized I didn't love him. In retrospect, it wasn't one day. It was the culmination of many days, little clues littering my life until finally I was wise enough to put them together as smart as Dupin or Sherlock. He said he loved me. What he meant was he needed to control me. At first, his interest in my day made my face glow, warmed by my appreciation of his care for me, that he found me so fascinating he needed to know all the details.

We would run on the beach, kissed by the wind. He'd inquire about my day and for a year, maybe two, it was endearing. Once Father took his interest in me seriously and approved of him – what was to disapprove of in the son of a railroad baron even richer than we were – things shifted. Oh, we had our daily walks along the beach but when I went into town, he would be there too. Because it was only one or two chance meetings I'd thought nothing of them. It slowly sank in after I'd seen his family's servants somewhere close whenever I was out. He always knew where I was.

The way he acted at the Flying Horse carousel filled in the rest. Any man looking my way was cause for worry. Would he fight them for no reason? What would happen to me if he thought I was looking back at a stranger? He had thrown that poor, innocent young man from the carousel for merely inquiring my name. Away from others, he was sweet as an entremets, showering me with kisses. He told me how nothing would ever sever our love. What had once sounded sweet had started to sound like a prison, one I no longer wanted part of.

Retreating to my rooms hadn't helped. If I didn't socialize, there would be a slew of little gifts sent to the house. There was nowhere to escape from him. Boxes, love notes, flowers covered my vanity to the point I could barely see the mahogany top. Reminders of him dotted all available space in my room, making it not mine anymore. Last night, after three separate gift bearers had arrived and I had not been lured out of my room, he finally swept in insisting on another walk in the surf. I couldn't say no, not with Father looking on. Concentrating on the insistent rhythm of the waves, the cry of the gulls wheeling overhead and chasing after them hoping for crumbs, the joy of others trying to enjoy the beach, none of it brought me any solace.

Heart heavy, I had approached Father last night to ask to break the engagement. Today found me hiding in my rooms with a split lip and a swollen eye. No one said no to Father. I cradled Violet to my chest, resting my sore cheek on the cat's furry head. Violet purred, rubbing against me, a soft comfort. A light knock at the door made me raise my face but I didn't invite whoever it was in. My maid would go away in time or tell me my father wanted me downstairs.

Instead, the door opened, and Mother swept in. I saw myself in my mother, the same long blond curls, and sky-blue eyes, only Mother had more lines than her age should have provided. Life with Father would do that to anyone. Would my life be any better? No, even

Father didn't follow Mother everywhere. My life would be worse, bound tighter than my corset to a man who needed to possess my every moment.

Mother swept across the room and folded her skirts under her as she sat on the window seat. "Annabelle Lee, I've sent a telegram to Lillie."

I raised my eyebrows. Aunt Lillie's name was not to be spoken in this house. Mother only whispered it to me rarely as if fearing I would be so swept away by my adventuress aunt's latest exploits, that I would forget myself and mention Aunt Lillie in front of Father. "Where is she now?"

"Cape Breton. She is expecting you."

I shivered. "I don't understand."

Mother heaved a sigh. "I would not wish my life on you, my darling. Your man is even worse than my own."

"But Father–"

"He'll be leaving for London shortly. He'll be gone for months." Mother smiled. Of course, she would. When his job took him overseas was the only reprieve she had.

"He'll notice I'm gone when he returns," I replied bitterly.

The conspiratorial expression on Mother's face lightened my heart. "I have a plan."

I caught his hand, pulling him along the beach, the wet sand cooling my toes. Father had been gone for a week before the perfect day arrived. Now that it was here, I felt swept away on freedom's warm breeze. Mother had been craftier than I had ever given her credit. Father had dimmed her light, but she had some of her sister, Lillie, in her. I did as well. Our plan would work. Once Mother had outlined her idea, I had built on it.

Mrs. Powell wasn't just a good cook for us. She had a knee that predicted weather better than anyone I knew. If she said today would bring rain, it would. The sun had been bright and sunny when I walked out with him but now clouds as gray and angry as my heart when I was with him had rolled in.

He tugged my sleeve and cast a glance at the sky. "Annabelle Lee, we should go, my love."

Oddly enough, he was still handsome to me even though I had more than enough of him. I would not weaken because of a pretty face. "No, I want to paint this when I return home."

"This?" He quirked up his eyebrows. "I love your art, beloved, but this is not pretty."

"Oh, but it is. Look at the grays and deep blues, the hints of a purple sunset. A stormy sea makes for wonderful art. You know it does. We can wait just a little longer."

"We didn't bring an umbrella," he argued.

"It's only a little water. We'll dry."

I might have underestimated the storm. Cold, wet winds lashed us. My dress stuck to my body tight as if sculpted there. Mother had suggested I run off with Aunt Lillie and change my name. My former love might not let that be. Father might send Pinkertons after me. No, Mother's plan was just the beginning. I had to be sure of my escape and this storm would be perfect for it, if only I didn't *actually* catch my death from it.

I was sniffling – fake – by the time he led me home and shivering violently – not fake – as I went inside. Mother had the servants lay in a fire in my rooms and I sat next to it cuddled in a heavy blanket gratefully. Tomorrow I would be sick. In a few days I would be gone. That's why I had to wait for Father to go overseas. He could not get a ship back in time. I would be in my tomb and he none the wiser. The hardest part would be my funeral. It would take acting skills beyond any Mother or I had evidenced so far but my freedom depended on it. We would prevail.

I slipped away so fast from my illness that I had but one day to fake being feverish and ranting when he insisted on being at my side. Mother insisted louder than he needed to leave me rest. In her grief, she had only two days of viewing, two days where I had to lie so very still, my breaths shallower than a puddle when anyone was nearby. It took Mr. Jackson, our butler, and two of the footmen to eject my former love from the parlor both days.

Our servants were Mother's first before becoming Father's upon their marriage – her money going to fund Father's ventures – and more loyal to her than they were to a man who treated them cruelly. They would keep our secret. Mother told me all the details of the church service and my former love's over the top show of grief, flinging himself on my casket in front of the altar and again before it was laid in the family mausoleum in the cemetery overlooking the sea.

Pangs of guilt nibbled my heart. I was not a monster and hated causing pain, but I would never be free of him otherwise. I could not live my life in a cage of his control. I packed up the last of my trunks when Mother came into my room for what would be the last time.

She had a heavy purse with her. "Money enough to keep you comfortable for a long time. Lillie will tell you best how to handle it and hide it since the banks won't deal with you."

No, banks were utterly unfair to women. I could open no accounts without my father's or husband's approval, such poppycock. I opened the purse, widening my eyes at what I found. "Where did you get all of this?"

"My father allowed me to sit in his office when he worked. I learned bookkeeping better than my brother. Your father is terrible at it. He has no idea how much I've squirreled away from his accounts, wondering one day if it might be needed. Now it is."

I tried to press the purse back in her hands, but she wouldn't take it. "I cannot accept your freedom, Mother."

A bitter laugh escaped her mouth. "There is none for me, but I am content to know you are free. Listen to Lillie, she'll teach you well."

Tears flooded my eyes. How could I leave her behind? I had no choice, but it tore my heart to do so. "Look for letters from Belle Champagne. Tell Father I'm one of your friend's daughters. I'll type them so he won't recognize my handwriting."

"You don't know how to type." Mother was crying now too.

"I'll learn."

She hugged me fiercely. Letting go was nearly impossible but all too soon me and my trunks were on a night train north, bearing me away from my life and my death.

It never fails to amaze me how long the years can be and so terribly short at the same time. I swore I had only blinked twice and I went from the naïve Belle Champagne to a grandmother of four. I shed Belle as a name early on – though she remained my journalistic byline all these years. Oh, the adventures she had written up and shared with the world. I took back part of my name as it fit me better and I was less fearful of being found out.

Those first years had been guilt-ridden and hard. Deceiving people as I did over something as big as faking my own death weighed heavily on me. I had no siblings to worry on and my father's entire reaction had been to say it would have mattered more if I'd been a son. His life went on unphased for ten more years.

His early death freed Mother. She sold the business, never remarried, and enjoyed jaunts with her sister Lillie and their young 'friend' Anne Leigh. I've had a few other surnames since. The longest, best, of them had been from my marriage to the sweetest self-made man of Scottish and Micmac descent. John had valued my intelligence and that of our daughters as well as our sons.

My life has been a rich medley of travel and adventure, walking the Roman avenues in Italy, crawling into the womb of an ancient cromlech in Wales and Ireland, touching a goddess in Greece, but nowhere was I happier than in our rambling home in Halifax.

Mother passed away a little more than a year ago and despite my thoughts over the matter, I arranged for the centenarian to rest in the stately mausoleum next to Father. Maybe she wanted a final view of the sea.

I traveled back last night with my daughter and her daughter to finish closing off Mother's house and prepare it for sale. I hadn't been able to face doing so last year; maybe it was my own mortality I hated facing. I had survived the birth of four children and three husbands, but every story had an ending. Bah, mine has more years waiting to be told.

"I'm going for a walk," I announced, dragging Brigid's attention away from one of Mother's trunks she was exploring with Ceridwen's 'help.' The four-year-old was more interested in tossing things about.

My daughter pushed her brown hair out of her eyes. "By yourself?"

"Unless you want an early evening walk in the cemetery." I smiled.

Brigid narrowed her eyes. "It's a strange time to visit grandma."

"It's not her I'm going to see."

Understanding flooded Brigid's face. She stood up to face me. "Ah, that old story Grandma used to tell about your first fiancé."

I winced. I hated thinking of him in those terms. Mother's story had haunted me for years. "I have to know if it's true, that he still sits every night by my grave."

"Surely he can't be."

I shook my head. "Mother swore he was."

"Well, I'm not letting you go to a cemetery at night alone." She scooped Ceridwen up.

I snorted. "I've done far more dangerous things."

"As a far younger woman." Brigid's sarcastic smirk was so like my own I could hardly be angry about it.

"Fair enough. Shall we?"

My daughter insisted on driving because she said I was too wild, and I didn't see as well at night anymore. Annoying but true.

The salty brine of the sea perfumed the summer air as we approached that beautiful mausoleum with its Egyptian columns and sun symbols, which provided no immortality no matter the hope. A shadow darkened the steps leading to the bronze tomb doors.

Brigid caught my wrist. "He's there," she whispered.

"So, he is."

How sad. A spear of guilt pierced me. Had I done this to him? Should I care? I hadn't forced him here decades after my 'death.' He was the one who forced me into such drastic action.

Brigid hefted Ceridwen against her hip and let me go forward on my own if I dared. Did I? Would he recognize me as I did him? Why should he? I was dead, moldering for decades behind the bronze mausoleum doors.

I strolled up to the tomb with the flowers plucked from mother's garden to place on the marble steps. "Oh sorry, I did not expect anyone here."

He looked up at me from where he sat reclined against one of the sphinxes guarding the way. Age had cut furrows into his face and his eyes gleamed fever bright.

"Nor I." He blinked. Was he trying to place me? Surely not.

"Are you here to sit with Judith too?" I set down my mother's flowers.

"Judith?" He shook his bald head. "No. My loves lies within."

"Oh?"

"Annabelle Lee. The angels were jealous of our love and stole her from our kingdom by the sea. They took her home so many years ago but nothing, not even death can sever our love," he proclaimed, proud as anything at this.

Brigid ghosted up alongside of me. Ceridwen shyly ducked her face against her mother's shoulder.

"Truly? Would she have wanted you to sit so long by a cold grave?"

He straightened up, eyeing me with such fury I had to rein in the urge to back away. "Of course. She would not have abandoned our love had our positions been reversed after that stormy night that claimed her."

No, I would not have sat by a grave for decades. I had lost loves but my life, my heart, did not grind to a stop nor would my true loves have wanted that for me. "She must have been a special woman," I said, testing how far he would carry this insanity.

"The best among them. As fair as you and yours are," He swept a hand to Brigid and Ceridwen. "you pale in comparison, hair of gold, eyes of summer sky, a heart so pure the angels wept to behold it, so they had to possess it. She's waiting for me." He sighed, looking skyward. "I never thought it would take so long."

I touched my hair. Most of the gold had faded to ivory. "You never looked for another love, a life outside of Annabelle Lee? It sounds to me, if she was so wonderful, she would have wanted you the best for you." Another twinge of guilt over causing this pain warred with the notion I had been right all along. Life with him would have been a miserable prison, harnessed to a delusional vision of the girl I had been.

He made a dismissive noise. "You don't understand Annabelle Lee at all."

I smiled, biting down hard on a laugh. "As you say. Well, it's getting dark, and we need to get this little one to bed." I stroked Ceridwen's cheek. "We'll spend time with Judith later and leave you to your visit."

"Thank you..." He trailed off, looking at me questioningly.

"Anne," I supplied.

A blissful look passed over his face. "You would have done well to know her, Anne."

"I'm sure."

We left him there, at the mausoleum by the sea in my old kingdom. In my head it was a queendom and I had done well enough by it, far better than he living in the cage into which he would have put me. This would be the last time I visited. Once Mother's house was sold up, I would have no reason to come back here. The mausoleum's care would be paid for because how could I do other? But there was no reason to sit and talk to the marble of the tomb. My mother was not here, just her shell. If I spoke to the wind anywhere in the world, she would hear me as clearly as if I were inside those doors seated on a cold iron bench.

I walked back to the car, the guilt shifting off of me. I might have been the trigger, but this display was pure mania. I slid into the car, keeping my silence as I cradled Ceridwen on my lap.

"That was not love," Brigid declared once we were underway.

"It's obsession," I concurred.

"You would have had a life in a gilded cage with that man."

I laughed at her indignant snarl even though nothing about this was funny. The cage he built for me might not even have been gilded, maybe painted in the blue and purple of a bruise when I couldn't be brought to heel. "And now you know why I ran so far and so fast."

My daughter smiled at me as my granddaughter snuggled against my breast. I stroked her back with my arthritic hand.

"Best decision of your life, Mother."

I glanced back at the fading cemetery and sighed. "My freedom was worth its price. I would trade it for nothing."

And so I would not. His obsession traded for my life of freedom and love? No, I had made the right decision all those years ago and I would make it again had life given me the chance. I would choose freedom every time.

Written by Kate Chopin in 1894 and published the same year in Vogue, "The Story of an Hour" describes the elegant Louise learning her husband, Brently, has been killed in a railroad disaster. She retreats to her bedroom to grieve but instead feels great rushes of joy, realizing she's free from every restraint of marriage. She delights in the next hour, inspired. In the original Louise has a so-called frail heart and upon seeing her husband uninjured, walking into their home, she is felled by "the joy that kills." Critics at the time believed such a controversial story needed Louise's demise in the final sentences. But Louise should have survived Brently, and exposed him too. For Louise, preferred name Liana, this should be the story of a future.

THE STORY OF A FUTURE
STACY BIERLEIN

KNOWING THAT I AM young and only a few years into marriage some care is taken in relaying the information to me. My name is Liana Fontaine. Shopkeepers often greet me by my sister's name, our physical resemblance being what it is. On those occasions I am called Mrs. Mallard, like the duck, the bird that both French and Englishman shoot down. I will not be shot down.

In my native France, films are being made. Letters from school friends hold wonder and enthusiasm. My husband finds the very idea of moving pictures strange, unsettling.

I want to say outright, if you adapt my story for film, the run time should be exactly an hour. The camera fades in as I am about to receive the news. I'm walking down the staircase from my bedroom suite. My husband's assistant, Mr Richards, is waiting at the threshold, his posture stiff, disturbingly so, always more fright than flight. The camera might close in on his facial expression. He is, today especially, an expressive man.

Mr Richards reaches for my hand as I arrive at the second to last step. An odd gesture, I think, as if the last two stairs are somehow more treacherous for me than the previous sixteen. His voice is a strange scratchy whisper, which I'm sure pleases my husband, who likes to be heard above others.

Because your film audience has not known me previously, they will not understand that a change has already taken place. Just yesterday I relocated the more serious outfits to the back of the dressing room. I'm wearing a pastel blue tea dress, Belgian glass buttons down the back that my husband's mother would consider frivolous, unacceptable. I've styled my hair up, but with fringe falling across my forehead, and in a moment of whimsy, I grabbed some freesias from the vase in my room, dried them, and pinned them to my waist. I believe I am taller than ever before, a now-solid confidence that had been fleeting. It is the *belle époque*, but of course I do not yet refer to these years this way.

I could not possibly have known the announcement I am about to hear, but my husband has been gone for days, my world already improved. In fact, I woke feeling oddly giddy, victorious, my intuition delightfully ahead of this flailing patriarchal world. Dutifully the staff gathers behind my husband's assistant, the decor no match for their sunken faces.

INT. Entrance Hall. Day. [camera close-in]
I'm so sorry to tell you, Madame Fontaine, *blah blah blah blah blah*, it is a great tragedy, the train, *blah blah blah* the authorities say *blah blah blah* nothing anyone could do.
[Mr Richards takes a deep breath]
The commissioner does not believe that Monsieur Fontaine is among the survivors. What we mean to tell you, with great regret Madame, I am so sorry, is that I'm afraid…Monsieur Fontaine, it is with my own despair that I tell you, he is gone.

At first my distress is obvious to them. It is painful, after all, to see Mr Richards struggle to deliver such news. The spectacle of a presumably good man in distress over such a deplorable one. The universe should be better than this.

I spend several moments looking hard at each of them, just staring. Emma, who does the cooking, Marco who helps me in the garden, Adele who does the shopping and the mending. It is a ridiculous thing to have a staff, their presence putting me in management capacities I never wanted, their tending to my rooms and my food when they have homes and stomachs of their own. They will be free now too. I bite my lower lip to prevent myself from wicked laughter, which of course looks to them like I am trying to hold back tears.

I would like to be alone in my room, I tell them. When my sister arrives (for surely, Josephine will not be kept away) you may all go home, as I'm sure you would prefer to be alone with your thoughts on such a momentous occasion. I know that Monsieur Fontaine is, *was*, I say slowly as their expressions fall even more, fond of you. I only ask that Mr Richards stay a few hours to handle the phone, should the newspapers call.

Because they are so lovely, they start to protest, Ella is sure I'll need her for meals, Adele will call the doctor if I need a sedative, surely Marco...but I hold up my hand and continue, I prefer to be alone now. Should visitors arrive – anyone at all – please send them away.

With that, I run up the stairs to our chambers, *my chambers*, close and lock the door. This hour I am about to spend alone in my suite will be a work of art.

INT. Bedroom Suite. Day. [camera wide on room]
Madame Fontaine pushes open the bedroom windows. From the eastern casements she sees the tops of trees all aquiver with new spring life. The scents of the previous nights' rains linger in the air. She hears the faint songs of birds twittering in the eaves. Patches of bright blue sky show between clouds. She cannot think of the word for this kind of cloud formation because only one word reverberates in her brain. *Free.*

She spins herself around the room like a little girl wearing a hoop skirt for the first time. Her pulse beats fast, every inch of her body relaxing. She dances a tango now, solo, but held by monstrous joy, the word coming from her mouth in whisper bursts. Free, free, free. *Free, free, free.* Free to fly out that window and do whatever she pleases. Body and soul free!

There are moving pictures in Paris, she thinks, bamboo flutes in far-away archipelagos.

She stops, noting for a moment that she will have to weep when the time comes. She will have to meet with the pastor and the funeral director, see her husband lying there in his favorite dark suit, hands folded in death. Or will she? His mother will insist that he is a prominent man, that the casket should be open. But his mother isn't the widow, is she? The decision belongs to her; the casket will be closed with sprays of roses on top. Oh, but wait, he had hated the smell of her rosewater. Well, she laughs, we do not have to worry about that now.

Madame Fontaine wonders what the decorum will be, how long she will have to wait before she boards a ship or a train to anywhere. To everywhere. She is sure there is enough money, she is careful about such things, but she will sell his collection of timepieces just to be sure. She takes her silver chatelaine handbag from her bedside table and goes to his bureau. She opens the maple box and starts shoving timepieces into her bag like a petty thief. The years ahead would belong to her absolutely.

Free, she whispers again as Josephine knocks on her door. Please let me in, Josephine begs. What are you doing in there? Please Sissy, for heaven's sake let me in.

Go away, she tells her sister. I am not cutting myself or making myself sick, I promise you. I only want to be alone with my emotions.

Her mind races along those vibrant days ahead of her. She does not want Josephine's drama slowing her down. She breathes a quick selfish prayer that her own life might be long, all the standards previously forced upon her abandoned as society women shake their heads, call her the crazy widow, a reputation that will allow her any behaviors she pleases.

Not that she is coming back here. Not when there are ships and carriages that might take her to the other side of the world. And why does she have to wait? She might make a quick voyage now while Mr Richards and the pastor prepare things.

She goes to the dressing room, selects a black coat dress with a modest bustle, throws it across the bed. It will take her some time to change, considering the delicate buttons on the tea dress, but she sings quietly as she works, *free free free*, free free free. She goes to the mirror, runs a finger across the lace on her collar, fixes her hair without fuss, then wraps her bag full of timepieces around her wrist.

INT. Upstairs Hall. Day. [camera close-in]
I am surprised to find tear-streaked Josephine still outside my door. I am going to be strong, I tell her. It is all going to be fine.

Josephine nods, wraps her hands around my waist, and we descend the stairs together.

Afternoon sun floods the hall. We hear Mr Richards on the phone in the study accepting condolences before he joins us at the bottom of the staircase. Suddenly there is a loud rattle of the latchkey. Someone is opening the front door.

My heart sinks even before my brain processes the reality.

It is Monsieur Barden Fontaine who enters, visibly travel fatigued, but composed in his usual dark suit carrying his Gladstone bag and an old umbrella. A change of plans had kept him away from the tragic event; he did not even know there had been one. He stands in the door shocked by Josephine's piercing cries.

Mr Richards makes quick motion to screen him from my view in case it is all too much for me. It is not. I walk to Barden, put my right hand on his cheek to be sure he is real, and say goodbye.

EXT. Courtyard. Dusk. [camera pulls back]
I breathe deeply, baby birds still singing as I cross the courtyard, carrying my youth and those pieces of time. Barden, Josephine, and Mr Richards are too stunned to call after me. I had spent that hour upstairs making the most exquisite plans. The world's subsequent spoiler is not going to deter me.

INT. Study. Evening. [camera wide on room]
When doctors arrive, they give Josephine a sedative to help her rest. That very evening they conclude that professionals will need to develop a comprehensive long-term treatment plan for Monsieur Fontaine's anger. He will continue with mood regulation therapies for many years, evaluation reports going to his mother and to the Mallards as Madame Fontaine cannot be reached. Misogyny remains imprinted on him, therefore the diagnoses are never good.

EXT. Seashore. Evening. [montage, multiple locations]
I do not disappear completely. I send my sister telegrams from the Islands, from the Americas, from Thailand and finally from Indonesia, where breezes of bamboo songs linger with great beauty. Here I discover the nutty, bewitching taste of *sate ayam,* and hold a camera for the first time. I fall deeply in love with the vibrant sounds of gamelan music.

It is here I learn to play with precision a two-headed drum.

In Christopher Marlowe's play Dido Queen of Carthage, Aeneas, fulfilling the prophecy set down by the gods, resumes his quest to found Rome, leaving his spurned lover Queen Dido of Carthage behind. She takes revenge on him by taking her own life...which causes her rejected suitor Iarbas to take his own life...which causes her sister who was in love with him to take her own life... In Dido's opinion this suicide pyre is not big enough for three. A change of plans is in order.

THIS PYRE ISN'T BIG ENOUGH FOR THE TWO OF US

CEALLACH STEVENS

SING O MUSE OF Venus' inability to mind her own damned business. Because this was it, the end of all. Aeneas now sailed for Rome.

Short-lived had been their love, but was a lifetime in the heart. Dido's proud, false Aeneas had been born to her on the tumultuous waves of Neptune. His honeyed words opened her to Cupid's arrow. The famously blind archer had Venus for his guide, and thus sealed Dido's doom.

For an oath she had sworn before Aeneas, to love none save her late Sychaeus. Slain by her King brother Pygmalion, she had fled into Libya, but in adversity did Dido thrive. Founding Carthage she herself had built the city's might. Its beauty famed throughout the word and abundance known to all. Great Kings of Africa sought her hand and fortune, but none would she love. Her duties as sovereign and favor of regal Juno were all she required.

Then guess what Cetus dragged in.

Cursed, treacherous arrow that pierced her breast! Fletched with feathers of a dove it struck Dido's long dormant heart and stoked love for none but Aeneas. Survivor of sacked Troy who passed Scylla and Charybdis with ease. Prophesized founder of Empires now adrift upon Neptune's unforgiving seas. Safety had she offered! Sanctuary for his weary men and women! This was his thanks to her, to leave her heart as solitary as when Cupid gave it aim.

That Jove-damned Shmuck.

How happy she had been and could have continued to be. With her Aeneas, Carthage could thrive under two shining rulers. Here their empire would flower and bear fruit. Rival kings would be conquered and, in time perhaps, an expedition would be made to found and conquer fabled Rome. Aeneas made her immortal with his kisses and his breath stoked her soul. She loved a once impossible love and had thought in poor faith that it was given to her in turn.

No. Such. Luck.

There went her love now, with Aeneas, out the sea. She turned from her window, summoned her attendants with all haste. All traces of Aeneas would be gathered, heaped into a pyre. Like a lighthouse it would shine out to be seen by his ship, so bright Aeneas sails would mirror its red. He would see and he would suffer, knowing his betrayal of her for Rome came not without cost.

For atop the Pyre, its crowning jewel, Dido herself would stand. Her curse would carry on the winds and fly on the foam to be the bane of his precious Rome! He who joined himself to her and took all her honor and love. Aeneas left her with naught but the scorn of Numidian Tyrants and Carthaginian men. For Aeneas she braved their hate and spurned their advances. Her honor lost, her name plummeting from grace even as her funeral pyre was kindled, she prayed, prayed for death.

Call her a drama Queen. Melpomene, Muse of Tragedy, had nothing on her.

Welcome, happy fire, flicking like the tongue of a loyal hound to kiss his mistress' unhappy feet. For a time they would be her companion until the sword in her hand would give a swift, merciful end.

A sword not unlike that clutched in the fist of her one time suitor Iarbas.

She looked to him. "Even before I've become ashes my avenger seeks to spring from them."

With an awkward thrust the sword was concealed behind his back, "Revenge, yes, of course my Queen."

Beside him her sister, the Princess Anna regarded the flames of the pyre with green eyes.

"You *are* both conspiring towards my vengeance?"

Both alike in sheepishness did Iarbas and Anna salute each other.

"My Queen is like the sun. What once blessed by her warmth can live without it?" offered Iarbas.

All reason and purple flowered prose left Dido's mind.

"All right, look, both of you. Aeneas broke my heart and ruined my reputation as a Queen. Because of that, I'm going to set myself on fire and kill myself with this sword. It's going to be super tragic and make that jerk feel really bad about breaking off our engagement to found Rome. If you two clowns kill yourselves right after I do, you're going to turn my masterpiece of a revenge-suicide into a big joke."

"But I cannot live without you!" protested Iarbas.

"Nor can I without my sister or Iarbas!" echoed Anna.

"This is my suicide pyre, okay? Mine. Aeneas will totally see it from his ship. I want him to stew in his regret, not spend the rest of his voyage wondering, 'who were those two idiots that jumped in Dido's fire,'" argued the Queen. "If you're going to kill yourselves at least give it a solid ten minutes and don't copy me."

"But you picked the most rad way to go out!" whined Anna. "No fair!"

"I'm the Queen, if my death isn't totally metal and poignant then there's no point," insisted Dido.

"There's already no point! If that dick doesn't care about you now he's not going to care about you when you're on fire!" snapped Iarbas.

"Yes he will! Watch!" Dido marched to the edge of the parapet, pointing boldly to the lighted pyre. "Hey asshole! Check out my rad suicide pyre! Good luck founding an empire that's totally getting kicked in the balls by Carthage in a thousand years!"

Cruel silence passed with none but the song of the sea for company.

"See, he didn't even notice," said Iarbas.

"To be fair I don't think they can hear that far out," observed Anna.

"Listen jerk-wad!" shouted Dido. "I'm cursing your dumb future Roman Empire to war and suffering! Carthage is going to have way cooler generals and we're going to own you harder than you've ever been owned! And you know what? We'll do it while riding Jove-damned war elephants because why not! I hope you're listening because my dying curse is the only warning your ass is going to get!"

The ship sailed on atop Neptune's indifferent waves.

"I don't think he heard you," repeated Anna.

"You know what, forget it. The dying curse still stands. Now for the last time, I am going to kill myself and I do not want you two turning this tragedy into a farce."

"Hold on, you're committing an over-the-top suicide because you got dumped by Aeneas, right? Well how come I'm not allowed to do the same when you dying is just like you're rejecting me again?" demanded Iarbas.

Sighing, Dido addressed her star-crossed attendant, her fingers massaging the bridge of her nose. "Because this is not about you Iarbas, and this is like the twelfth time I've told you no. At this point an over-the-top death for you wouldn't be tragic, it would just be pathetic."

"And if you kill yourself I'll have to kill myself," added Anna.

"Why?" asked Iarbas.

"Because she likes you, you walnut," groaned Dido.

"Sister!" protested Anna, throwing her hands over her mouth.

"Come on, I know the only reason you told me I should get with Aeneas was so Iarbas would give up on me and get with you," huffed Dido.

"For the last time, I'm not into you Anna!" exclaimed Iarbas.

"Oh, gee, sure sucks when that shoe's on your foot, doesn't it," Dido said irately. "By the way pot, I should introduce you to my friend kettle, they're also black."

"It doesn't change the fact that you killing yourself for Aeneas when the kingdom needs you is dumb!" said Iarbas.

"I swore to love none other than my late husband, I rejected proposals from every king from here to Troy. Once word gets out that I not only broke my vow but the guy I broke it for dumped me because the gods told him to, we're going to have a lot of angry kings at our door and a city with no faith in its Queen. This–" Dido spoke, her arm stretched aloft towards welcoming flames, "–is the last honorable way out, okay? I'm not doing it because it's going to be fun and I think other people should join in. Just look after Carthage and try not to do anything stupid for at least ten minutes after I light myself on fire."

"Well, if you think we're so incapable of sound decisions, why are you dying and leaving us in charge?" demanded Anna.

"I don't want to! I didn't want to fall in love again, but one minute you're helping war refugees who washed up on your shore and the next Eros is using your heart for target practice. Because of that I can either wait for a bunch of angry rejected kings to bring their armies and wreck the city, or I can stop them from doing that by eternally peace-ing out!"

"Wait, what was that bit about target practice?" asked Iarbas.

"You know, Eros, the one who shoots you in the heart and makes you fall in love," said Dido.

"So if the gods made you fall in love *and* the gods also told Aeneas to leave you," reasoned Iarbas. "They had it in for Carthage from the start. The second Aeneas showed up and brought his celestial drama with him there was no way out for us."

"And if there really isn't any way out why shouldn't we get to make our deaths as over-the-top as yours?" protested Anna.

"Hold on, I'm thinking," said Dido.

With their strings held by the gods, each Carthaginian had played their part. Dido a tragic love for their hero king and Iarbas the jealous rival. For Anna a confidant's part suited best, and so admirably did she play. Now the curtains drew on this scene and they would rise upon Aeneas. Brave true Aeneas would carry a heavy heart in both hands, his stoicism to be admired. He would be a hero to men, a symbol of sacrificed love for duty. And what role would there be left for Dido's memory but a Queen whose love drove her to mania. Rational man, irrational woman, a way of being justified through their shared fable.

The gods would go with Aeneas, seeing his journey to its end. He would be the hero to justify their precious Rome. Aeneas the one to mint its values through his voyage. The gods would guide the vessel as a child a toy boat in a pond. But with that guidance lost, no matter how untrained, would not the boat either ground or flounder?

"We can't fight off every neighboring kingdom I ever turned down a proposal from. We also can't stop Aeneas from founding Rome because that's a sure-fire way to have Jupiter start throwing lightening at us. Dying stops the invasion, but leaves Carthage in your hands and you two already told me how that's going to end..." Dido mused, her thoughts taking form through her lips. "I think I know a way out."

"We all jump in the pyre together?" suggested Anna.

"No, we're done with the pyre. The gods made me fall in love with Aeneas as a way to get him the ships and resources he needed to go found Rome. And if Venus and Eros make everyone fall in love than that must go for the two of you and all those foreign kings I turned down," reasoned Dido. "So if we all have a common enemy, why don't we all get together and go ham on that common enemy?"

"Queen Dido," said Iarbas, "Are you suggesting we rally the surrounding kingdoms and fight the gods?"

"Not all the gods, just one specific cow who has been a pain in all of our necks," said Dido.

Once more did Queen Dido turn to the sea, declaring for all who might hear, "While all the other gods are focused on Rome, we're gonna climb Mount Olympus. Then once we get to the top, we're going to free ourselves from this love-curse."

"The gods are immortal, how would we do that?" asked Anna.

Quenching the fire's thirst with water Dido announced, "By punching Venus in the boob!"

In the concluding scene of Joseph Conrad's Heart of Darkness, Marlow, having sought out the avaricious Kurtz in the Congo and witnessed his death, visits the woman Kurtz had been engaged to marry, referred to in the text only as 'the Intended.' Marlow, believing it to be an act of kindness, goes against his self-professed hatred of dishonesty and tells the Intended that Kurtz's last words (in reality, 'the horror, the horror') were her name. He does so to protect the delicate world of delusions he believes women to live in, never seeming to realize that his story has revealed the world men live in to be every bit as delusional and much more destructive.

UNINTENDED

JOSEPH S WALKER

HE WAS A STAMMERER, this Mr Marlow, uncertain of himself in the confines of walls, lost in a room filled with soft surfaces, where the floor did not rock beneath his boots. The dim light discomfited him, as did my raven attire. From the moment I entered the room, he desired nothing more than to be free of it.

Perhaps this is why he lied, though men, to be sure, always have a reason, while seeming to need none. The idea that Mr Kurtz expended his final breath on my name! It is a patent absurdity. I would sooner believe he recited Mr Carroll's *Jabberwock*.

I indulged myself in the briefest of fantasies, imagining Mr Marlow's reaction if I expressed my disbelief, if I challenged his meticulously constructed narrative. If, horror of horrors, I laughed. How thoroughly it would destroy him! He cannot imagine how he needs me in these widow's reeds, pining away for the beloved departed. He cannot imagine how he needs me here in this quiet, this so very civilized, room.

I took pity on him, and stayed still, the innocent bearer of all the world's evils.

We must pity men, once we see how they suffer in their self-imposed exile. For they live in a world of their own, and there has never been anything like it, and never can be. They enter it early, waving swords made of wood, wearing hats folded from the day's *Times*, which told breathlessly of the exploits of their fathers, who wielded more formidable weapons.

The world of men has no beauty, but it whispers to them of beauty. It has no love, but it whispers to them of love. It's a world of possession. My money. My land. My servants.

My intended.

Kurtz. The very name a blow. A bludgeon taken to the world, and all done in my name, all done in the name of this big soft *civilized* room, all done in the name of the pretty cages they've built us. I let Mr Marlow sweat and stammer. He was not comfortable in that room, but he clung to it. Without it he would have no reason to exist.

I could wreck his world so easily. I could whisper in his ear the fact we have lived with since creation: a woman with a bank account, and even the most minimal manual dexterity, has no need of any man.

Eventually I allowed him to flee. I even watched from the window.

Where Mr Marlow sees the garb of mourning, I see mighty armor which will protect me for the rest of days. I have made *Kurtz* into a shelter and a shield.

When Marlow was gone I turned to the garden (not *my* garden). I turned to books (not *my* books). Here in the light at the heart of my darkness they will suffice, until the world changes.

The legend goes that in the ninth century, Pope Joan became the world's first and only woman pope. An educated and clever woman, she successfully disguised herself as a man and infiltrated the bastion of the Church, then rose to its very pinnacle. Rumor has it she took many male lovers, and her fall from grace was swift and brutal when she collapsed in a procession and gave birth. Joan is said to have died soon after, and the cardinals created a new ritual to ensure that all future popes were born male. While one of those things still happens here, the other very much does not.

HER HOLINESS
JONATHAN TITCHENAL

I COULD HAVE DONE so much good.

I mean. I was the Pope.

You have to understand, the Church at the time was basically a dunghill on fire. You'd go from town to town and hear stories about Pope Officius electing a ten-year-old bishop in the city of Todi, or Bishop Dyskinesius praying to Jupiter and the other demons when he diced with his whores. Charlemagne's empire was gone, and the kleptocrats who were running Italy had turned the Holy Roman Church into a pornocracy. It was mass chaos. You could have got a dog elected bishop if you had the swords and cash.

My mother named me Theodora. This is going to get confusing really quickly, because not only was *her* name Theodora, there are a *lot* of Theodoras in Italy at this time. Honestly, the Byzantines are even worse. Walk into a crowded convent near Constantinople and shout "Irene!" and watch the heads turn, like gulls hearing the fishmonger's cart going by. So let's go ahead and call me Joan. This still leaves a rash of Theodoras, but we'll just have to grin and bear it. Theodora's husband, a bristling ogre named John Crescentius, named his son Crescentius II, so things could always be worse.

Things can *always* be worse. You should see the Pope they've got in now. Put it this way: Remember when Pope Stephen VI exhumed the decaying corpse of his predecessor, Pope Formosus, just so he could prop the ghastly thing up in the Papal chair and put it on trial? Those were the good old days. Between the horror show Cadaver Synod and the actual, literal brothel Marozia's bastard nephew Octavius – excuse me, John XIII – has set up in the Lateran, there was one very brief, bright spot.

That was me.

My lover has told me of the great learning in the East, in Constantinople and the lands of the Muslims. In Christendom we had Charlemagne, Carolus Magnus, Karl der Grosse, and that was it. The lights of learning flickered fitfully, tended by didactic pedants like Alcuin and his successors, who, to their credit, were trying their best. When Carolus' squabbling offspring split their lands, and then split them again, they paved the way for the Northmen to come sailing into town and turn it all into picturesque ruins. The kleptocrats moved in not long after.

My father, to his misfortune, passed the intelligence test. He knew how to hold a sword the right way round, and which end of the arrow goes in the other man. He was swept up by the rising Crescentii for one of their numerous skirmishes with the Counts of Tusculum – and anyone else who got in their way – and never came home. I don't remember his name, or what he smelled like.

Not long after, my mother began spending time with the local bishop. Quite a lot of time, in fact. They would sit close together, the firelight throwing their shadows out behind them, speaking in hushed voices. This went on for quite a long time. If my mother was confessing, she had a lot to get off her shoulders.

Then, later, less talking.

It wasn't uncommon for bishops to have mistresses, children, or even wives at that time. No one questioned what Bishop Liudolf was doing at my mother's house every evening, yet I couldn't help noticing how differently he acted when he was with her. Out in the street, he spoke in a harsh, barking Tuscan accent, like most of his fellow churchmen. A little higher-pitched than the average man, but the clergy rarely sprouted from the most burly and virile mother's sons.

(Irene, leaning over my shoulder: "And what's wrong with burly and virile?" A purr in her voice both playful and serious, a whiff of something in her scent that says, "Careful now, little Theo. I shan't hurt you, but oh mother, I can make you beg for mercy." She can. She has. She does.)

But we were talking about Bishop Liudolf.

Inside, sitting by the fire with my mother, Liudolf was another person. His voice was soft and kind, his words rolling gentle and smooth as river-washed stones. He moved differently. He even ate differently, I came to realize. Only there. Only with my mother.

But it was none of those things, really. Oh, I might have cottoned on eventually, but the key for that particular lock was, as so often for me, in his smell. I remember the day he swept past me on his way out the door, and I breathed in the scent, really breathed it in above the fire and the pitch and the dung and the animal smells that infested everything everywhere at all times. Her scent.

Not my mother's but another woman's.

She saw it in my eyes, of course. I've always been a terrible liar.

Irene tells me they call that irony.

Liudolf knelt down, her dark eyes level with my own. "Are you going to tell anybody?"

"No."

"My name is Liutgard. Do you want to get married and have children, like your older sister?"

Looking back, I'm pretty sure she knew the answer to this one already, but I didn't. "I don't know."

She tilted her head. She was not pretty, not handsome, just a person. "What do you want to be when you grow up, Theodora?"

I flashed on an image I had seen the previous year. Two battered, blood-stained soldiers carrying a litter. On the litter, a body feathered with arrows. Smell of sour sweat, blood, old hay. It was not my father, but that was who I thought of.

"Alive," I said.

"Good answer. Your mother told me you were bright."

I wanted to bring them both to Rome later, but they wouldn't come. Not because you couldn't swing a bridle without hitting a Crescentii or Tusculanii, but because of the pestilential Roman summers.

Two years ago they died of a fever. Together at the end, huddled beside the fire, cold despite the heat within them both.

Perhaps I do understand irony.

As you may have surmised by now, Liutgard was not the only churchman who had to pretend to shave in the mornings. When the lights went out in Saxony and Frankland and Italy, many towns found themselves with a shortage of men. Worse, the men who arrived to fill these vacancies were more akin to the Northmen – the people Irene calls the Rus – than the farmers and drovers whose flyblown bodies sometimes disappeared mysteriously during the worst famines. These were men who used scrolls as kindling. They had a use for the church – to keep their new serfs in line – but no interest in joining it.

I don't know where it started. Perhaps it began spontaneously in a number of places, a little miracle handed down from a God to whom, despite being halfway to Heaven, I've never spoken. By the time Liutgard found a teacher for me, things were rolling along nicely. Vows of chastity? No problem. I'd seen the men people like my sister married. Devotion to good works? Anything was better than the tide we were holding back. Endless hours of prayer? Okay, a little dull, but I only ever saw one person die during the benediction, and he was very old. No arrows. No ogres. It was a good enough life, in this vale of tears they call the world.

That was how I thought of it then.

You look up, your eyes aching in the guttering light of a single candle, and suddenly years have passed you by like whirling autumn leaves, and you're a woman. You're a man.

I was lucky. I'm small and flat-chested. When my morning toilet is complete, I look like an underfed young man, of which there are roughly an infinite number on this suffering Earth. I've spoken to others, both in the Church and out, and for some the binding and loosing never ends. Others were less lucky. Rumors have filtered into the Lateran. When I was the Pope – yes, we'll get to that – I did what I could to quash those stories. But things were heating up, even before I died.

My biggest concern moving up the holy ladder was, oddly enough, basically the same as I would have had, had I remained Theodora and not become Berengar. I ended up in Athens, a city known for its variety, and despite being a churchman I received a number of startling offers from men who were, in many cases, not ogres. Some were quite charming. I have been assured by high-ranking members of this Most Holy and Apostolic Church that sodomy is a sin, but then so is wrath, and yet half the Church hates the other half with a fire undying. So I was quiet, and studious, and good, and one day I found myself made a bishop, complete with ring and crosier – not to mention a hundredweight of doubt. The miter heavy on my head, my dreams teeming with hostility. I kept flashing on that image, that body feathered with arrows. Waking on my pallet at Lauds, sweat beaded on my forehead. There was something, some weight inside me, like a dark pregnancy.

Loneliness.

My lover told me that.

Life was safe, and food was plentiful – if you were a bishop – and no one was shooting arrows at me, and I thought this was what life had to offer. Lying on my hard pallet, shifting from one position to another, the Kingdom of Heaven seemed echoing and hollow, a basilica of porphyry, and ambergris, and jade, empty and unoccupied.

And then Pope Agapetus died.

Rumor, like a pestilence, is self-perpetuating. Official Church doctrine held that he died from a fall. One day, after Vespers, Count Rodoald of Porto confided in me that he had heard this was true; Agapetus had fallen on a knife. Several times.

Much later, Bishop Eusebius told me that Agapetus had indeed fallen on a knife. A knife wielded by his own hand.

Loneliness.

What all this meant for me was that I had to leave Athens and make the perilous journey to Rome for the conclave. We went in a procession, not for religious reasons, but to protect ourselves from the wolves on two legs who prowled about the edges of every enclave, every town. Bright, cold days of racing clouds. Damp nights upon the ground. Thin sun through the trees. And then one day the great walls loomed ahead. Rome, mother of cities. Rome, seat of the Holy Roman Empire. Rome, heart and soul of Christendom.

It was a dump.

Names float out of the past, like the whispers of ghosts. Augustus. Tiberius. Marcus Aurelius. All long gone. Poor Rome had been sacked and sacked again, her gold and silver carted away, her monuments toppled. As our procession made its way through the remains of the gate, I saw men grinding up a statue to use the stone for concrete.

A body, feathered with arrows.

Surely this can't be all. This can't be all there is.

We were traveling along the Via Sacra when it happened. There was no sense of gangs or armies coming together, not from my vantage point. Shouting, bodies pressing around me, and then clashing steel. More shouting, screams, men running one direction and another. A big fight ahead – no – behind – no–

From out of a cross-street came a wedge-shaped phalanx of men in armor and helmets. Real armor, chainmail and all. Real helmets, each one the same. As they cut through the rabble on their way toward us, I realized something I had always known, but never had the context to explain to myself. I hated – and still hate – weapons of all kinds. Swords, axes, polearms, bows, they all sicken me. I came to this realization just there, just then, because before that moment I had never seen a weapon wielded with any skill. I'd seen any number of weapons used badly, slashing or clubbing or stabbing with the frantic, terrified wildness of an animal facing death. These men were nothing like that. Their broad, straight swords cut and stabbed with deadly precision, the operators displaying neither anger nor fear nor any other discernable emotion, simply the one-pointed focus of a craftsman absorbed in a job.

I still hate weapons. But those men were beautiful.

They cut their way through to us and formed up around the procession, swords facing out hedgehog-fashion. I stepped backward to give their leader room to swing and tripped over the hem of my own robe. God's face.

The man saw me fall from the corner of his eye, whirled round and grabbed my robes in one strong fist. He yanked me to my feet and I stumbled forward, almost falling into him. For one moment we were standing very, very close.

And all at once, I knew.

Perhaps it was a scent. I've always been very good with scent. Perhaps it was something in the set of the body, the ice-blue eyes, the hand on my robes – fingers long and strong. Perhaps it was none of those things. But I knew.

We stood for a frozen moment, in the middle of a whirlwind of death, and she read the knowing in my eyes.

And I read the knowing in hers.

She cleared her throat, suddenly awkward and vulnerable. "We're...we're here to escort you to the conclave. I am Doukas of Odessa, captain of Varangs." She looked around at the carnage, as if seeing it for the first time. "Let's get you inside, Your Excellency."

"Berengar," I said, hating the name as it came from my mouth.

I thought about the name that came from her mouth. I thought about her mouth. I wondered what it would look like when it smiled.

We exchanged another frozen look.

Then events crashed back in on us and the Varangs were protecting us in the rear as we fled the riot, their swords and axes leaving corpses behind like breadcrumbs.

They put us up in fine houses near the Lateran. I don't know who was evicted to make room for us, but I never saw any of them. Standing in my room, looking out the window at the Castel Sant Angelo, I felt the world shifting beneath me. Someone told me that Liutprand of Cremona described Marozia, the Senatrix of Rome, as 'a shameless strumpet.' I wonder what it would be like to be a shameless strumpet. It sounds very freeing.

Of course she came in. She had her helmet and chainmail off, and she'd...well, thrown water on her face, at least. Her head was shaved to stubble, save for two wispy strands that started just above her ears and hung down around her chin. She was not handsome or pretty, just a person. There were scars on her hands. She was coated in sweat, and dust, and the blood of other men, and she stank.

She was gorgeous.

We looked at each other.

"Do they know?" I said. "Your soldiers?"

"My countrymen? Yes, most of them. Where I come from, it's not so unusual. The Romans? No."

"Romans?" I looked round at the window, confused.

"The Eastern Romans. My commanders come from Constantinople, the center of the world."

"I was always told Rome – I mean, this city – is the center of the world."

She came to stand next to me at the window. "Does it look that way to you?"

We surveyed the wreckage of the great city. "Not really," I said. I glanced at her, at the smooth muscles of her shoulders. "Tell me of Constantinople, Doukas."

"Irene," she said.

"Theodora."

She went out and came back with a jug of wine and two clay mugs. We drew our chairs together and she spoke of Constantinople, shimmering bastion of learning and culture on the Bosphorus. As she spoke, I found myself longing for a life far from the Church, a life of learning and exploration in lands where careful scribes had preserved what the ancient Greeks and Romans knew of the workings of this world-machine. As the wine warmed me from inside, I imagined having such a life.

I spoke to Irene of the things that had left impressions upon me: the smells and sounds of my village, the scent of my mother, the smoke of cookfires rising past the Acropolis in the golden Athens sunset.

And then words came from me that I had thought without knowing them. The petty, small thoughts of my fellow churchmen. The ignorance of my mother, my sister, my teachers, myself.

"You're frightened," Irene said. "You've been frightened a long time."

"I'm not frightened," I said, and knew it was a lie.

I include that quiet, contemplative interlude because so much of what came after was dominated by angry, shouting men. You might think, if the leaders of the Church are holy men, their collective decisions would be imbued with sanctity and truth. The assembled holiness at any given papal conclave ought to promote ideas of a grace and loftiness unimagined by the sinful laity, right?

No.

Assemble a collection of the angriest people you can find. Shut them up in a room with no windows, little food, and primitive eliminatory facilities, and then ask them collectively to make a unanimous decision about the single most important and polarizing issue of their lives. The acoustics in that room were atrocious. I can still hear the shouts echoing and re-echoing, one atop another atop another atop another. I will not speak here of the smells.

As I was from neither Rome nor its suburbs, and had no opinions about who the next Pope ought to be, I was able to stand at the back of the room and observe the carnage. I had traveled a bit prior to this visit to Rome, and knew a few bishops by sight, and they me, but no one solicited my opinion about anything, and I had no clout in the Church, happily. At one point I bumped, literally, into an acquaintance, Bishop Arsenius.

"Berengar!" he said over the hubbub. "Come into this alcove where the clangor of men may not disturb us. How do you fare?"

"God is merciful," I said. "This is my first experience of such things. How long do you think it will last?"

He appeared to turn one boss eye toward the center of the throng. "Someone knows," he said. "God knows. Too many factions. No one likes anyone else's candidate." He turned his attention back to me. "Likely they'll pick someone no one cares much for or against. Everyone knows Marozia is only waiting for Octavianus to reach his eighteenth year before she thrusts him into the papal seat. Much good may it do him. Or us."

"Do you know many of these people?"

Again that boss eye, scanning the room almost as a deer scans the horizon. "Most of them."

"And?"

"Some are all right on their own. Collectively, they couldn't pour piss from a boot." He grinned at me from under his bushy red beard. "They'll do something sensibly insane and let God take care of the rest."

"Will he?"

"God," Arsenius said, "or Marozia."

My only consolation during these days of being shut up with unwashed bodies and angry voices came in the evenings, when I would retire to my apartments on the Lateran, and Irene would join me. The broiling Roman summer was over, and through my second-floor windows there came at intervals a cooling breeze. Irene and I would draw our chairs close and speak of Greek learning, the days of Carolus, theories of the nations beyond the Saracens, religious practices of far lands.

Over the days, our chairs grew ever closer, in mirror of our minds.

Irene tells me the Byzantines have a word for this as well, but I disremember it.

On one evening, as the sinking sun threw a carpet of gold across the world, I found that we had drawn very close indeed. I could feel the breath moving through my lungs, slow and regular, though my heart beat so fast. I looked into Irene's faded blue eyes with an expression which, she later informed me, resembled that of a poleaxed deer.

She sighed. "I'm going to have to teach you everything, aren't I?"

"You are."

She did.

"The food is appalling," Arsenius said, and threw down a crust of black bread. "That's on purpose, you know."

"Oh?"

"Yes. The city prefects are trying to hurry the conclave's decision. John Crescentius was heard saying he'd have masons remove the conclave roof if we didn't reach a decision soon."

"Would he?"

"Who knows? They've done that sort of thing before. I, for one, don't relish the idea of being exposed to the elements day in and day out whilst fauna crawl all over my shoes." His roving eye seemed to fix on a mouse that had found his crust of bread. "Well, more fauna."

"Are the cardinal bishops any closer to a decision?"

This time we both looked toward the center of the room, where two men were inches from one another's red faces, stabbing fingers emphatically as they shouted over each other's argument. Behind them, on both sides, other shouting faces egged them on.

"Not really," Arsenius said.

"What will happen?"

He gave a Gallic shrug. "Enough of them – of us, I suppose – will get tired of being shut up in a shit-smelling hole together, and they'll choose a compromise candidate. Anything to get back to their dioceses and mistresses."

"That seems terribly cynical."

Arsenius turned his attention to me. "You sound different. Something happen to you?"

I blinked, caught off guard. "I don't know what you mean."

"Fall in love, did you?"

I opened my mouth to say something, but nothing came out.

Arsenius grinned. "Don't fuss yourself. Happens to the best of us. Just remember it's a Roman dalliance, lad. When the shouting is done and all this is over, you're going home to Athens. And you can't take her with you."

"When all of this is over," Irene said. "I'm going back to Constantinople. I could take you with me."

We lay together on the narrow pallet, Irene wrapped around me like protective armor. The westering sun had already slid behind the hills, and a spectral twilight filled the apartments.

"What would your people think of you bringing home a bishop?" I said sleepily.

She laughed. "You would have to stop being a bishop, Theo."

"What, then? Your wife?"

A pause as she considered it. "If you like. My lover, anyway." Her strong arms and legs, entwined with mine. "Would you?"

I paused, considering it.

"Yes," I said. "Yes, I would."

A different sort of hubbub at the conclave that day. The factions seemed to have changed; people were conferring with people they had previously been shouting at. Voices were still raised, but they sounded tired, and I couldn't blame them. This dank chamber had become hateful to them, and they wanted out. These arguments had a rote quality to them, people going through the motions for the sake of, presumably, God. One candidate or another had finally been settled on, and bishops from whose lips spittle had flown just days before were subdued, resigned. As my eyes moved from face to face in the pale candlelight, I could see no one who looked triumphant, no one who looked pleased or self-satisfied.

I looked around for Arsenius and saw him looking back at me from across the room. His expression was unreadable.

An unsettling weight took hold in the pit of my stomach. A dread, I knew not of what.

I started across the room toward Arsenius. As I did, he raised his hand and pointed a finger at me. For a moment, I thought he was warning me away, but then the bishops around him turned and pointed their fingers at me, too.

I stopped where I was, confused.

As I stood there, another clutch of bishops turned and pointed, as one, toward me. Then another. Then another.

I looked around. In every direction, from every corner, the bishops were looking at me, fingers raised to point accusingly in my direction. For one insane moment, I was certain I had been found out, that they knew I was female, that they would now descend upon me and tear me to pieces. Then I heard what they were shouting.

"Papa!"

"Papa!"

"Papa!"

The conclave was over. They had made their decision.

Irene simply stared at me.

"It wasn't my doing," I said. "I didn't want this."

"I believe you."

"No one could decide on a candidate. All the factions hated one another. The Crescentii and the Counts of– "

"So they chose a compromise candidate."

"Yes."

"And that was you."

"Well...yes."

"You're the Pope now."

"Well, officially– "

"My lover is the Pope." Irene sat down heavily in a chair. "The Pope. Why you?"

"No one could think of anything bad to say about me. And Arsenius likes me."

"So why isn't Arsenius the Pope?"

"Not everyone likes Arsenius."

"God's face." Irene scrubbed a hand down her cheek. "Come here."

I went and sat in the crook of her lap. She wrapped her arms around me and drew me close. I touched my forehead to hers, warm where I was cold. I smelled her scent, musky and animal and alive. In an hour, I would be the most holy person in Christendom. I wished that hour would extend out forever, like Xeno's paradox, leaving me in Irene's embrace until Judgement Day.

"What are we going to do?" she said.

"I don't know."

And so a conclave of hostile, alien, ill-smelling men made me the Pope. After interminable embarrassing rituals of lustration and censing and being shouted at in Latin, they set me upon the papal chair, a lone navigator at the helm of a ship, and left me alone for a time. I sat there, looking down at the empty stone floor, and wondered what God was thinking.

I was interrupted in my reverie by the sound of tramping feet, marching in unison. I looked up to see a box on poles making its way down the hall toward me. Six giant men in Crescentii livery were carrying a palanquin, walking in step to avoid jostling the unseen passenger. When they were within six feet of the steps, they set their burden down and retreated to the far wall to stand at parade rest.

The curtain of the palanquin parted, and the Senatrix of Rome emerged, slippered feet stepping down onto the dank flagstones. I had never seen her up close before. So this was what a shameless strumpet looked like. A painted Jezebel. A merciless harlot.

To be honest, she looked a bit tired.

Below the paint and make-up, beneath the tiara and wig, lay the face of a middle-aged woman with many cares on her mind. She was not quite a wreck, as Arsenius had described her, or if she was, she was the wreck of something great. She knew power, and the fear of men was not in her.

She gathered her skirts in both hands and climbed the steps leading up to the throne, gazing at me from beneath heavy black eye paint. When she was level with me – actually above me, for I was seated and she was not – she executed a tiny, ironic bow. "Your Holiness."

"Your Grace."

Peering over her shoulder, I saw a bearded face, hideously scarred and fearsome, looking up at us from within the palanquin.

Marozia turned to follow my gaze. "Oh," she said. "That's just my husband. Pay him no mind."

I had heard tales of John Crescentius. In that moment, I had no doubt my glimpse of the butcher of Rome had been engineered deliberately. I glanced at the six giants in their gleaming armor. They and he and she and I were alone in this room. Anything could happen.

Something inside me went cold. Not with terror, though terror filled me up like too much water in a jug. Just cold.

I might die here.

I felt calm.

I wondered if this was what Irene felt when she went into battle.

"What may I do for you, Your Grace?" I asked.

She padded around me, walking behind the throne and coming around my other side, leaning down so our eyes were level. "You're rather young for a bishop," she said.

"How old is Octavianus, Your Grace?" I asked.

"Ouch. Fair answered. And do please leave off the appellations, Your Holiness. Do I sense a question within your question?"

I held her eyes, saying nothing.

"I am not here to have you removed and replaced with my layabout nephew. I've promised him the papacy when he reaches the age of eighteen. You still have a few years." She leaned in a bit closer. "Provided you understand the rules of the game."

"And those are?"

"As laid down by Carolus Magnus, it is the duty of the ruler to reign, to fight to protect the people, to enforce the laws. It is the duty of the Most Holy to pray to God for the well-being of the people. And the ruler."

"I would be more than happy to pray for you, Your Grace." I felt like I was taking steps across a thin carpet of ice, each footfall an invitation to a cracking, as of paint laid too heavily on an aging face. A shattering. And then an icy plunge.

We stared into each other's eyes for a time.

I thought: *She knows. She knows what I am.*

"You will find," Marozia said at last, "that you need my help, if you wish to retain your position upon this lofty throne. Alberic and the Counts of Tusculum will come for you when they learn you are in league with me and John Crescentius, which they will. It would behoove you to actually *be* in league with us, yes?"

"I have no quarrel with you," I said.

"Nor I with you." She crossed her arms and straightened up.

"To be honest, I barely know who you are. So let us work together to shepherd the people of Rome forward toward Heaven, shall we? You will take my counsel, when I give it, and I will keep your secrets, should you have any." She smiled like a knife. "Even the Pontifex Maximus should have a father – or mother – confessor, don't you think?"

I opened my mouth, not sure of what I would say. What I said was, "As it happens, I do have a secret to confide in you, Your Grace."

She cocked her head, startled. "Do you, then?"

"Yes. I do." I crooked my finger, motioning her closer. I felt giddy with adrenaline. I was the Pope. I was playing cat and mouse with the Senatrix of Rome. Nothing felt real.

Marozia leaned down again, her face close to mine. Behind her carefully cultivated handsomeness, I could see the traces of the beautiful young woman who had ensnared the Crescentii. I wondered who had kissed those painted lips, and if she ever wished it had been someone else.

"My secret," I said, "is this: I truly want to help the people of this city. I want nothing for myself." An image of Irene flashed into my mind. "I just want to help."

The Senatrix stared into me, still so close, her perfume cloying in my nose. Her lips curled in a small smile. It made her briefly young again, and I thought again of who might have kissed that young-old face. In another life. In another city.

Marozia straightened once more and lifted her chin. "As you entrust me with such a dangerous secret, Your Holiness, I can only return the favor. The truth is, so do I." Her smile widened, but the light left it. "The only difference is that I know what keeps mankind alive, and you don't. God give you good day, Your Holiness."

"God give you good day, Your Grace."

She descended the steps and climbed back into the palanquin. The giant men lifted it and took it away, feet echoing away down the passage as they marched in step.

Then the throne room was empty, and some part of me wondered if it had happened at all.

But I could still smell Marozia's perfume, like a ghost in the pale afternoon light.

"We have an hour."

"Oh, an entire hour?"

"Don't joke. I had to brutalize the rituals to get this much time with you."

Irene looked at me. "And what happens in an hour?"

"The clergy arrives for the procession along the Via Sacra, to the Lateran."

"And what happens then?"

"I'll be formally installed in the Lateran."

"And what hap– "

"Stop it!"

"Why are you doing this, Theo?"

"What do you mean?"

Irene came to me then, and in an odd mirror of Marozia, bent to bring her face level with mine. "My Varangs and I will be leaving after the ceremony. We could go now. You and I could go now, while we still have a chance. Once you're on that lofty throne, it will be hard to see you, harder to see you alone, maybe impossible to spirit you away without half of Rome knowing who you went with and where. Why are you going through with this? I thought you didn't want this."

"I didn't."

"So?"

"But it happened."

"So?"

"If not me, my love, then who? I've seen the other candidates. I've smelled them. At best, they would be yes-men for Marozia until Octavianus comes of age. At worst..."

Irene crossed her arms. "And this affects Constantinople how?"

"It doesn't."

"God damn it!" Irene threw up her hands. She turned away, then turned back, as if unable to let me out of her sight. "Are you really choosing this dirty little city – this dirty little throne – over me?"

"I'm not choosing anything."

"That's a choice, too, Theo."

"I can do some real good here," I said, and the image that came into my mind was not the body feathered with arrows, but the face of Liutgard, looking down on me with kindness. "I've never really done good things. I've never really done bad things. Perhaps there is a God, and He–"

Irene snorted.

"And He put me in this position for a reason. Who am I to deny that?"

"And what did your God have in mind for me, when He let me fall in love with an idealist?"

"Irene, I don't know."

She took a deep breath, chest rising and falling beneath her chainmail. "Me neither."

She made to turn away again, but I grasped her shoulder, feeling the smooth muscles even beneath her armor. I turned her toward me and, rising up on my toes, kissed her.

We held the kiss until my feet began to ache, and I dropped back onto my heels.

Irene looked at me for a long moment, saying nothing. Then she retrieved her sword from the table and strapped it about her. "I can keep my people here for another week, perhaps," she said. "If you need me, send word."

"How?"

"You're cleverer than you give yourself credit for," she said, buckling her sword belt and heading for the door. "I'm sure you'll figure out a way."

"I love you," I said, but I didn't say it loudly enough, and she didn't hear me.

The procession made its way toward the Via Sacra, followed endlessly by a pulsing, shifting, screaming mass that was the great god Crowd. Arsenius was leaning in my ear, trying to be heard above the beat of the noise, but it wouldn't have mattered anyway. My mind was elsewhere. My feet steered the palfrey beneath me. My blood pulsed in my body and my ghost remained in its shell, but I felt caught, insubstantial, lost between one world and another.

In one world, I sat upon a throne much too high, and did deeds of greater or lesser good for those screaming people in this screaming world.

In another world, I fled with my beloved to another place, and someone else sat upon that throne. Would they do better? Would–

My horse checked as something snagged upon my robes. Looking down, I saw that it was four fingers and a thumb. Someone had stepped forward and grasped my papal robes in one strong, dirty hand. I gazed down into a face that might well have been John Crescentius, thirty years earlier. I had seen him from a distance. Now we locked eyes for the first time.

Octavianus. The sixteen-year-old nephew of the painted Jezebel who ruled Rome.

Some people have closed faces. They give nothing at all of themselves away, which can be information in itself. Some people have simply unreadable faces, painted with expressions that could mean one of a million things. Octavianus, on the other hand, was transparent as a cup of morning dew.

I understood several things all at once. The Crescentii and the Counts of Tusculum thought they were playing John Crescentius. Crescentius thought he was playing Senatrix Marozia. Marozia thought she was playing her grotty little bastard of a nephew. And Octavianus was playing her. God's balls.

He smiled at me. Then the smile opened into a shout. "A woman! This pretender is a woman!"

Popes don't carry weapons. I hate weapons.

I would have gladly skewered the boy at that moment.

On cue, the shout was taken up – of course this had been planned – on all sides. "A woman! A woman profanes the Church of the Most Holy! Get the woman!"

"She's–" Octavianus began, then a mailed fist knocked him sprawling to the mud. Irene grabbed me. "Come on! Hurry!"

"You were following me?"

"Shut up. There's going to be a riot."

Rome never needed much excuse to riot. Already people were punching other people in the streets. The procession had fled in every direction as the chaos ensued, and by morning, half the city would be on fire. And by the end of the next conclave–

"Where are you taking me?"

Irene yanked me into a narrow side alley. "Where would you have me take you, Your Holiness?"

I yanked the robes over my head, revealing the plain clothes of a traveler beneath. "Wherever thou listeth, my love."

She kissed me so hard I was afraid my lips would bleed. "Let's go."

They said later that I was found out because I went into labor. They said later I died on the spot. People say a lot of things. In a sense, I did die on the spot. Whoever stood in the doorway between one world and another is gone now. I can see her, distantly, when I stand on a high promontory and look out across toward the hills beyond Constantinople.

My lover bears more scars than she used to. Some of them are obvious.

I bear a scar or two myself.

We lie, together, some nights, neither of us sleeping. There is all the time in the world for sleeping. Instead:

"Would you have stayed? If it hadn't come to that? Would you have left me to come back here alone?"

"I don't know."

"Would you have wanted to?"

"I don't know."

Not satisfying answers, but honest. With Irene, always honest. And she takes me in her arms, and she smells like sweat and work and life and death and for a moment, just for a moment, everything almost makes sense.

And then I giggle against her stomach, and she has to ask me why. And I have to tell her.

In the wake of the scandal, the Papacy instituted a new policy.

For every new pontiff, part of his ritual elevation involves him being seated upon a reclining porphyry chair – this is all true – with a keyhole-shaped opening in the bottom. While he sits there, as if lying down, the least-lucky deacon in the entire Church has the official task of reaching up through the hole, up under the papal robes and making publicly known the results thereof.

As my lover and I drift off into sleep, I comfort myself with the knowledge that, perhaps even at this moment, Octavianus is sitting, a *very* readable expression on his face, as someone announces to the most holy and august assembly in Rome:

"HE HAS TESTICLES!"

For the last 200 years, the most well-known guise of Pandora's myth has been as cautionary tale for feminine curiosity. Earliest traces suggest she was a primeval Earth Goddess, yet as societal power in Ancient Greece shifted from matriarchy to patriarchy, Pandora was given a new origin story. Zeus was said to have formed her from clay as the first mortal woman, and she is then sent to Earth with a deadly gift for mankind. Zeus intends her as bride for Epimetheus, brother to Prometheus, renowned for having stolen fire from the gods. The jar contains a punishment, and when Pandora opens it, death and illness are released into the world. Pandora's gift has its own story within a story. Originally an earthen jar (pithos), a sixteenth century poet named Erasmus mistranslated the word in Latin for box (pyxis). This error in translation has endured as the infamous "Pandora's Box."

THE PRICE FOR FIRE
MELISSA COFFEY

"But I will give men as the price for fire an evil thing, in which they may all be glad of heart while they embrace their own destruction."
– Hesiod, *Works and Days*

YOU THINK YOU KNOW me, but you do not.

I wear the tattered threads of a myth, frayed and tangled through the centuries. You think I represent the immutable curse of ignorant feminine curiosity. You think I released illness and death into the world because I couldn't resist opening a box to see what was inside. You think I walked into this story as a hapless little girl.

A little girl, cast as the downfall of mankind: who would believe that? Not my daughter. Not Pyrrha. How she would throw her head back, and laugh.

Hidden behind countless, nameless tellings, beneath the bloom and wither of civilizations, there lie clues to my story. Clues, wedged between the bones of those silenced and those with power to speak. Excavate the old names for fragments of truth. Trace the slip of a pen, mistranslating a word. Those long-bearded poets, who were soon calling my jar a box; do you think they could be trusted in all details? How a story is told depends on who is doing the telling.

I was not a girl. I was a woman. The first woman.

Let me speak; let me untangle the thread.

I was the thing flesh-made that the world had yet no name for. I had a father, but no mother, and perhaps that's where the trouble began. My father made me, only to betray me. My body, a strategy for revenge.

I know that now.

Cast an eye to the sky on that long ago day, and you might say I fell from the heavens. I was made there, it's true; fashioned from clay, face and form inspired by goddesses. But I did not fall. Hermes carried me in his golden-winged embrace, setting me down under an olive tree. In my arms, I clasp a large earthen jar, sealed with intricate designs. Sealed tight as a secret.

Before me stands a house. I mount its steps, knock upon the door. What else could I do?

The man's eyes, as he opens the door, tell me I am beautiful. How could I not be – I am intended as a gift to this man, who has disappeared from many versions of my story; this man who accepted me greedily without asking my name. Despite warnings from Prometheus, his brother. Bright Prometheus, who stole fire from the Gods to light the hearths of men. Prometheus, the fire-bringer. It was he who sought my name.

Have you guessed it yet?

Newly-made as I was, I did not know my name until it fell from my tongue.

Pandora.

His brother ogles me, while Prometheus stands, tasting my name in his mouth.

"Your name means all-gifted," he says. He is wary. *"Who sent you?"*
I am the gift, but also the gift-bearer.

I hand his brother the jar. "A wedding gift, from my father, great Zeus himself. It's not to be opened until we marry. When we are husband and wife," I say. But my gaze is on Prometheus.

So many new words. I am giddy with them. Or is it the burn of Prometheus' hand on my arm? The heat, imprinted on my skin, as he bids me sit, asks if I desire food and wine, as his brother Epimetheus licks his lips, dull eyes sliding from the jar to me, and back again?

Greedy, impatient Epimetheus.

He could not wait for the wedding to open Zeus' gift, for the wedding night to bed his bride. Sleeping but three nights under his roof, I wake, to find him trying to open the jar. Protesting, I rise to stop him. He pushes me down, body heavy on mine. Coarse hands tearing my gown. I struggle, screaming, pushing him off me. The jar is the only heavy object in the room. The jar, breaking over his head, silences his roar of indignation.

There is a whirling and a screeching. Strange winged things with beaks like knives rise out of the jar. A torrent of darkness engulfs me.

Those that dwell in the house of Epimetheus, all those weighty, earth-bound men, are howling my father's name when I wake again. There is only silence in reply from the skies above. Despite their warm hearths, the men are afflicted now with disease and illness. With death. My father has forsaken them, as he'd forsaken his daughter, too.

Epimetheus points his finger towards me, away from his greed; my curiosity is blamed. Their eyes, as they avoid mine, still tell me I am beautiful. But I am a woman, bringer of evil things, and not to be trusted. Only one man's eyes meet mine, only he acknowledges the truth, for he knows his brother's true nature.

The myths say I was the price for fire. I could not alter the destiny deemed for me, but after the jar was opened, my story was mine to make. The abandoned creation found a new purpose.

I married Epimetheus, but it was not he I ever loved.

Let me speak; let me untangle the thread.

Motherless though I was, I bore one daughter, Pyrrha. The first daughter, she would be mother to all future women. Pyrrha. Radiant, always laughing, with hair like flames. Her name meant *fire*.

Who do you think was her father?

With the slip of a pen, a jar becomes a box. A woman becomes a little girl. A perpetrator is erased from the story. Blame is shifted from a man to a woman. An entire gender, generation after generation, scapegoated for being *too curious*.

Look, but don't touch. Don't ask questions. Listen, don't speak.

Men have always tried to take what was not given to them freely. Fire and treasure. Cities and queens. Entire countries.

How a story is told depends on who is doing the telling.

I am Pandora. I was the first woman.

Let me speak.

The story of Cinderella is known and loved by all: a sweet, downtrodden girl meets a charming prince, and one glass slipper later, they live happily ever after. But what about those wicked stepsisters? Do they ever learn to be kind? Do they find their own happily-ever-after's? Or do they remain their wicked, selfish selves? What's the rest of the story?

SWEET EVERYTHING'S

PATSY PRATT-HERZOG

DRISANA TRIPPED, AND THE container of flour flew out of her hands. It burst open and enveloped the back room of the bakeshop in a thick white cloud. She sat down in the middle of the mess and tried very hard not to cry. A few months ago, she would have thrown a kicking, screaming fit, but tears and flour made paste, and she didn't want to get stuck to the floor...again.

She shook her head. All those years, she'd tormented Cinderella, sending her to fetch, cook, wash, and clean. Until recently, she'd never fully appreciated how difficult it all was. Drisana found it oddly comforting to think Cinderella might be proud of her. *It took becoming divorced and penniless, but at least she'd finally learned something.*

"Are you all right?"

Peter, the bakery owner, looked at her through the settling cloud of flour with a concerned expression. He was a kindly man with warm brown eyes and a cute little round belly, and no matter how she wrecked things, he never shouted at her.

"No. I'm not all right. You took me in. You gave me a chance when no one else would, and how do I repay your kindness?" A tear rolled down her powdery cheek. "By making a mess of things over and over again."

"Now, now." He gently helped her to her feet. "There's no sense in crying over spilled flour."

"Why do you put up with me?" she asked, sniffling.

So far in her tenure at the bakery, she had spilled every substance in the kitchen at least ten times and nearly set Peter on fire... Twice. She certainly wouldn't have tolerated such a useless, clumsy servant in her days as Lady of the manor.

He smiled and gently touched her flour-smeared cheek. "Because everyone deserves their happily ever after; your day will come, Drisana, you'll see. Often happiness is right in front of us; we just have to be brave enough to reach out and grab it."

Happiness... Up until a few months ago, she had been Mrs Leo Teplov, the wife of a wealthy merchant. That should have led to happiness, but the beastly man had grown bored with their arranged marriage and cast her out.

No. She straightened her spine. *You will be honest, if only with yourself. You were perfectly horrid to Leo. That's why he threw you out. You spent all his money on frippery, parties, and fancy gowns, then shrieked like a shrew when he tried to make you behave reasonably. Face it, Drisana. It was all your fault.*

After all, she'd done, she wasn't even certain someone like her deserved true happiness.

"Would you like me to help clean up?" Peter asked.

Drisana shook her head tearfully and turned away to wash her face before the flour could glue her eyelashes shut.

Peter was still standing there when she returned with the broom. She attacked the flour vigorously, driving him back to the front of the shop so he wouldn't see her cry. Cleaning the mess gave her a chance to get herself under control, and once she'd tidied up, she went to apologize for her moment of self-pity. This was her life now. She was no longer Lady of the manor. She was a shop-girl who lived above a bakery, and she'd best come to accept that.

The front of the bakery was a wondrous place. There were display cases filled with cookies, cakes, candies, and bread in all their fragrant and colorful glory. Peter was a marvelous baker, the best in the entire Kingdom. People would travel for hours to purchase his delicious goods, and the shop was always crowded with customers. She wasn't allowed to work on finished products yet, but she helped mix the batters and frostings, and she could manage to bake cookies now without burning them, at least most of the time. The slightly singed ones, she saved for the local street urchins, who didn't seem to mind in the least.

The front bell tolled, and a hush fell over the shop as the Grand Duke strolled through the doors. Drisana crouched down and tried to make herself invisible behind the bread case. The last time they'd spoken, she'd been trying to shove her foot into Cinderella's shoe. Not precisely her finest hour.

The Grand Duke was a frequent patron of the bakery, and he was always quite friendly with Peter. They laughed and talked like old friends as he collected his usual selection of tea cakes. Drisana stood up with a sigh of relief when he left, but who should walk into the shop next? None other than her sister, Anastazie.

Anastazie's face lit with malicious glee when she saw Drisana standing behind the counter. "There you are, *dear sister*," she cooed, shaking her head. "Mother told me I'd find you here, but I simply refused to believe it. My sister...a shop-girl!"

It wasn't as if she'd had anyplace else to go. Mother had made it quite clear she would not abide the shame of a divorced daughter living under her roof, and they hadn't spoken since. "What do you want, Anastazie?"

"Why to order my wedding cake, of course." Anastazie pulled off her glove and shoved a big sparkling diamond in Drisana's face. "You've missed a lot of news while you've been here grubbing for the masses. Duke Blokovich has asked me to be his wife, and I couldn't think of anyone I wanted more to make my cake than you, *dear sister*."

Peter was suddenly by her side. He put a comforting arm around her shoulders. "Well, you've come to the right place. Drisana would be thrilled to make your cake. She's the most talented baker I've ever seen. She'll own this shop soon if I'm not careful."

Drisana looked up at him in astonishment, and he gave her a subtle wink.

"What kind of cake would you like to order?" he asked.

As Drisana looked on in stunned silence, Anastazie started blathering about flavors and frosting and six tiers with swans and pink roses, lots and lots of pink roses, while Peter nodded and made notes.

Anastazie shot her a pointed glare. "And you'd better not bungle it up. I'll be back to check on your progress." Then, with a final smirk and a flounce of skirts, Anastazie left without even offering an invitation to the wedding.

As soon as the door closed behind her, Drisana looked up at Peter with wide, terrified eyes. "I can't possibly make that cake! I can't even frost the doughnuts right!"

"I'll help you, of course," he said with a gentle smile, "but your sister doesn't have to know that, now does she?"

Anastazie's wedding was in two days, so they got to work straight away on the cake. Things started out disastrous, as usual, with Drisana dropping eggs and spilling milk. Still, Peter didn't give up on her, and they got the chocolate, strawberry, lemon, cherry, orange, and vanilla layers of the cake all baked and stacked. He beamed proudly at her as she helped him drive in the last stick to hold it all together.

"Now for the icing," he said.

She got out the small tubs of colored frosting for the decorations and put them on the counter. Then certain they'd need it, she climbed up the ladder to pull down the spare container of white frosting they kept on the top shelf.

Peter came up behind her. "Let me help you with that."

She had her hands on the tub, but they were greasy, and the tub slipped through her fingers and tipped. The lid popped off, and a wave of frosting cascaded down from the shelf and landed right on top of Peter's head. He covered his eyes with his hands when he saw it coming, and when he drew them away, he was left with a white frosting beard and snowy hair.

Drisana laughed and then clapped her hands over her mouth.

"You think that's funny, do you?" Peter asked.

"You look like one of Snow White's dwarves," she giggled, and scurried down the ladder.

When she reached the bottom, he took a handful of frosting and gave her a matching beard of her own. "Now we just need five more," he said with a grin, licking his fingers.

As Drisana looked up into the warm chocolate of his eyes, she realized that the happiness she so desired was right in front of her, just waiting to be grabbed.

Peter must have seen something change in her expression as the truth finally dawned on her. "At last," he sighed, cupping her sticky chin in his hands.

"But why?" Drisana asked, stunned. "I'm a menace in the kitchen, I haven't any dowry, and I'm not even pretty."

"You are beautiful," he said tenderly, "and you have brought me more joy in the last three months than I ever thought possible."

She laughed. "By almost setting you on fire?"

"By bumbling your way right into my heart," he replied, leaning down for a kiss.

Drisana closed her eyes and turned her face up to his in giddy anticipation.

"Just look at this mess!"

They started, jerking apart at the sound of Anastazie's shrill voice. Hands on hips, her sister glared furiously at them from the doorway. "You brainless twit, I knew you'd bungle it up! I should have known better than to patronize a tawdry little establishment like this."

Peter gave Anastazie a calculating look. "I don't know about you, Drisana, but she strikes me as a little *grumpy*, don't you think?" And before she could stop him, he lobbed a handful of frosting at her glowering sister.

White goo dripping from her chin, Anastazie shrieked in outrage. "You horrible man! I'll ruin you for this! You'll be closed by the end of the week!"

"I take it that means your cake order is canceled?" Peter asked with an unrepentant grin as Anastazie turned and stormed out the door.

Drisana was no longer smiling. "Oh, Peter. You don't know her like I do. She means what she says." She shook her head. "I always make a mess of everything, and now I've cost you your business!

I've never known anyone as wonderful as you. I'll make it right, I promise! I'll go talk to her. I'll even grovel if I have to!" She turned, but he caught her hands before she could race after Anastazie.

"Drisana," he said soothingly, "your sister can do me no harm. You see, my darling, I am not merely a humble baker. I am the youngest brother of the Grand Duke."

"The brother...of the...of the...you mean he's your..." She couldn't even finish the thought, let alone the sentence.

"Life at court was not for me," Peter said with a gentle smile. "I just wanted to be a baker like my grandmother." He looked down into her eyes. "But now there's something else I greatly desire." Peter squeezed her hands. "Would you do the honor of becoming my bride?"

With a squeal of delight, Drisana flung herself into his arms and kissed him, sending frosting flying. "Yes! Yes! Oh, yes!" she said between kisses, but then she drew away and gave him a serious look. "On one condition."

"Anything, my darling Drisana," he promised.

"Fire me?" she asked with a grin.

He laughed. "Agreed."

And they lived happily ever after, which just goes to prove not every girl needs a glass slipper to find true love.

Sometimes all it takes is a little frosting.

The greatest love story of Jane Eyre is not that between Jane and Mr Rochester but Jane and her dearest bosom friend, Helen Burns. In the original tale, that love is cut short when Helen succumbs to consumption and that loss shrinks Jane, diminishes her self-worth, so when she finally meets Rochester, she allows herself to be abused in the name of companionship. Helen Highwater is the tale of a Miss Burns who, instead of succumbing gratefully to the fate she believes she deserves, rejects God, her fate, and the gentle grace of death and, instead, allows Jane's love to transform her. Literally.

HELEN HIGHWATER
SADIE FOX CURTIS

I WAKE UP FROM Hell and I'm on fire. Quite literally alight. Before anyone else can save me, before the bed curtains catch, I smother the flames with my thick, woolen blanket and shake the ash to the floor.

It's quiet, well before dawn, though the light in the room has changed since last night. I remember flickers of candlelight, sweat on my upper lip from the fireplace, the closeness of a body next to mine, snuggled deep under the covers. She was curled into me like a comma, a second skin. I had been too hot with her there but, moments from Death, it was fitting, it seemed to me, to be this uncomfortable. I was, after all, primed to meet my Maker and to allow Him to peel my swollen skin before the kingdom of heaven.

Except, when I Left, He wasn't there. Rather, there was a choice. (Or a promise – I can't quite recall. There was music at odds with sense and tonality; a pressing of hands that felt dangerous). And when I woke, I did so neither in the sky or deep below the Earth but here, in the nursery, nearly as I was before.

As I uncurled my toes and gently loosed the stays at my throat, I noticed the absences before all else. No pain, no heat, no cough, no fear. Everything had simply sloughed off in the night like a layer of soot or sin. A crumbling-down of past failings, though invisible to the eye. I was left pale and clean and unmarked. Made anew. Like I had never been in life, I was now, in Death – or what passed as Death in this near-waking state – a being without cause for anxiety.

Except one.

She was still at my side, clutched to my form like an undersea thing, her calloused hands tucked into the folds of my nightclothes. Like life-lines. Had she not felt warm and sticky and weighted against my side – pink, round, delicious – I might have imagined she was the cause of this great change. Without her obvious life-force, I would have chastised myself for sleeping with Death near the night through.

Now, I worried I would wake her and that, seeing me, she would flee. I had neither looking glass nor windowpane close by in which to reflect and yet, I could sense the all-over changes. My eyes felt cold in my head, and too large for my skull. My bones had stretched in the night, smoothing out the wrinkles of my neck, elbow folds, forehead. My jaw had loosened to allow for more teeth, and sharper ones. Their very tips brushed my lower lip and sliced them clean open. They healed over at once, but the memory of pain remained.

A thrill overtook my caution and I slipped a hand beneath the covers to stroke her spine, the soft curve of her hip, nestled against my own, lupine haunch. She stirred yet remained asleep and I chanced a shift in position, rolling onto my back so as to contemplate the ceiling and my own fate.

Sometime, in the pitch of night, I had undergone a change. I had no memory of its action – nor would I; my mind was gloriously blank in this regard and my sharp senses agreed it would remain so – but I knew, indubitably, of its happening. I recalled nothing but a humid fog followed by a tingling of the extremities not unlike the bite of snow. And then floating, floating on the salt sea of my imagination, pain an array of sharp rocks hidden and exposed by the tides.

Someone had been here. Someone or – some*thing*. I had been visited in the night, on the brink of expiry. Someone had weighed my soul and decided me Unworthy and had spit me back into the half-life of which I had known I was most deserving. Despite my prayers and my attempts at piety, I remained a wicked girl. God had seen me and rejected me at His doors. Strangely, I did not feel empty and bereft as I had once determined I would. Instead, I was–

Renewed.

The door by my head creaked open and with a rustle of stiff skirts, Miss Temple arrived. I opened my mouth to speak, to test my lung power, perhaps, or to ask for a draught of clean water, when she spied me and her kind, unlined face collapsed into a complexity of emotion I could not unfold at once.

"Helen," she said, with a hoarseness that told of little sleep and too much fire in the throat – it was at that moment my understanding began to shift and awaken. "At last."

She rushed to my bedside, her apron shimmering with a crimson wetness that both intrigued me and left me recoiling. As she knelt by my side, she took up my hands in hers and wrung them, leaning forward to press her cold lips against the skin.

"I am pleased to see you are Awake." The properness of that adjective was as clear as the daylight beginning to paint the corners of the sky. "How are you feeling now, dearest?"

"I am...well." My voice was changed, too. Slow. Sonorous. Like the bell that signaled us to Mass, turned somehow upside down. "What news is there of Lowood, of the students?" Perhaps an account of the day would rattle free a memory of the evening prior so that I might begin to piece together the shattered edges of my existence.

Instead of a response – or perhaps *as* one – Miss Temple rushed to the windows and began tugging closed the thick fabric there, forging a bond, as she would soon reveal, between the day outside and the night within. Once finished, she whirled around and clapped together her fine hands, one of which glimmered in the firelight. A ruby-and-gold oval ring sat upon her middle finger like a sacred text. Of what it spoke, I did not yet know.

"Now, let's awaken our Jane so we can begin to plan in earnest."

To my endless amusement, Jane was fascinated. A quick pupil, as

I'd observed from the classroom, Jane Eyre was as eager to apply herself to this new path as she'd been to conquer French, drawing, comportment, and literature.

She'd awoken scared, I'm ashamed to say. My very skin had not felt safe to her and so she'd arisen with a heart clenched in fear. I cherished her so and never wished to see her harmed, but Miss Temple – Maria, as she insisted we both call her – soothed me, saying the elasticity of her memory would soon return. She would replace that memory – jolting awake in a monster's arms, expecting those of her most cherished friend, screaming herself faint with powerful lungs – with one of triumph. Soon it would be as if she'd never felt a moment of sickness or regret or fear, no matter how short-lasting.

"You have been Awakened," Maria taught me, "to fulfill your destiny to God." At my disapproving look, she held aloft an ivory hand. "Your God may look different to you now with your new eyes, Helen – and to you, Jane, with your new understanding – but I assure you that He is just as real and powerful, just as benevolent and welcoming, as you've been taught all your young lives."

"But Miss – but *Maria*," Jane began, excitement filling her up, tipping over the brim of her vessel, "isn't this – what we desire – at odds with our condescension? Aren't we to be humbled before Him in order to serve as promised?"

It was a good question and I was glad she'd asked it, but impatience was rippling my skin, flowing through the hair that had sprung rapidly from the pores on my arms and legs, from my forehead and the backs of my knees. I needed to be outside the sick room, and soon. I was needed here at Lowood, and in the world beyond. Delays like these would become anathema to me.

"Jane, the lessons are the same. First, you must examine your heart and see what lies within. Then, you must ask yourself to be cleansed of sin in the face of God. He will ask you to take action, and that's what you shall do."

"But the Brocklehursts. And Cook–"

"Are not the temples of God they claim. You are the messengers now and you proclaim the Word."

Jane jumped down from her chair, satisfied. It warmed me to see the blaze in her eyes, the fervor returned after years of learning docility. Domesticity. She was a sword, my Jane, and I hoped to be the force behind her swing.

We began with the schoolroom. It seemed natural to start there. It was a mercy. The girls who'd fallen ill were taken first, to spare them the suffering of collapsed and damaged lungs, the lifelong weakness of limb and mind. Maria and I broke them quickly and individually, sparing one the pain of the other, the fear of the very short-term future. For the first time, I could sense His presence in my work; I never knew how hungry I'd been at Lowood, how sparse had been the food, the warmth. Now, deeply satisfied by the sacrifice of the weak girls, a calm began to settle over a nervousness I had not before discerned.

Jane scoffed, said I looked beatific when I should, instead, embrace my rage. She made me laugh, sweet sword. I tried to be firm with her, to settle my mouth in a gentle but disproving countenance, but no matter my admonitions to practice grace, she had returned to the feral fly-away child she'd been upon arrival at our institution. And secretly, I was glad. Unbeknownst to her, I *was* furious. I had believed my path was lined with gold, that by humbling myself and striving toward perfection, I was made decent in the eyes of God. Now I knew that God called Himself another name and did not care that I had scraped myself thin for Him. What He wanted was a fat sacrifice of blood and fire and to offer those things, I needed to be made of them.

After the sick girls were Healed, we built a small line of defense. We chose the heartiest girls, the ones with sly wit and thick bones and no relations. We chose them for our family and they, in turn, chose others still until we stood twelve-strong. Until we, along with Maria and one other teacher, a Miss Millfield, were a community united against outside prejudice.

And then we waited. We were full and healthy. We slept during the daylight hours, or read with the curtains drawn. At night, we danced, we sang, we cleaned, we rejoiced. We stripped ourselves bare and marked upon each other's skin the symbols of our covenant. We practiced and we prayed. And most of all, we waited.

Months passed. When at last, drawn by greed and cruelty (and perhaps the pointed absence of written communication, Maria mused), the Brocklehursts came to visit. Edith was delighted when the daughters arrived wearing their finest regalia, plump with a recent feast and glittering with jewels. She no doubt imagined herself in feathers and furs once the youngest were taken care of. I, for one, had eyes for no one but Mr Brocklehurst for he had had eyes, once, for no one but my Jane. I would burn for an eternity recalling my words to her after his public humiliation of her. I was ashamed, now, of how I'd begged her to consider her faults and turn the other cheek rather than imagining him as he was now, skewered like a beast and dripping into the open flame, fat hissing pleasantly.

Once the family was dispatched, our shackles fell free finally. Maria assured us they were symbolic but no less powerful for being unreal. We took up their slaughter like a mantle. Our family – for that's what we were now – operated as one.

At night, wrapped in my arms like a gift, Jane complained of being an outlier. "Am I so unworthy?" she begged tearfully. I kissed away each salty stream, savoring the exquisite way she squirmed at the touch of my roving tongue. "Dearest, no," I reassured her, and again. "You are the strongest of us, save, perhaps, Maria, and she is already Turned. It is with you, as you are, that our fate is protected. Once we are secured a future, clever girl–" Here, it must be confessed, I lost myself in the fall of her hair, "–I will recreate you in His image."

"And we shall be married?" Her eyes were galaxies. I understood; before this change, I had not imagined a world in which love was the purpose of matrimony.

When at last she turned eighteen, Jane and Maria spent several months poring over advertisements for governess and teacher positions, roles Jane could easily fill with her clever brain, her capful of accomplishments, her glorious face scrubbed clean of rouge and other ornament.

Soon, Jane secured a position at a large estate called Thornfield.

Her letters were fervent, frequent. She wrote of numbers: rooms, staff, stables. She spoke of humbling herself before the master of the house, a Mr Rochester, whose bloviated idea of manhood and fatherhood made him the perfect mark. He noticed Jane only in so much as she reflected his own ego back to him. He found her a fascinating slip of a woman. A pious mirror. He played games with her, invited her to sit fireside and listen to him pontificate about the world and his woes. My Jane sat obscurely, hands itching for a pencil, a needle, a sword. She listened and planned and worked to set her face in a guileless pose so as not to reveal her disgust, her glee.

"In another life," she wrote, "I see myself beating my breast at night, barely able to fathom my distress at not having him. He is everything I thought myself unallowed to want and now that I know this life – our life – I feel pity for the poor Jane who thought herself beneath even him."

At Lowood, we covered the furniture in bolts of cloth, cleansing the institution of everything it was and readying it for sale. We secured horses and luggage and supplies for the journey. Maria walked to the post daily, awaiting the message that would alight us on our path; I bathed to shed the old skin that was peeling off in sheets and rubbed a lemon-rose balm into the creamy new flesh that emerged.

Each of us felt ourselves on the brink of this new life, and it breathed fire into our very limbs. Edith wore jewels of Augusta Brocklehurst at her throat and wrists and made us laugh with her impromptu theater. Alice and Clara stitched us all fine cloaks – thick wool lined with soft silks. Louise tanned leather strips to secure our boots tight against the wind. Elizabeth lined a case with velvet and carefully packed an apothecary of herbs and flowers and spices and teas. I sharpened the kitchen knives and fashioned pouches for them to hang at our waists.

When the letter came, we stood together as one and prayed for the health of Lowood and its future residents. Then, at the stroke of ten, we clambered into our carriages, and set off for Thornfield Hall.

Jane welcomed us, some days later, with the housekeeper, a Miss Fairfax, in a dazzled state. Jane had been preparing her tea nightly, and lacing it with a strong hallucinogen to keep her docile. She ushered us in under cover of night and we streamed silently upstairs to occupy the second-floor rooms. Maria and Edith retired to the kitchens to decide what to do with the staff while Jane put Miss Fairfax to bed. That left me to dispatch Rochester, a task I did not anticipate with any joy – he was not an innocent like those in the Lowood sickrooms so he did not warrant the deep, sacred ritual that sacrifice deserved.

I crept to his chambers with no light to guide me, my traveling skirts trailing behind me like a detached shadow. His bedroom was silent, striped with moonlight in variegated blues and greys. The man himself was a mountain atop his bed, the great rise and fall of his chest like a volcano readying itself for eruption. I studied what I could see of his face in the moonglow that shone softly upon him. He wasn't an attractive man, but his brow was large and intelligent and his brows had a wicked tilt that hinted at conquest. It should have been a shame to destroy him; it *would* have been, had the world been set up properly for women like me, like us. Jane, Maria, Edith. Women with talent and promise. Women who could have managed a fortune as well as a household or occupation but were denied the opportunity by chance – or curse – of birth.

My new limbs sometimes startled me. I had but to think of leaping atop Rochester and there I was, straddling his tremendous form like I would an ill-bred stallion. He awoke at once and ascertained the situation with ease. He reached out an arm, lightning-quick, but my reflexes were quicker. I pinned his wrist to the nightstand without consequence.

"Please." He swallowed noisily and it was this, not his tone which was flat, detached, that alerted me to his fear. "I have a child–"

"The child shall be spared."

"And a – a wife." This was news. Jane had not mentioned a wife in her letters. From his expression, though, I did not doubt her existence.

"Where is she?"

He pressed his lips against the words but a flicker of his eyes betrayed him. As if cued, a thump from above, followed by a ragged moan. Not the whisper of an apparition but full-bodied, blood-rich.

"Maria," I called softly. I could hear the approach and fade of footsteps, Maria's smart boots tapping down the hall and then up the creaking stairs.

"Shall we begin?" I met his eyes and Rochester, believing me mad, began to struggle.

Ownership of Thornfield passed to Bertha's son, James, after Rochester's death. Once Maria discovered Bertha shut away in the attic, she sent away her caretaker, Grace, with a handsome settlement and a story for the inevitable lawyers who would seek order.

The story was this: Rochester had gone mad after a brain fever caught in the West Indies. He'd jailed his wife, Bertha, after which he had run mad with infection, slaughtering his staff and doping his housekeeper with opiates. Once he'd discovered Bertha was with child, he tried to murder her, believing his unborn son to be a demon. In a fit, he slit his own throat and was found by his daughter's governess, Jane.

Bertha herself was not mad, of course, though Grace Poole had tried to bestow the diagnosis before her removal. Bertha was one of us, a woman who simply burned with the fire of God. When Maria found her, heavy with child, unkempt, starving, she loosed her ropes immediately and fell weeping against Bertha's breast.

Today, the two are inseparable and raise James together, having turned the top-most floor from an attic prison into a moon-bright nursery. Every night, we hear them dance across the floorboards to songs of their own devising, James's sweet, shrill voice rising wordlessly to mingle with theirs.

Rochester's daughter, Adele, we sent to live with Jane's cousins, Mary and Diana Rivers, padded with half the fortune left to Jane by her uncle, a John Eyre, who'd left the entirety of his worth to his orphaned niece.

As for Jane herself – she is one of us at last, settled into her final form by my own hand, Christmas last. She is resplendent in scarlet robes of velvet or thin silk dresses the color of peacocks and under which she wears nothing but the mother-of-pearl skin into which she was reborn.

At dawn, we retire to our small bed, preferring to sleep in a tight crib rather than sprawled in one of the family rooms with an acre of bed-space between us. I have the nightmare less and less frequently now, the one where I fall asleep consumptive and awake in the arms of Heaven, my body weak and my heart full of spun glass, eternity spread before me like a dull bolt of linen, limitless, unending.

I used to wake gasping, only to have my Jane soothe me back slumber with her deft hands and soft lips. Now, I sleep the day in her arms, two iridescent butterflies in a cocoon of soft darkness. A world we made together.

In John Luther Long's 1898 short story "Madame Butterfly", a young geisha in Nagasaki marries an American naval officer, who proceeds to isolate her from her family and then abandon her, pregnant, for an American wife. In the short story, Cio-Cio-San survives her attempted seppuku and disappears with her friend and her son; when it became an opera, she died. What if, with all her training, wit and intelligence as a geisha, she never fell for Pinkerton's slick promises in the first place?

METAMORPHOSIS

NARRELLE M HARRIS

A SALT BREEZE SIGHED inland when the American ships arrived, carrying with it a briny tang, with a hint of fish, and exotic foreign harbors. The shouts of those tall sailors bringing their ships into harbor came on the breeze, too. Cio-Cio watched them from her window as they clambered over the deck and underneath their flag. The officers did not clamber, of course, so smart in their dark blue uniforms, their faces pale and strange.

In the days that followed, she heard them in the streets. All of them, confident and loud, so sure of their place in the world; and of their place in Nagasaki, as though it belonged to them.

Within a week, the American lieutenant came to see her, acting like he already knew her answer. He didn't speak her language except for a few words, badly pronounced. He said them haltingly, and laughed merrily at every mistake he made, as though her language were a trifle and not her trade. Although only young, Cio-Cio was a gifted conversationalist of great delicacy, beauty, and wit; a dancer, singer, musician. She was not a courtesan; those licenses were forbidden to geishas.

And here he was, brought by Goro, the marriage broker, suggesting marriage. Cio-Cio would make his stay in Nagasaki magical, the

American said. Someone to come home to, he said. Someone to care for him.

He seemed to think this was enough, that she be of service to him. That seemed enough for her parents, too – the prestige of an American husband, a naval officer, Lieutenant Benjamin Franklin Pinkerton.

But Cio-Cio had spoken to her sister geishas, and the courtesans too, and knew what happened when an American sailor took a geisha wife, no matter how gentle his speech or how admiring his glance. Cio-Cio was young, but she knew she deserved more than to decorate his home and his bed for his short stay in this harbor, more than promises with no more longevity than that of the butterfly for which she was named.

Cio-Cio had overheard the advice Pinkerton's friend Sayre had given him, thinking she spoke no English. Nagasaki geishas had grace and intelligence, and so many talents, and with their port so full of great men from around the world, she had learned to be graceful and clever in several tongues, and how to hold her own while she listened. Her silence was meant to help her be a perfect hostess, to know best what words and music would please her guest.

Her elegant silence taught her many things, besides.

"Marry her, Ben, just for now," Sayre had said. "It's good to have a wife while you're in a foreign port. All the comforts of home, eh, and no risk of the pox." His laugh was sly. "It's not like a Japanese marriage counts back in California. Easy enough to divorce her when your time here's up."

Ben Pinkerton smiled. He laughed, too. Pinkerton, so pink, like the cherry blossoms in Nagasaki's gardens; as pink as his long pale face. His eyes sparkled at the suggestion of a disposable wife.

Ben. He would better go by Benjamin here, in Japan, but she would not be the one to tell him. Not when he smiled at his friend's sly joke that she could be wed and then discarded as though she meant nothing. That she was to serve him only, with nothing truly in return. A roof over her head, which she already had, and then to spread her legs for him in wifely duties: 'wife' to this American only a slightly more dignified name than 'prostitute.'

And oh, the absence of dignified names for the one called *Ben*. She would not tell him, and perhaps nobody would. That sound could mean so many things in her language, but Sayre had said it as *Ben-just-for-now*, and now to her it was redolent of *benjo* – lavatory – and then the suggestion of *excrement* – *daiben*. His distasteful offer and his contempt for her written even in his name.

No, she would not marry this American, so pink, with his soiled name and how he laughed at what he thought was her ignorance.

Cio-Cio's friend Suzuki has whispered another name in her ear, in any case. The Americans had brought back with them a Japanese prince, Yamadori, who longed for a Japanese wife now he was home from his many years with the people in those United States. Unfortunately for the prince, some families considered him not entirely suitable as a husband, with his foreign habits. But Cio-Cio thought otherwise.

Cio-Cio-San would tell Goro to go to Yamadori. And if Yamadori did not want her, she was young and beautiful. She would still wait for a suitor who would value her, not fleetingly as a butterfly, but as a woman of talent, wit, and worth.

Cassandra's gift of foresight offers huge appeal to the modern reader, who share her knowledge of how the story ends. Clytemnestra and her axe also read differently to modern viewers, trained by Sigourney Weaver, Linda Hamilton and Uma Thurman to shout 'you go, girl!' when a tough woman picks up a weapon. It's easy to sympathize with Clytemnestra taking the axe to Agamemnon once you know her full story (sadly her surviving children won't agree!); but it's impossible to be on her side when she kills Cassandra. Even Euripides knew the Trojan women got a raw deal. There are various versions of this story, but Cassandra is always condemned to die alongside Agamemnon as if she was his sidekick, not his slave. Allowing Clytemnestra the opportunity to free Cassandra feels a little bit like saving them both.

CASSANDRA GETS A FUTURE
TANSY RAYNER ROBERTS

CASSANDRA HAS ALWAYS KNOWN that the gods exist. You don't have to see something to know that it's there, screwing your life up from the moment you are born.

Chosen of Apollo, they used to say about her. Which was perhaps a kind way of saying: "Too bright, too quick, suspiciously clever. What a waste of a princess: no one will ever marry her."

Cassandra does not believe in magic. She does not see literal visions of the future. She's just the only member of her family who grasps how consequences work.

"This will end badly," she says when her brother Paris brings home the queen of another country, both dizzy in love and hoping no one will mind.

"This doesn't look good for us," she says when the armies of half the world encamp themselves on the beach of Troy, because it turns out the husband of Queen Helen had a lot of friends, and all of them have been itching to teach a lesson to the beautiful, gold-rich city from across the sea.

"He won't take this lying down," she says when her brother Hector returns from a battle, having accidentally killed the wrong man in a duel – Achilles still lives, and his love lies bleeding on the sand.

It's not a magic trick, to see the future. It's not a gift from the gods. It's common bloody sense.

Cassandra's curse is that she can't shut up about it. She says the things no one wants to hear, even after a lifetime of knowing it makes her unlikeable.

"It's done," she tells her mother, as the siege wears on. Hector is dead at Achilles' hand, leaving them without a halfway competent general. The stores are running low. "We won't survive another winter."

"Oh, Cassandra," sighs the queen. "You always think the world is about to end. Have faith in your brothers. Have faith in the gods."

The gods have never done Cassandra any favors, and she's running out of brothers.

Cassandra's little brother Troilus has known nothing but siege. He was a baby when the stolen queen came to live with them; five years old when the war began.

Now he is twelve and thinks he knows everything.

"Why do you hate the war so much?" he asks her. "War is how we achieve glory and serve the gods."

Cassandra sighs. Whatever she says, he will not hear.

She does not say: they have already killed us.

She does not say: our city is drained; if they left our shores now, we would still collapse into dust and starvation.

See, she has some restraint.

What she does say is: "Darling Troilus. The best and worst thing that can happen to a prince like you in a battle is that you will die, and ballads will be written about you. After the battle is lost, your mother and sisters will be herded into a line while our enemies argue over which of the royal women they each wish to own. If we survive the first rape, they'll drag us home in chains to scrub their laundry and pour their wine until the world ends. That's what war means for women."

Troilus pats her arm. "I'll protect you, Cassandra. I'll never let that happen to you."

Sweet boy. If only he had been born into another family, he might have gone places. Done something with his life.

"I wouldn't worry about it," she tells him, because she can already see the pattern of his blood spilled out on the stones of the courtyard. It is not a vision of the gods; no prediction. And yet the image of it stays with her for days.

Cassandra cannot literally see the future.

That is why she has no idea that there are soldiers hiding inside that ugly horse statue, ready to burst out and kill them all.

As a person who sees consequences, and is rarely wrong about them, the sudden appearance of a wooden horse does raise some fairly obvious questions, but no one wants to hear her thoughts on the matter.

"Why would the kings of all those countries who hate us decide that now is the time to honor our gods with gifts?" she asks, as the men of Troy haul the wooden horse inside the city.

"Oh Cassandra," says Paris, already dying from an arrow wound he took days ago, because he thinks he knows better than every healer in the city. "Why can't you let us have one nice thing?"

"You're the worst," she tells him, and drinks three cups of wine while her mother's back is turned.

Paris dies of fever from his wound gone bad. This could be a good opportunity to send his stolen wife home. But Cassandra's father has learned nothing in ten years, and so the old king gives Helen to another of his sons before the day is even over.

"Kicking her out would have been more productive," Cassandra mutters as the wedding cakes are baked, the garlands strung. She eyes the wooden horse that sits so meekly in the center of the room, knowing somehow that it means trouble. It means the end of everything.

"Have some compassion," says her mother. "Would you have your sister-in-law suffer at the hands of those awful kings?"

Cassandra says: "Better her than us," knowing that no one is listening.

There are soldiers in that wooden horse. Surprise!

The gates of the city swings open, bolts loosened in the dead of night by one of the invaders. The kings of those other countries storm through with their army.

Old King Priam breathes his last before his sons are butchered, so he never has to acknowledge his terrible decisions.

Cassandra finds herself in a line of royal women, eyed up by their invaders.

Helen weeps silently, while they wait to be claimed by their enemies. Cassandra's mother Queen Hecuba comforts the weeping foreign queen who actually thought Paris, of all people, was a good bet. "You could not have known, my dear," Hecuba murmurs.

"Really?" says Cassandra. "*Really?*"

"I hear you are chosen and beloved of Apollo," says Agamemnon, the king who won Cassandra as his lucky door prize.

"I hear you've forced yourself upon several of his priestesses since the war began," Cassandra mutters in return.

Agamemnon gives her an odd look, and she realizes to her bewilderment that he heard what she said. Worse, he paid attention to her words. She's so used to being unheard and invisible in her family, who rarely wait for her to finish a sentence before drifting on to their next disastrous decision.

"Oh," Agamemnon says: a large man, ageing into bulk and enriched by his own confidence after taking ten years to win a war. "My wife's going to *love* you."

"That seems unlikely," says Cassandra.

She pretends to be too seasick to submit to Agamemnon's bulky advances in bed. They call her his concubine, regardless. A pretty word for an ugly job.

Cassandra speaks little on the voyage to Argos. It is too disorienting, to have people listen when she speaks. She does encourage Agamemnon's people to share any gossip they have about their king, his wife, their people.

"You sacrificed your daughter to the gods for a good wind to Troy?" she says to Agamemnon, one night. "What did your wife have to say about that?"

"She was furious," he says. "Cursed my name from one end of the city to the other in between bouts of weeping, and murder threats. My Clytemnestra does not understand important matters of men and war. But it's been ten years. I'm sure she's forgiven me."

"I suspect you have drastically misread this situation," says Cassandra.

Cassandra does not need god-given visions of the future to see it unspooling before her when Queen Clytemnestra meets them at the palace gates. They are led across a newly-dyed carpet of purple-red, as if their feet tread upon the blood-soaked history of this family.

There are axes everywhere. It is what you might call a recurring motif.

Agamemnon struts off to his bath, happy to be home in his own palace. Cassandra watches him go, knowing she will never see him alive again.

She waits in a small antechamber for her own fate. Prays a little, though her conversations with gods have never been especially productive.

"Now would be a wonderful time to show me you exist, to prove none of my suffering has been a colossal waste of time."

No visions of Apollo. No golden fruit or showers of unearthly light. If it is true that the gods chose Cassandra as their beloved, then they have a funny way of showing it.

Supper is brought to her: wine and cheese and fruit. Classy, she thinks, but unnecessary. At this point, she'd rather go to her death on an empty stomach.

When the queen comes – another surprise, really, that Clytemnestra would see to Cassandra's disposal personally – she carries her own axe. A beautiful woman, with a hardness to her face. Odd to think that she is sister to Helen, who was all softness and tears.

Cassandra wonders if Clytemnestra still weeps for her murdered daughter. Perhaps over the years she has comforted herself with vengeful thoughts, boiled hard and sharpened to an edge.

The queen's feet are bare; she has come directly from her husband's bath. The axe has been washed clean, but there are flecks of blood upon those bare feet.

"What should I do with you, daughter of Troy?" asks Queen Clytemnestra. First rule of leadership: never ask a question if you do not already know the answer.

Cassandra knows her place; she kneels before the queen. "I was brought here against my will. But I would be a good asset for the ruler of this city. I am quick-witted, and I have a mind for strategy."

Clytemnestra seems amused. "Did not your family just lose a war?"

"*They* never listened to my advice. You should try it. Start a trend."

"You think I should suffer my husband's concubine to live?"

"Your husband's prisoner," Cassandra corrects. "That is your choice, of course. You are a queen. You have the axe."

The longest moment passes.

Finally, Clytemnestra says: "I hear you are chosen and beloved of Apollo."

"I wouldn't worry about that," says Cassandra. "He doesn't."

Another long moment; and the axe lowers more gently than Cassandra had predicted. "Come with me," says Queen Clytemnestra. "I want to show you something."

The shrine is small, out of the way. Tucked into a corner of the palace where few people pass, or congregate. Clearly not a monument to a favorite god. Cassandra does not recognize the symbols carved on the outside, nor the statues.

Inside the shrine, the walls are damp. Everything smells of must and neglect. Cassandra almost barks her knee on a low statue. "What is this place?"

"My husband lost a boy he loved in his youth," says Clytemnestra. "He built this tomb in his honor. Don't let it warm your sympathies; he built one twice the size for his favorite mare."

"Why am I here?" asks Cassandra. "Agamemnon never loved me," she adds, feeling the urge to clarify the matter. "I'm not sure he knew my name."

"I have been told you can see the future," says Clytemnestra.

The words *that is a common misconception* rise on to Cassandra's tongue and for once she swallows them down, says nothing. Perhaps it's not too late to learn vocal restraint.

"I thought you might be able to help me with something," the queen continues.

Deep into the shrine, a stone mound serves as a tomb. It is not as dark in here as it should be; they carry no lantern, but there is a blue-ish glow emanating from the far side of the tomb.

"This light appeared the day we got word my husband was sailing home," says Clytemnestra. "I knew in that moment I was going to kill him. Before that, I was rather holding out hope that your kinsmen might do it for me."

"He hid behind Achilles for most of the war," Cassandra says absently. "And there were all those priestesses to ravish, gods to offend. He's been a busy fellow."

"Glad to hear my daughter was sacrificed for something important," says Clytemnestra, her voice sharp as an axe.

They are both angry women, Cassandra realizes. Not angry at each other, but running in parallel, side by side. The man they both hated and feared is dead, but this will never make them friends.

"What did you want to show me?" she asks. Surely, Clytemnestra would not bring her all this way to strike her dead, when there is all that convenient blood-colored carpet out there in the hallway, ready to catch Cassandra's headless corpse.

"This," says Clytemnestra, and shifts her weight at the stone lid of the tomb. Already loosened, it slides across. Blue light spills out, sharper than any candle lamp.

Cassandra leans in, fascinated at the color and brightness. She has seen a lot in her short life, but nothing quite like this. Within the blue light, she can see images flickering, thick and fast. It is exactly as she thought visions from the gods might be if she actually saw them: distinct pictures, magically clear. Full of detail.

She sees a city made of silver. Ships sailing through the sky. People made of metal, alongside those of flesh and blood. Women walking at the side of men, speaking and being heard with voices of equal weight. Extraordinary clothes. Mouthwatering food.

She sees it unfold before her, and she wants it.

"Is that the future?" Cassandra breathes.

"*A* future," says Clytemnestra. "I believe so."

"How did you find this?"

"People disappearing, here and there over the last few weeks. Yesterday, it was reported to me that three slaves entered this shrine and never left. I investigated." Clytemnestra shrugged. "Twelve in all have gone missing."

"You think they climbed in here?" A portal, then, some kind of magic door from the present to the impossible future. Cassandra's hands ache to touch the brilliant images; she restrains herself, not wanting to disturb the visions. "They went through to this other place?"

"I don't know for certain. But I believe so."

Cassandra knows, in that moment. She turns to face the queen, her eyes wide. "You don't know what will happen if I go through there. Do you?"

"I do not," the queen says softly. "And neither do you. Perhaps it is an illusion, or a trick. Perhaps the voyage will steal the air from your lungs. Perhaps your death will be crueler than if I cut you down with my axe. I don't know."

"I don't know, either," Cassandra murmurs. It's been so long since she asked a question and did not immediately see the most obvious, inevitable answer spooling out ahead of her. It is a strange thing, the unpredictable.

"I do know this," says Clytemnestra. "A queen is always under scrutiny. I cannot show weakness before my court. I cannot pardon the concubine of my traitor husband. If you step outside this shrine, the future is set: I must swing my axe, and soak your blood into the carpet."

"Yes," says Cassandra, gazing into the glowing blue light. "I know."

"You have all the information I can provide," says Clytemnestra. "To make your choice. I will leave you to contemplate your future."

"And you'll be waiting right outside, with your axe."

Clytemnestra smiles. "I see we understand each other. Good fortune to you, daughter of Troy."

"Good fortune to you," Cassandra replies.

Clytemnestra's smile becomes brittle. "I have killed the father of my living children. I think we both know there will be consequences for such an act. My future closes around me like a funeral pyre."

"Are you not tempted to escape into the unknown yourself?" Cassandra asks.

"I am the queen," Clytemnestra replies, as if she never even considered the alternative. "Better the queen of a known country, than nobody in a new land."

Cassandra has been ignored her whole life, but she has never been nobody; she's rather keen to know how it feels. Slowly, she reaches out a hand to disturb the surface of the light within the tomb. It ripples invitingly.

She hears footsteps as Clytemnestra walks away.

Both hands now; Cassandra dips her hand into the cool blue light. Something tugs on her, holding her fast. Images flicker. Ships in the sky, female equality, bright silver mechanical limbs, platform heels, raw fish rolled in pretty patterns.

There is so much to look forward to.

Cassandra leans in and grasps the future tightly.

She has no idea what will happen next.

Isn't it wonderful?

Outside the shrine, Clytemnestra waits for a few moments. She does not look back to confirm Cassandra's choice. She saw this consequence as soon as she decided to share the secret of the tomb.

Clytemnestra, queen of Argos, is good at predicting outcomes. From a young age, she has been very aware of cause and effect. Of consequence, and inevitability.

Her reign will be short; she has always known that to be true. But she has never been one to shirk from responsibility.

She bows her head for a moment, remembering her daughter Iphigenia. She would be the same age as Cassandra now, if she had lived. Perhaps Iphigenia would also have been enticed by a glorious, magical future of flying ships...if anyone had ever given her the choice.

The moment has passed; the day ahead will be a busy one.

Clytemnestra lifts her axe, straightens her crown, and returns to work.

Women of all ages and stations are diminished and degraded in classic fairy tales and popular children's stories. Young women, beautiful and virtuous, must be rescued by handsome young men, preferably of rich and royal birth, instead of relying upon their own resources to combat abuse and injustice. Old women, bitter of heart and grotesque of visage, are witches and cruel stepmothers, never kindly mentors or sages. These familiar narratives are especially pernicious because they are typically heard or read during the formative years when girls create their own identities. Wouldn't it be liberating if female role models were instead smart, courageous, and independent? Wouldn't it be encouraging if the young aspired to become wise, compassionate, and kick-ass elders?

SNAPPILY EVER AFTER
ANN S EPSTEIN

Prologue

Womenfolk do you feel mistreated?
Overlooked, demonized, and defeated?
In literature reviled?
Cheated, defiled?
Tis time those old tales were deleted!

Herewith in the tales that ensue
Noted females are given their due
Lame brains stereotyped?
Beauty over-hyped?
We visit their unfair stories anew

Chapter 1

Given the choices at hand
The Little Mermaid eschews life on land
"I want him," she doth shout
"The guy with the spout!"
Then she joins Moby-Dick's punk rock band

Chapter 2

Doing aerial yoga from a tower rafter
Rapunzel explodes with raucous laughter
She shreds all her frocks
Crops off her long locks
And dwells happily alone ever after

Chapter 3

Her country by fanatics beset
Snow White rallies to the threat
Elected President
She reforms government
Naming seven Little People to her cabinet

Chapter 4

Sleeping Beauty, a.k.a. Briar Rose
Fakes somnambulism as a pose
Her palace mates snore gravidly
While the princess reads avidly
Not what the naive prince doth suppose

Chapter 5

Cinderella dislikes the royalty scene
Her charmless husband arouses her spleen
With nary a wince
She beheads hubby prince
And rules o'er the realm as solo Queen

Chapter 6

Why must every stepmother be bad
Henpecking a girl's hapless dad?
That nasty reputation
Merits rehabilitation
Henceforth, we declare all stepmothers rad

Chapter 7

Resisting social pressure to be thin
Alice sits down to tea with a grin
Snarfs up the Queen's tarts
Emits loud staccato farts
Vows she'll never go on a diet again

Chapter 8

When the Hardy Boys call her a jerk
Nancy Drew reacts with a smirk
Joins the FBI
Becomes a CIA spy
And hires Frank and Joe to do her leg work

Chapter 9

Frisking amidst lambs, kids, and shoats
Edelweiss twined round ankles and throats
Heidi plucks mountain roses
And when Peter proposes
Opts to cavort with sheep, pigs, and goats

Chapter 10

When the wolf, his sweet talk doth spew
Grandma eviscerates him without further ado
Simmers him with spuds
Carrots, marijuana buds
Feeds Little Red Riding Hood trippy wolf stew

Chapter 11

When Beauty rejecting all that is mod
Professes love for Beast's hairy bod
Beast becomes a comely "He"
The hunky prince he used to be
Whereupon Beauty spurns his preening facade

Chapter 12

The Wicked Witch subverts the word pretty
TikTok's top meme is her witty ditty
"Dark chin hair is in
Gnarly warts, bright green skin
Vote me the Supermodel of Emerald City"

Epilogue

Are not these updated tales exciting
Their defiant feminist spirit delighting?
Indeed, every author knows
That making poetry or prose
Entails at least ninety percent rewriting

No more shall woeful heroines epitomize us
Neither sacrifice, sully, nor sanitize us
Let's re-envision ourselves
Take dusty tomes off the shelves
Tis time to reward and revise us

Beautiful socialite Anna betrays the husband she married at eighteen with dashing cavalry officer Vronsky, and is cast out of high society. Both eventually attempt suicide, Anna successfully. Meanwhile, sweet eighteen-year-old Kitty – whom Vronsky had courted, and who was once 'not merely under Anna's sway, but in love with her' – recovers from her heartbreak. She dutifully marries Konstantin Levin, an eccentric but respectable gentleman nearly twice her age, and gives birth to her first child. But perhaps we can imagine another story, one in which Anna had more choices, one in which passion joins and heals rather than tearing apart.

LILAC
BÉATRICE DE CHARMOY

Kitty had been seeing Anna every day and was in love with her, and had always imagined her in lilac.

Anna Karenina, Part I, Chapter 22
(trans. Rosemary Edmonds)

BEFORE IT WAS ANYTHING, it was a knocking at Anna's bedroom window in the middle of the night.

She woke with a shudder and lay wide-eyed in the dark, motionless, wondering what had awakened her.

Then she heard it. A thud as something knocked into the wood of the window frame. A few seconds later, a sharp sound, something hard hitting the glass pane itself.

Anna slid out of bed, tiptoed towards the window, smoothed the front of her nightgown, and ran a hand through her hair. Then, gingerly, she twisted the knob and swung open the window.

Silence. The night spread like a blanket over the sleeping city. A cool breeze blew into the bedroom, rustling the curtains. Wagon wheels, far off. Then, a cry.

"Anna!"

Startled, she searched for the voice. There, only steps from the house, wrapped in furs and smiling gently – was none other than Princess Ekaterina Alexandrovna Shcherbatskaya. Whose name, Anna reminded herself, was Levina now.

"Kitty!"

"Oh, I'm so glad it was you I awakened, and not that...man. Vronsky," giggled Kitty.

"I was expecting a bird," whispered Anna, slowly, softly. *Birdsong.* She had never paid particular notice to Kitty's voice before, but now it seemed uncommonly lovely.

"Oh dear, I'm afraid you got me instead."

"Is Konstantin Dmitrievich with you?"

Kitty giggled again. "At this hour?"

"Shall I..." something prickled in Anna's throat. "I'll come down and let you in. But – oh, I'm in my nightgown!"

"What of it?" Kitty laughed, waving a dismissive hand, "We are friends. No need to dress for a ball."

Anna smiled, and inched the window shut before rushing down the stairs.

When she opened the door she found Kitty waiting, a bouquet of wildflowers in her arms, cheeks red from driving in the wind and dimpled with exuberant joy. Anna had been preparing at least a semblance of an eloquent welcome as she turned the key and unhooked the latch; but, seeing the flowers, she broke into tears.

"Oh...oh, Kitty...you are so kind...kinder than anyone..."

Kitty dropped the bouquet then, and wrapped her slight arms around her friend's neck; her furs, half-undone, draped themselves over Anna's shoulders. Anna crumpled in her arms. A moment passed. Kitty broke away to close the door behind her. Anna sighed.

"Kitty, dear...what were you thinking, visiting at this hour of the night?"

Kitty hesitated. "It seems so silly now that I say it, but...ever since your visit at Dolly's I have had a strange feeling that I had to see you again somehow...as if to settle something with myself. And then last night I dreamed – I dreamed I was with you, and it was so clear to me that I had to see you as soon as possible..." She blushed, and raised her hands to her face in embarrassment. "Maybe it's all stupid. But I'm glad to see you even so. As for the method...forgive me for this, but I couldn't bear to have Count Vronsky thinking I came to call on him."

"I understand." Anna whispered. "But you shouldn't have taken the trouble, he barely comes here anymore..." Scarcely had the words left her mouth than Anna began to cry once more.

"Oh, Anna! My God, what has he done to you?" Kitty, flustered and concerned, grabbed Anna's hands and pulled them close to her chest. "Anna. You are so dear to me."

"I was sure you must hate me, after everything...after..." Anna choked on her words.

"How could I hate you? I have always admired and adored you, since before we met, and now more than ever. As for that awful man...I should have warned you. He hurts everyone he touches."

"It is not his fault. I have done this to myself. I have been so stupid, so blind..." Anna fell back into a chair. Hot tears rolled down her cheeks.

Kitty knelt by her side, holding her hand. Thinking, oh, even when she is miserable she is so elegant. Graceful. Like a swan. For a moment there was silence. Kitty inched closer. "Come with me," she whispered. "Let's disappear. I will take you home. You cannot stay here."

"And I cannot leave."

"But of course you can. You must."

Anna leaned back in her chair. The curve of her trembling lips, the nape of her pale neck woven with the coal-black strands of her hair, her frail wrists – the whole of her seemed to glow softly, divinely in the dim candlelight.

"I cannot. He would never forgive me."

"You need some relief."

"A good lover would not need relief," Anna sobbed.

"Everyone needs relief. That is something we must all forgive ourselves for."

"You are an idealist."

There was a pause.

"Come with me," Kitty whispered again. "Just a few days."

Silence.

"I refuse to leave you here. Look, you're shivering."

Anna closed her eyes. Sighed. Gave in. "All right, you angel. For you, I will go."

She left only a note in the nursery explaining herself – to Annushka, not to Vronsky.

They drove to the station and waited together, talking about nothing; when the train came they sat down together, arranging their things around them, as if it were the most natural thing in the world for two ladies to find themselves here, a few hours before dawn.

Kitty, who had been traveling all night, was asleep before they had even made it out of Moscow; but Anna wasn't at all tired and looked out the window the whole time, smiling down every once in a while at her sleeping companion.

Kitty awoke as dawn was breaking. Before she could get her bearings, her eye was caught by the woman sitting beside her. Anna's dark hair was loose around her face and neck, and her throat was bare. Her gaze was soft, her lips parted; but her eyes glittered with that secret fire everyone found so fascinating in her. Kitty had never seen a creature more ravishing.

"Good morning," Anna smiled.

"Beautiful, isn't it?" Kitty gestured at the horizon, at the clouds tinged pink and yellow.

"Lovely. I haven't been awake at dawn for the longest time."

Soon they arrived at the station, where they found a carriage waiting for them. Arriving at the estate, they walked arm in arm up the well-tended garden path to the front door of the Levin house. Kitty knocked, Anna standing behind her.

Konstantin Dmitrievich swung open the door, half-dressed for the coming day's work, one boot on and the other on the floor beside him.

"Why, hello!" he smiled, genial, kind. "I didn't expect you to be back from town this early!"

"Oh, Kostya. I have wonderful news! Our lovely friend from Moscow is to stay with us a few days. It'll do her a world of good, don't you think?"

"Of course." But his tone was different, suddenly. Konstantin peered over Kitty's shoulder at Anna.

Suddenly self-conscious, Anna pulled her coat tightly around her. Her cheeks reddened with embarrassment as she apologized for the state of her attire – she hadn't had much time to dress before leaving.

Seeing her, disheveled as she was, so different from the cool and collected society woman she had seemed to be in Moscow, Levin's features were softened by pity. He knew that the woman before him was Anna as she was, and not Anna as she would have liked to be; the contrast was striking. He looked down at the ground in contemplation. Only those who suffer horribly, he thought, could ever resort to artificiality so extreme it turns a mourner into a socialite... He nodded gently. "Yes, of course. How wonderful. I do hope you enjoy yourself here."

Anna smiled. "I hope for the same, Monsieur. My deepest thanks for your hospitality."

Levin pulled on his second boot and reached for his coat. "I assure you, it is my pleasure. Now, if you will excuse me..." He slipped the coat over his shoulders and paused to give his wife a kiss on the cheek before striding out the door and towards the fields.

"Oh dear," sighed Kitty as soon as he was out of earshot. "I'm afraid he forgot to ask us in. He can be rather absent-minded, but it's all in good faith, you know." She giggled. "I hope he hasn't offended you. People don't behave quite as they do in Moscow, down here. You know how it is."

"He is a lovely man, Kitty. You are very lucky."

Kitty smiled. She seemed positively to glow.

The two were barely in the door before she exclaimed: "Oh, you must meet Mitya!"

Anna remembered, of course, the news of Kitty having given

birth. She remembered the moment she had been told. The odd sort of feeling that had filled her chest even as she had smiled so widely, even as she had gasped so politely and made all her little exclamations of joy and surprise. That flower of a girl, now a mother...

She had felt a familiar sort of disconnect. A rift between the voice on the outside which gushed polite exclamations, and the voice on the inside, which was silent. No, not silent: sighing. A long, haunting sigh.

It was a happy thing, really. Or rather, it should have been. A son! Good news, at least, at a time when such things were so scarce and so precious. And the thought of Kitty a mother, happy and in love, shining in her domesticity, should at least have been a comfort to her.

And yet the feeling had remained. The sigh. It was heavy, Anna remembered. She had needed to sit down soon afterwards, and found it difficult to breathe. It was draining; it was a kind of longing. Like a terrifying great magnet drawing her forward and outward, she knew not where. It was like homesickness.

Kitty dragged her up a flight of stairs and into a bright clean room. That feeling, Anna realized, that sigh – it was gone now. With Kitty's hand in hers she smiled and laughed and felt no disconnect, no artificiality. The early sunlight streamed into the room through a large window. Kitty bent down and lifted the bundle named Mitya out of his cradle.

The child stirred, fists waving languorously through the sunlit air, eyelids fluttering. And Anna, looking down at the creature, the infant Kitty held so gently on her hip in her slender arms, felt truly happy, filled with the feeling in a way she hadn't been in a long time, and even proud, if a touch wistful.

"He's beautiful," she breathed, cupping his soft cheek affectionately in her hand. "I'm so glad he's healthy."

Kitty smiled. It was a smile Anna had never seen on her before, a strong smile, proud, confident: a mother's smile.

Kitty pressed her lips to the child's downy forehead, and the boy grinned a honey-sweet, toothless grin. Anna felt her heart swell.

"Sometimes I wish I could have been a better mother," Anna sighed.

Even as she said it she knew she shouldn't have. She held a hand over her mouth and blushed. What place did such confessions have between two friends like themselves? And at a moment like this, a moment that should have been so happy! Even if it hadn't been such an awfully, dreadfully intimate thing to say – she shouldn't have ruined Kitty's mood so. As she watched Kitty's face fall, her brows furrow and her soft lips curl into a frown, Anna felt a stiffening pang of regret. Kitty was so lovely when she was happy.

And yet it was something about the light, somehow, that drew the confession from her. Something about the light and the way it fell through the window and shone like gold on the locks of hair that tumbled over Kitty's shoulders; the way it made her lips glisten, the way it outlined her delicate eyelashes and the youthful curve of her cheek, the way it made her bright eyes shine ever brighter.

"Oh, but Anna, you will help me with little Mitya, won't you?" Kitty asked, breaking the brief, eternal silence.

Anna didn't know what to say.

"It's been so hard for you, all of it. But I think you were – you are still – a wonderful mother," she went on. "All you need is a fair chance, really. Wouldn't you say?"

Anna was speechless. Gently, Kitty lifted the bundle in her arms, held the baby out for Anna to take.

Anna reached out and cradled the child. She didn't speak, not yet. But slowly, slowly, a smile spread across her face. A strong smile, proud, confident. A mother's smile.

And Kitty smiled too, bright and sunny and youthful – because it was then that she knew, finally, that Anna would be all right. The woman she remembered – that woman who glowed and sparkled and stole everyone's hearts at balls and on train carriages – she still existed. After all that had happened, after all she had done and all that had been done to her, this was still the woman Kitty knew, admired, even loved. And here they both were. Together.

And so it was. They made a habit of it, a sort of ritual. Kitty would come – at a decent hour, now, fearing nothing – to do errands and make calls around town, and call at Anna's first of all, before seeing even Dolly or her parents or anyone else.

They wrote to each other – every week at first, then every other day or more. Sweet, empty letters, full of trivial news and pressed flowers and well-wishes. When Kitty arrived the two of them would read to each other in the evenings, play quatre-mains, sometimes sing. Anna began to look forward to those visits like nothing else. She had everything dusted and polished, bought flowers, prepared menus days in advance, with a sort of nostalgia for the thrill of *soirées* and society. They would dance, sometimes, when it was late and they were giddy with laughter, twirling and tripping through the drawing-room, stumbling into sofa legs and lampshades.

Anna remembered that Kitty had once said something about lilac dresses, and began to wear the color more often, half-hoping Kitty would notice.

Once Kitty, calling on the Tsverskoys, ran into Vronsky. She recognized him at once, and went pale; but he noticed her before she could do anything, and she went to him and made pleasant conversation. She avoided mentioning Anna. Nothing came of it in the end.

In Moscow, Kitty bought dresses, shoes, things from the market. Then, a few days after arriving, she would declare that she had finished all her business here and was ready to go home, and the two of them would head out to the countryside together. And another few days having gone by, whenever she felt that she should, Anna would take the train back to Moscow alone. And so on.

But Anna never really wanted to leave, and she began to stay longer and longer, until she barely ever went back herself. She began to take little Annie with her to the country, and only went along with Kitty when she went into town to do her errands, city life becoming less and less familiar to both of them; slowly losing a world that had never truly been theirs.

Anna had always glowed in society, had always thought herself at her best surrounded by servants and ball gowns; but she soon grew to love the country. Here, far from it all, there was sunlight. The city sky was too often grey, cloudy, fogged-over and soot-black. In the country, in the Levins' fields and orchards, the sun shone; when it rained it rained, but after the rain there was always a rainbow. It was honest weather; the clouds in town were too ominous, loomed too darkly all the time, haunting every summer day.

Rare was a straightforward crisp winter afternoon in the city, the kind of afternoon it had been when Levin saw Kitty skating and knew at once he would marry her. Anna heard about this, and many other stories too, the three of them sitting wrapped in rough, thick blankets around the fireplace; she smiled when they told her these things, felt her heart stir a little, like the earth does when the rivers thaw in the springtime.

Seryozha, Anna's son, was rarely mentioned. But one day, a few months after the first visit, Kitty broached the topic with a new sense of resolve.

"You miss him," she frowned. Solemn.

"Yes."

"I could go to him." A decisive tone. "To Alexey Alexandrovich. I'll tell him everything. He forgives you. He will have pity."

"I don't want pity. I want liberty."

"I know...I know."

"He has refused me too many times already. I can't bear to hope for anything."

"Just let me try," Kitty implored.

Anna conceded.

To everyone's surprise, Kitty showed herself to be a more brilliant negotiator than any of the dozens of petition-bearers Karenin saw every day; and they made an arrangement for Anna to meet her son once, to test the waters. Seryozha was first overwhelmed, but then overjoyed. Anna and her husband even talked, civilly. They agreed it would not be the last time. Anna felt as if something cold and heavy had been lifted out of her ribcage.

Time in Moscow had passed slowly, endlessly waiting, endlessly hoping for release from this waiting, this suffocating sense of dread.

But in the countryside, with the poetic rhythm of the days from dawn to dusk, and with the pleasant, regular journey to Moscow and back, time flew by on silver wings.

Spring had been a blur, soft greens and blues, mud and birdsong; summer was a single, vaguely remembered sun-drenched afternoon, a picnic in the grass and Kitty dressed in white. They watched the sun set in the evenings, the three of them and Mitya, the sky orange and azure and blood-red and lilac. Anna saw her own son more often. Then, in the blink of an eye, spring and summer were gone, and autumn – rain, smell of earth, the birch leaves a rich saffron – was already nearing its end.

"Will you stay for Christmas and the New Year, then?" Kitty asked her one night as the two of them sat together in the nursery, giving Mitya a bath. Little Annie slept beside them.

"I would love to," Anna nodded. "If you'll have me, that is."

"But of course! We are family."

Mitya whimpered. Anna scooped him up, held him to her breast as Kitty soaked a cloth in the bathwater. The child giggled.

"He is getting so big now," Anna whispered. "Healthy and beautiful. You must be proud."

"Oh, I am," replied Kitty, softly. "I have never been so proud in all my life. Sometimes it makes me want to cry, I am so happy."

Anna smiled at that, and began to sing softly to the child.

That was when it happened.

The cry came from outside. The voice of a peasant woman, calling to Konstantin. They both heard it, couldn't help but hear it.

"It's Count Vronsky, sir! He's come!"

Kitty froze. Anna went on singing, as if she had not heard, or not quite understood what she had heard.

"Anna." Kitty spoke in a whisper.

The singing trailed off.

"Anna, he's come to get you."

Anna was deathly pale, now, the reality of it sinking its claws into her heart. "What does he want?" But of course she knew what he wanted. His trophy back.

"We must go." Kitty grimaced. "Whatever he wants, I won't let him take it from you."

"And what? Leave poor Konstantin to confront him? There will be a duel, death...he will think I have run off with someone, perhaps even..." Mitya began to cry. Anna rocked him softly in her arms.

"Kostya is a reasonable man. He is kind, and knows how to be diplomatic. He will convince him to forgive you, to forget."

Anna shook her head. "You do not know Alexey Kirillovich. I asked him to forget, too, at the beginning... He will not. He is stubborn. And besides, I am his prize. An impossible conquest. He may not love me anymore, but he wants me on display." There was a scornful curl in Anna's lip, a look of harsh contempt on her face.

Kitty shivered; she had never seen that look before. They never talked so openly about these things, always avoided mentioning his name.

Beyond the darkening frame of the window, the sound of a carriage approaching could be heard, a horse whinnying.

Kitty grabbed Anna's wrist, sudden and desperate. She spoke quickly, breathlessly. "We have no time. We must go, trust me. Get blankets, coats, anything we need. I have some money with me. I'll fetch some things from the kitchen. We must leave out the back door, get the carriage ready and go, as fast as we can. Kostya will keep the Count waiting. He will understand."

It was all moving too quickly to resist the flow; so Anna did as she was told. Gently, she settled a sleeping Mitya into his cradle. Kostya and the women would look after him, and Annie too, while they were gone. She hoped it would not be for very long. She gathered blankets and coats, hats and gloves. Winter was approaching, and there was frost on the windows in the mornings already. She picked up as much as she could carry, and met Kitty silently at the door.

The two slipped out, looking around to make sure the Count was nowhere in sight, and ran to the stables. And then they were off as fast as the horses could carry them, the carriage – a large, four-wheeled affair with a leather top – thumping along the road, their backs to the sunset.

"I talked to Agafea Mihalovna in the kitchen," whispered Kitty. "She will ask to speak to Kostya about something, will say it's urgent. She will tell him to say you are at a cure in Switzerland, recovering from a bout of illness; and that I am in Moscow. As far as the Count is to know, this carriage is driven by peasants, carrying beets and carrots to the market. We will not be pursued."

Anna was struck by this, and struggled to come up with a response. Kitty was no longer a child, she realized. And what a brilliant woman she had become.

"Still, it's better to go quickly, just in case. The Count may be suspicious. I do not trust him."

"Thank you," Anna breathed at last, still trying to get her bearings. "I would be lost without you."

Kitty only smiled. "It's nothing."

"Where do you plan to take us?"

"I'm not all too sure, unless you have an idea. Away, anyhow, somewhere you can be safe. We'll stop in some town or other, when we're tired."

Anna laughed, and remarked jokingly on how romantic it all was. "Isn't it so strange? You, whisking me away from him in your carriage. You're so brave, so heroic. My Ivanhoe. My knight in shining armor." She sighed dramatically, posing as if in an opera.

Kitty only blushed, pretended to be busy with the horses, something tangled in the reins.

They rode for hours, not daring to stop for fear that Vronsky would appear in pursuit. Finally, both of them yawning and aching from bumping along the road so long, they saw a sign by the wayside, an inn – clean beds and hot breakfast in the morning. Lights blazed in the windows of a quaint-looking house behind a row of birches.

"We'll stop here for the night," murmured Kitty. Anna nodded.

The innkeepers, husband and wife, were warm and welcoming, offered them tea and cakes, and marveled at such beautiful young girls – "You flatter me," Anna laughed – traveling alone so late at night.

"It's an elopement," joked Anna.

"How scandalous! And who is the lucky gentleman?"

Kitty only shook her head, smiling. "Don't listen to her. We are going to a cousin's wedding, and we want to get there quickly – we meant to leave earlier, but were kept back by something unexpected," she explained. "We mustn't be late!"

And the innkeepers – none too curious, when it came down to it, as to what exactly had brought them here – simply nodded, and wished happiness to the bride and groom.

"There is only one room left," the wife, grey-haired and kindly, pointed out when they had finished their tea. "I hope that's all right."

"Oh, we don't mind at all," smiled Anna, waving it off. "We can't be picky, so late at night. We can only thank you for your hospitality."

The room was cozy and pretty, with a warm fire and thick beams of dark wood across the ceiling, and flowers on the tables, and an old, broad canopy bed. Anna and Kitty washed their faces, untied their dresses, and lay down under welcoming blankets, sighing with relief.

"I hope Mitya and Annie are all right," whispered Kitty in the dark.

"I'm sure they're just fine." Anna turned on her side to face Kitty, a soft silhouette and nothing more. "Konstantin will take good care of them."

"Oh, Kostya. He is a good man, and a wonderful father. I could not have hoped for a better husband."

"You warm my heart, both of you. You are so genuine, so kind to each other. Sometimes I think yours is the only love that exists."

Kitty was silent for a moment. "Kostya says things like that too, sometimes."

"You don't agree?" Anna asked curiously.

"I don't know." Kitty's words were barely spoken, barely more than a breath. "I think there must be more than one love in the world... even just in one person's heart. Love can't be alone."

"Maybe that is the right way to think about it. I thought the Count was the only love I would ever know. My great love. And look how that's turned out."

A pause. "I'm sorry."

"Don't be, you have done too much for me already."

"I wish I could do more."

"You're very sweet." Kitty couldn't see Anna smile, but could hear it in her voice. "You are far better than I am."

"Not better," protested Kitty. "Only luckier."

Anna sighed. "Perhaps." A moment's thought, then: "I was eighteen, too, when I married Alexey. But it was not love, not ever. We had...bouts of tenderness, perhaps, but for the most part we were cold to each other. We both resented each other for the loss of the lives we could have had if we hadn't been married. Always talking to the wall behind each others' heads. He is a good man – it is not him I blame – but our union was impossible. It made me wretched. Now, looking at you and Kostya...it is so lovely. It gives me hope."

"What for?" Kitty was delighted, fascinated by this hint at the story of Anna's life.

"Oh, I don't know. For happiness."

"I hope for that too. For your happiness."

"You are so lovely, Kitty. What would I do without you?" And, reaching forward in the dark, she kissed Kitty on the cheek, softly.

Long silence. Soft breathing. Slow rise and fall of chests.

"Anna."

"Yes?"

"May I...could I tell you something?"

"Of course."

"Promise you won't laugh at me."

Anna smiled into the dark again. "I promise."

Kitty hesitated. "Ever since I met you..." trailed off, started again. "Ever since I met you, I have had the deepest tenderness in my heart for you... For years...I have looked up at you and thought, oh, how lucky I am to have known you... I was so worried for you, and now I am so happy, and I can only thank you." She paused there, gathering her courage to go on.

"You mustn't thank me, I owe you too much," Anna whispered.

"No, it is I who owes you. You make me feel so lovely. When you smile, I feel somehow that my heart...has been polished, and is shining, like a brass kettle."

"Oh, Kitty."

"Anna...what I am trying to tell you is – everyone I know has always liked you terribly, even from the first glance, and I am no different. I am saying that...I must confess...like so many others before me..." A final intake of breath. "I am helplessly, completely, pathetically in love with you."

Anna didn't know what to say. So she only reached out, and cupped Kitty's soft cheek in her hand.

"You are too young to love me," Anna whispered.

"What difference does it make?"

"You love Kostya."

"What difference does it make? I love Kostya and I love you, and Mitya, and the farm, and the city, and spring and summer and autumn and even winter. I love it all. My heart was made to love."

Anna nodded. Spoke slowly. "I understand. Yes, I understand."

A pause. Then Kitty smiled. "You looked ravishing today."

Anna laughed. "I was only in a peasant's dress. But thank you."

"I love you." Kitty laughed, too, hearing herself say it, and said it again: "I love you. I love you. I've said it. I'm so glad I've said it."

And when Anna pressed her lips to Kitty's, it was the most natural thing in the world.

Anna pressed her lips to Kitty's, and hands were stroking cheeks and combing through soft hair. Kisses on lips and necks and jawlines, shoulders and collarbones. Bodies intertwined, and they couldn't bear to be apart, eyelids fluttering, entanglement and exhilaration.

And the whole world seemed to fall away and leave only the two of them there, in a soft bed under sweet-smelling blankets in the center of the vast universe, skin and bones spun into constellations, faces full of light. The night cupped their love in her velvet hands, and they fell asleep in each other's arms.

When morning came, the two began to plot.

They both knew that the story of the spa cure wouldn't be enough to keep Vronsky off their trail for long, not after he'd already come all the way to the Levins'. They needed something better.

"He won't ever stop haunting me. Not until I'm dead," Anna sighed, shaking her head.

"Well then, we'll have to make him believe you are." Even Kitty was surprised at how easily the idea came to her.

"Dead?"

Kitty had a plan in mind already, and it was absurd enough that it might just work.

"You'll never be able to show your face in Moscow or Petersburg ever again," Kitty warned.

"I'm a ruined woman as it is. It's just as well," Anna laughed, but Kitty knew she was being sincere.

They wrote letters. They wrote to Konstantin, of course, and Alexey Karenin. And Dolly and Stiva, too – "But he'll talk, Anna!" "But he's my brother!" – and a friend or two from Petersburg. And they informed them of the plan.

Konstantin wrote back with news of Vronsky's whereabouts. He had gone back to Moscow, but expected Anna back within a week, and was ready to go to Switzerland himself if she didn't arrive on time; Konstantin had done his best to buy them a few days. Karenin wrote back saying such a plan was all folly and idiocy, but that he would help if they'd like, with the legal records and such. The Oblonskys wrote back baffled and amazed.

If they went quickly enough, it would all be on time. A letter addressed to Saint-Moritz, had Konstantin sent one, would arrive in a few days. Then a carriage ride to the station, and afterwards the journey from Bern to Warsaw, where the train stopped. Kitty tried to remember how long it had taken her, when she had been to the waters. They would have to time it all very precisely.

Kitty knew someone at the station in Warsaw, she explained. A good woman, honest, hardworking. A friend of Konstantin's brother, Nikolai. She'd seen her twice – once at Nikolai's funeral, where she had been solemn and silent; and once when she had stopped at their estate for the night, on her way to some business or other in Petersburg. Then she had been loud and boisterous, fiery and full of conversation. They would ask for her help. She would tell them who to talk to, where to go, how to arrange everything – she would know.

They ate quickly, and dressed warmly for their journey. As she was paying for their stay, Kitty asked the matronly woman who had welcomed them the night before for directions to the nearest train station; the information obtained, Kitty thanked her for everything, and the two of them drove off.

The journey was uneventful, for the most part. They paid to stable their horses in Gatchina, and took the first train Westward. They were cautious, making sure not to be recognized. They refined their plans, going through every detail until neither could have any doubt, any step of the way, what must be done. During the day they drank tea, and laughed together. At night, they slept in each other's arms. Let anyone who noticed their intimacy think them to be cousins, or sisters, or whatever suited them.

It took them three days, in all, to get to Warsaw.

Once there, everything was a blur. Kitty took Anna's hand, and they wove through the crowds on the platform and down a flight of grimy stairs into the underbelly of the station. There, everything was work, and sweat, shovels and crates and coal dust. Kitty asked around, and soon enough they found her – Zoya, who had been the friend of Nikolai Levin, short and bony but gruff-looking. Her skin was pale, but her hands were coated with jet-black coal grime. She had pretty green eyes and a tough jaw, with her hair in a tight bun, wearing a pair of men's overalls rolled at the ankles and tied with a rope around her skinny waist.

She was thrilled to see Kitty, smiling wide, her dirt-smeared cheeks shining.

"Goodness! I wasn't expecting you! What in Hell's name are you doing down here?" She laughed, heartily. "And who's this?"

So Kitty explained, and Anna nodded curtly every once in a while, and finally covered her face in shame at all the trouble she had caused.

"Hey, don't get all wrought up about it!" Zoya smile kindly. "I know what it's like. Men, men, men. But I can help you! I know exactly where to go – you'll have to talk to Olya from the kitchens for the pig's blood, and Sasha for wood chips to fill the sacks – and I'll set it all up myself! We'll have it ready by the time the next train goes by, yes indeed!"

Anna was moved, found it difficult to speak. Everything well-bred in her was begging to refuse the offer, knowing it was too much – too much! And for something so absurd! But where else could she turn? She couldn't bear to go back to that awful house and wait for that man who didn't love her anymore, who cared only for his own pride. Yes, that would truly be too much. She remembered the state she had been in, all those weeks alone like a ghost, before Kitty had come for her.

"Please, tell me," she said finally, eyes glistening with gratitude. "Tell me, what can I do for you? How can I repay you?"

Zoya shrugged. "Don't worry about it, dear. I'm happy enough just to help you out, anything I can do for a friend."

Anna shook her head. "Please, let me thank you, somehow."

"I told you, don't fret about it. Or, well, if you must – I suppose I might ask for a kiss on the cheek from a pretty woman such as yourself." A laugh, a glint in the eye, and Anna bent down and kissed her on both cheeks. Zoya laughed. "Now look what I've done – you've got coal all over you."

"Are you sure I can't give you anything? I haven't got my purse with me now, but I have a brother, with money and land; and my husband..."

"No-o-o!" Zoya cut her off, wagging a coal-blackened finger. "I'm not that kind of girl. A kiss and a smile and I'll be just fine."

Anna blushed, then, and smiled shyly.

And so the plan was put into action. Burlap sacks were filled with wood chips. Anna handed over a dress she had brought with her, lumpily covering the sacks; then Zoya loaded all of it into a cart, covered it with a sheet of canvas, and filled the cart with coal to keep it hidden. They gathered the knife-sharpener and the sweet-seller, and mapped out a perfect collision – the distraction. Meanwhile, a skin-and-bones kid, face smeared with coal, nodded along as Zoya explained to him how to dart in and wrench the burlap marionette from the cart, and fling it under the tracks without attracting unwanted glances. An equally skinny girl, who seemed to appear from nowhere, was given her own instructions, along with a bucket full of pig's blood.

And then, almost too soon, the hour had come. Anna and Kitty drew their shawls over their heads, afraid they might be recognized, and left the station, planning on staying the night before leaving Warsaw in the morning. Separate trains – Kitty to Moscow, to keep up their alibi; and Anna back to Gatchina, and then to drive back to the Levin estate. They found a room in an inn, and waited with hearts pounding for news from the station.

When the news finally came, it could not have been better. The execution was flawless. Zoya came to tell them about it herself – how real it had looked, the shadows falling just right; and how the sweet-seller had rung his bell like a madman and the knife-sharpener had called out for everyone to leave the area before anybody could get too close a look at it. Someone had even fainted on the platform, she gushed: it was perfect.

Anna Karenina was dead.

Yes, everything was as it should have been. The funeral was planned immediately. The casket would be closed – of course, after such mutilation. Karenin had even offered to pursue Vronsky in court for driving his wife to suicide – and Anna had nearly broken into tears at this generosity, though she refused the offer. Let him live his life, she thought; it's not my business anymore.

That night, sleeping again in the same room, Anna held Kitty's hand, and was oddly silent.

"Is something wrong, Anna?" Kitty whispered.

"It's just so morbid, do you know?" A sigh. "My funeral, you're writing invitations for my funeral. And I feel so guilty. All this for my sake." A tear might have rolled down Anna's cheek, but it was too dark in the room for Kitty to see it.

"You're alive, and you're going to come home and be with us. That's all that counts. Trust me."

"Listen, Kitty...I need you to know. Today, on that platform, I saw myself die – I saw what could have been my death. The weeks before you came for me, in that carriage at midnight... Those were the darkest weeks of my life. I...God forgive me...I was ready to slit my wrists, hang myself, drink down a bottle of morphine, anything. All it would have taken was one last thing – a letter, a word, even a look. I am so, so lucky you arrived in time."

"Oh, Anna..."

"So lucky," she repeated, and cupped Kitty's face, and kissed her softly on the lips.

"I will not see you until after the funeral," Kitty whispered.

"I know." Anna smiled. "But it won't be long. And then I will be free. We'll both be."

"Yes." Kitty smiled back, and Anna felt it more than she saw it in the dark, heard the brush of Kitty's cheek against the pillow.

"It's so strange, but I feel somehow that this is the beginning of my life, Kitty," sighed Anna. "All I ever wanted. The beginning of what life was supposed to be."

"How was it supposed to be?" Kitty was delighted, curious. "Tell me what it's going to be like."

"Oh, we'll be together, and we'll go out in the sun all the time, and eat sweet things no matter the season," Anna whispered. "And Kostya will be there, and Mitya and Annie will grow tall and strong and lively, and we'll all sit and watch the sun set. And Alexey will come with Seryozha, and they will all play together. And we'll watch them, and be happy."

"That's beautiful," sighed Kitty.

"You're beautiful." Anna said it lightly, but meant it. Kitty turned her face into the pillow, blushing, and smiled again.

A pause.

"It will be so strange, so strange to be there," whispered Kitty. "The funeral, I mean."

"It is so strange to talk about it," Anna whispered back, shaking her head. "All of this is strange. You, me. Death. Life."

"Do you love it?"

"What?" Anna tilted her head dreamily, not thinking, wanting only to talk a little longer, to lie like this a little longer.

"Just...this. The strangeness of it all."

"Do I love it?"

"Yes, do you?"

Both of them were breathing gently, sounds of outside, sounds of themselves. Everything warm, soft, quiet. Did she love it?

"Of course," she whispered. "It keeps me alive."

AUTHOR BIOS

ALI COYLE *(The Magician's Children)* is a science educator by day, a fiction writer by night, and has been an unapologetic daydreamer since birth. Whilst studying physics at university, Ali chose to interpret the "scientists can't write" stereotype as a personal challenge and has been writing down their daydreams ever since. Some of those daydreams lead to Ali's triptych of novellas, *Chrysalides*, published with Improbable Press in 2023. You can find Ali on Twitter @AliCoyleWrites and at https://alicoylewrites.wordpress.com.

ANN S EPSTEIN *(Snappily Ever After)* writes novels, stories, poems, memoir, and essays. Her novels are *On the Shore*, *Tazia and Gemma*, *A Brain. A Heart. The Nerve.*, *The Great Stork Derby*, *One Person's Loss*, and *The Sister Knot*. Her other award-winning work appears in *North American Review*, *Sewanee Review*, *PRISM International*, *Ascent*, and elsewhere. She also has a PhD in developmental psychology, an MFA in fiber art, and certification as an end-of-life doula where she applies her literary skills to help people write their life reviews and ethical wills. Read more about Ann's writing at her website https://www.asewovenwords.com.

APARNA KAPUR *(My Gratitude Journal)* has been involved in Indian children's publishing for over a decade. As an editor, she has worked on a monthly science magazine, comic books and picture books. She has co-authored a novel, Ruckus on the Road; and has written several picture books, including *Ghum-Ghum Gharial's Glorious Adventure*, *The Button Box* and *What the Dark Sounds Like*. She has recently completed a master's degree in Wild Writing. She is often found poring over a book or pouring herself a large cup of coffee.

ARI OCHOA CONTRERAS *(A Heart of Stained Glass)* Ari Ochoa Contreras (they/xe), is a writer in process that likes dancing to old music and history, one of their goals in mind is to bring to the world stories about the human condition told through the intersectionality of being queer and Latine. Find more of xyr work in the JUVEN Press, Healthline Zine, Graveyard Zine, #Enbylife, Hooligan Mag and at Instagram in @Ari_gibberish.

ATLIN MERRICK *(Editor)* is the commissioning editor for *Anna Karenina Isn't Dead* and for Improbable Press. She's the author of articles and essays, as well as two short story collections: *Sherlock Holmes and John Watson: The Day They Met* (writing as Wendy C Fries) and *Sherlock Holmes and John Watson: The Night They Met* as Atlin Merrick. She's so proud of the stories Improbable received for this anthology, and hopes you'll find her on Tumblr at atlinmerrick.tumblr.com.

BÉATRICE de CHARMOY *(Lilac)* is a writer, activist, statistician, and part-time Tolstoy scholar. They hold three passports, speak six languages (and counting), and thrive at the intersection of politics, data, and art. In 2020, they gave the title *Anna Karenina Isn't Dead* to an online story collection based on Tolstoy's first true novel. The rest is history.

CEALLACH STEVENS *(This Pyre Isn't Big Enough For The Two of Us)* is a walking disaster masquerading as a human and is trying their best. Currently living with their cat Pangur Ban, they enjoy waking up, doing things and then going back to sleep. Their writing was first featured in Improbable Press' anthology *Dark Cheer: Cryptids Emerging (Volume Blue)*.

CHRISTINA LADD (she/her) *(Lady Godiva in the Garden)* is a writer, reviewer, and editor who lives in Minneapolis. She will eventually die crushed under a pile of books, but until then she survives on a worrisome amount of tea and pizza. You can find more of her work at christinaladd. com.

CLAUDIA CARANFA *(Cover Artist)* is an illustrator, cover artist and fanartist based in Italy. She has a master's degree in visual arts from the Academy of Fine Arts of L'Aquila, Italy. During the first years of her artistic path, she focused on traditional techniques – oils, acrylics and pencils. In 2009 she began experimenting with digital painting, and gradually shifted towards a more illustrative style, influenced by imaginative realism, pop surrealism, and dark surrealism, as well as pop culture, movies, TV shows and books. Her art explores the human figure, the boundary between human and inhuman (where inhuman can be machine, alien, animal, monstrous, or ethereal) and the world of the subconscious. She has participated in several group exhibitions with her traditional paintings, and currently works as a freelance illustrator and cover artist for publishers and independent authors, mostly from the United Kingdom, United States, and Italy. You can find Claudia at: https://kittrose.jimdofree.com.

DANA M EVANS (*Annabelle Lee Escaped the Sea*) has been writing almost all of her life. Careers as a foot and ankle surgeon and a biology professor allow her to color her stories with medicine and science. She also enjoys setting them in places she's lived or traveled to. She's been a lifelong devotee of history and folklore. Her students call her campus office Nerdvana thanks to all her sci-fi, anime and comic book memorabilia filling it. Her works can be found in *Nothing but Red: The Anthology Inspired by the Death of Du'a Khalil*, and the *Young Explorer's Adventure Guide, Volume 5* anthologies, and she can be found online @DanaMEvans13 on both Blue Sky and Twitter.

DANNYE CHASE (*Love Knot*) is a queer, married mom of three who lives in the US Pacific Northwest. Her mother taught her to love "The Highwayman" as a child, and would have loved seeing Bess triumph. Dannye claims to write in many genres, but her son suspects it all boils down to either romance or horror... or somehow both. Dannye's short fiction has appeared in magazines, anthologies, and podcasts. You can find her at DannyeChase.com and on Twitter as DannyeChase.

GEORGE IVANOFF (*My Last Duke*) is an Australia based author who usually writes for kids and teens. He's written over 100 books, ranging from the interactive fiction of the *You Choose* series to the nonfiction *Survival Guides*. Sometimes he has a go at writing grown-up stuff. So far he's done okay, with stories appearing in numerous magazines and anthologies including *Clamour and Mischief, Dark Cheer, Dead Red Heart* and *[untitled]*. Check out George's web site at: georgeivanoff.com.au.

JACK FENNELL *(The Leopard Queen)* is a writer and researcher who teaches at the University of Limerick, Ireland. He is the editor of two anthologies, *A Brilliant Void* (2018) and *It Rose Up* (2021), collecting lesser-known Irish science fiction and fantasy stories respectively. His own fiction has appeared in *Silver Apples Magazine, Archive of the Odd*, and the anthologies *The Only One in the World, Who Sleuthed It?* and *Clamour and Mischief.* He also contributed translations to *The Short Fiction of Flann O'Brien* (2013), and was the winner of the 2022 European Science Fiction Society award for Best Translator.

JESSE FRIEND *(There Was an Old Woman)* is an emerging writer known for her compelling short stories. Her work has achieved recognition in various competitions, and previous publications include the Sheepshead Review's inaugural Summer 2021 issue. She's currently writing her first novel.

J M CYRUS *(A Call to Arms)* is a London speculative fiction writer. She writes whenever there's a chance, and reads even when there isn't one. With a master's degree in Reception Theory, and a thesis on the reader's imagination, she feels academically validated to essentially play make-believe in her head. Her work has appeared or is forthcoming in literary and speculative fiction publications, including an anthology from *Patchwork Raven*, Erro Press' journal *Flint*, as well as online on *AntipodeanSF, Sci-Fi Shorts, Medusa's Kitchen* and *Orion's Beau.* This poem was her first ever submission. Say hello at: jmcyrus.writer@gmail.com or at https://jmcyrus.carrd.co.

JONATHAN TITCHENAL *(Her Holiness)* was a passionate reader and writer of fiction for well over a decade. This was nice because it meant being able to get out all the unprintable stuff and get on to the fun stuff—actually, that's not true, it was all fun stuff. His work has appeared in *The End of the World As We Know It* from Das Krakenhaus publishing and *A Lonely & Curious Country* from Ulthar Press. Jonathan passed away in June 2020, but his friends and family continue to seek publication for his writing, including a completed epic fantasy novel.

JOSEPH S WALKER *(Unintended)* lives in Indiana and teaches college literature and composition. His short fiction has appeared in *Alfred Hitchcock's Mystery Magazine, Ellery Queen's Mystery Magazine, Mystery Weekly, Tough*, and a number of other magazines and anthologies, including *The Best American Mystery and Suspense* and three consecutive editions of *The Best Mystery Stories of the Year*. He has been nominated for the Edgar Award and the Derringer Award and has won the Bill Crider Prize for Short Fiction. He also won the Al Blanchard Award in 2019 and 2021. Follow him on Twitter @JSWalkerAuthor and visit his website at https://jswalkerauthor.com/

KENZIE LAPPIN *(And Wendy)* is a writer with short stories in publications such as Wizards In Space Literary Magazine, Brigid's Gate Press, Belanger Books, WordFire Press, Air And Nothingness Press, and more. Check her out on Twitter at @KenzieLappin.

LENA NG *(Made for a Monster)* lives in Toronto, Canada. Her short stories have appeared in publications including Amazing Stories and Flame Tree's *Asian Ghost Stories* and *Weird Horror Stories*. Her stories have been performed for podcasts such as *Gallery of Curiosities, Creepy Pod, Utopia Science Fiction, Love Letters to Poe*, and *Horrifying Tales of Wonder*. "Under an Autumn Moon" is her short story collection.

MELISSA COFFEY *(The Price for Fire)* is an Australian writer and editor, based in Melbourne. A former theatre director, their poetry and fiction often explores desire, agency, and sexuality, sometimes through a feminist lens. Their work is published in *The Ekphrastic Review, Aurora Journal, Last Girls Club, Exist Otherwise, Writing in a Woman's Voice* and *Not Very Quiet*. They are intrigued by the subversive potential of myth and fairy tale to interrogate patriarchy and reimagine the feminine experience. Melissa is working on several chapbooks and a novella. Find them on Twitter @CuriousSeeds.

MIRANDA JUBB *(Beyond the Wall(paper))* lives in Bristol in the UK with her family and assorted animals. This is her first publication although she has been writing all her life; her childhood ambition was to sell her own books from a stand outside her house. Also wicker baskets. She squeezes writing in between taking care of her household, attempting to garden, and reading whatever she can. You can find her on Twitter/X @dreemywyrd, Bluesky @mirandamiranda or http://dreemywyrd.blogspot.com/.

NELLY SHULMAN *(Madame)* is a writer based in Berlin. Her work has appeared on JewishFiction.net, in the Vine Leaves Press Anthology of the Best 2021 Flash Fiction and in the various literary magazines. She is a winner of three writing awards and can be found at nellyshulman.blog.

NHU LE *(Three Make a Tiger)* is a Vietnamese-American writer. Born in Saigon but now based in New York, she is interested in Southeast Asia-inspired speculative fiction that scrutinizes narratives of empire, family, gender, and memory. She is also an applied anthropologist, and in this role persuades companies to send her to new cities to indulge in her three passions: deconstructing culture, eating a lot, and daydreaming up new tales. *Three Make a Tiger* is her first published short story. You can find her at qnhule.com and on Instagram @newnhu1010.

PATSY PRATT-HERZOG *(Sweet Everything's)* is an emerging freelance writer from Southwestern Ohio. Her favorite writing genres are sci-fi and fantasy. She lives in the burbs with her husband, Tim, and a chunky cat named Buddy. When not writing, she enjoys painting and riding roller coasters. Publishing credits include short stories in *Suspicious Activities, From A Cat's Viewpoint II, Halloween Party 2019, Detective Mysteries Short Stories, Bodies in the Library Short Stories, Misspelled: an anthology of magic gone awry*, and *Accursed: a Horror Anthology*. Visit her blog at https://patsyprattherzog.wordpress.com/featured-publications/ or tweet her at @PatsyAPH.

SADIE FOX CURTIS *(Helen Highwater)* is a modern witch with an ancient heart who writes about deep magic, light mischief, and hot makeouts. She lives with her partner, two cats, and a couple of freeloading ghosts in the Midwest (though she dreams of smelling salt water in her hair and picking lemons from her backyard tree someday). Her work has appeared in Apparition Literary Magazine, The Last Girls Club 'zine, and on Vocal (writing as Maisie Krash). She's working on her second novel. Follow Sadie on Instagram at @sadiefoxcurtis or at sadiefoxcurtis.com.

SAMIR SIRK MORATÓ *(Gorgoneion Knot)* is a scientist, artist, and flesh heap. They are a 2022 Brave New Weird shortlister and a F(r)iction Fall 2022 Flash Fiction finalist. Some of their published and forthcoming work can be found in TOWER Magazine, Seize the Press, ergot., and Catapult.

SHERYL CLOUGH *(Limits of Perfection—remembering Mrs. Cleaver)* learned to swim in the glacier-fed Skykomish River, in the foothills of the Cascade Mountains. After finishing an MFA at the University of Alaska Fairbanks, Sheryl moved to a bluff overlooking an arm of the Salish Sea, where eagles fly overhead daily. She has worked as a paralegal, whitewater river guide, Upward Bound teacher and college instructor, and has writen two published chapbooks. Sheryl also edited and published two collections of other poets' work under her imprint Write Wing Publishing. Her writing appears in *Sierra, Bacopa, Poet's Touchstone, Adelaide Independent Daily News, Third Wednesday* and others. Sheryl and her chess master husband, Bill McGeary, support the Whidbey Camano Land Trust. Contact Sheryl at Scatchetpoet@gmail.com.

S M LAWSON *(Dancing by the Red Sea)* discovered her love of writing later in life, but is enjoying every minute of it. She is a proud feminist, mom, fanfiction author, and all around nerd.

STACY BIERLEIN *(The Story of a Future)* is the author of the story collection *A Vacation on the Island of Ex-Boyfriends* and an editor of the acclaimed fiction anthologies *A Stranger Among Us* and *Men Undressed.* She lives in Southern California where she is an advocate for survivors of stalking and post-separation abuse. Her Instagram is @StyleFileFour.

STEPHEN D ROGERS *(Greater Expectations)* is the author of *Shot to Death* and more than 800 shorter works. His website, www.StephenDRogers.com, includes a list of new and upcoming titles as well as other timely information.

TANSY RAYNER ROBERTS *(Cassandra Gets a Future)* is an author of historically-inspired SF, fantasy and gaslamp fiction. Her books include the short story collections *Love & Romanpunk* (2011), and *Gorgons Deserve Nice Things* (2023). Tansy won the Hugo twice, for Best Fan Writer and Best Fancast for the Galactic Suburbia podcast. She is on Instagram, Bluesky & Threads as @tansyrr and her website is tansyrr.com.

YVONNE KNOP *(To the Editor of the Strand Magazine)* was born and raised in Germany. They have been a translator, researcher, teacher, and scholar. They have survived a blizzard in Minneapolis, the food in a British local pub, and survived a well-nigh plane crash. For years, Yvonne Knop was searching for queer novels that depict life with all its facets; from the absurd and hilarious to the tragic and mournfully. After having read all novels there are fitting this category, they decided to write their own stories to expand the list. You can find them on Instagram as @yvonne.knop.

ZACHARY ROSENBERG *(That Which Yields)* is a horror and SFF writer living in Florida. By night, he crafts horrifying and fantastical stories and by day he practices law which is even scarier. His work is out or forthcoming in multiple anthologies and publications such as Seize the Press, The Deadlands, and the Magazine of Fantasy & Science Fiction. Find him on Twitter at @ZachRoseWriter.

GET MORE GREAT STORIES
IMPROBABLEPRESS.COM

From ancient gods rising, to road trips on the trail of cryptids,
from romance to mystery to adventure,
Improbable Press specialises in sharing the voices and tall tales
of women, LGBTQIA+, BIPOC, disabled, and neurodiverse
people.

Come along for the ride.

Sign up for our newsletter *Spark* at improbablepress.com
Find us on Twitter @so_improbable
Instagram @improbablepress

Improbable
PRESS